TRIAL AND RETRIBUTION VI

Lynda La Plante

WINDSOR
PARAGON

First published 2002
by
Macmillan
This Large Print edition published 2004
by
BBC Audiobooks Ltd
by arrangement with
Macmillan
an imprint of Pan Macmillan Ltd

ISBN 0 7540 9542 8   (Windsor Hardcover)
ISBN 0 7540 9428 6   (Paragon Softcover)

British Library Cataloguing in Publication Data available

Printed and bound in Great Britain by
Antony Rowe Ltd., Chippenham, Wiltshire

ctive
first
fore
ickly
stent
to
and
the

Chief
pport
for
other
new
boyfr

Whe   are
teste   they
are w

Pages damaged 23-34.

I would like to dedicate this book to Antoinette Tucker. Antoinette is always a constant source of encouragement to all of us at LPP. Her energy and enthusiasm never waver and we are all fortunate to know such a brave, beautiful lady.

ACKNOWLEDGEMENTS

I would like to say how much I appreciate the talents of my leading actors Kate Buffery and David Hayman. They have maintained the high standard of *Trial and Retribution* through their performances and are encouraging and helpful to all the actors joining the series.

Trial and Retribution VI has been very honoured to welcome back the talents of Dorian Lough, George Pensotti, N'deaye Baa-Clements, Jacqueline Tong, Richard Durden, James Simmons, Sheila Donald, Barbara Thorn, Michael Simkins and those of the guest stars James Fox, Corin Redgrave, Bella Emberg, Tim McInnerny and Con O'Neill. My thanks to all those whose professionalism and dedication made it such a special series to work on.

We are so lucky to have formed such a strong team over the years of making the series of *Trial and Retribution*. Our thanks go to the very talented and dedicated crew, led by executive producer, Lorraine Goodman. Special thanks to Simon Kossoff, the director of photography; Bill Bryce, the production designer; Joanna Eatwell, the costume designer and Carol Cooper, the make-up designer. Thank you also to Les Healey and his assistant in the edit suite, Milena Tasso.

The staunch and terrific back-up from the La Plante script editing staff makes my life so much easier. Thanks to head of development, Jason McCreight, and script editor Jocelyn 'hamburger and fries' Cornforth. Further thanks must be directed to my chief executive Liz Thorburn, my PA George Ryan, my researcher Lucy Hillard and our new team member Eleni Kyriacou.

My sister Gill Titchmarsh's casting remains, as it has throughout our career together, a major input into the show as she leaves no rep theatre or drama school unturned! May I also thank Gill's casting assistant, Chrissie McMurrich.

I would like to thank Susie Tullett and all at Premier Maxworks Public Relations.

Thanks to Jonathan Channon and the team at EMI, and of course to Evelyn Glennie and Greg Malcangi for their inspired and imaginative soundtrack.

I also wish to thank Nick Elliott and Jenny Reeks, who have been so much a part of the success of La Plante Productions. They remain supportive of us and are a constant encouragement, along with David Liddiment of the ITV Network Centre.

Thanks to my literary agent Gill Coleridge and to Imogen Taylor, my editor at Pan Macmillan who publish all my novels, and thanks to Philippa McEwan.

I would also like to say thank you to Stephen Ross, Andrew Bennet-Smith, George Brook, Julie Phelps and to all at Ross Bennet-Smith.

A big thank you to my agent, Duncan Heath, and the lovely Sue Rodgers.

I would also like to say a very big thank you to Mark Devereux, whose constant support and guidance, along with that of the members of his team at Olswang, Julia Palca, Nigel McCorry and Linda Francis, has been so important to the success of LPP.

I would like to say thank you for the continued support of all at the Nine Network, Australia, especially to John Stephens and Geraldine Easter.

Special thanks to our wonderful team of advisors: Jackie Malton, Dr Liz Wilson, Dr Ian Hill and David Martin-Sperry.

I would like to sincerely thank the following for all their generosity and assistance during the research and making of Trial and Retribution VI: DI Morgan O'Grady; Chris Porter, BSc Hons forensic manager; DCI Paul McAleenan; Callum Sutherland, crime scene manager; David Pryor, senior forensic scientist; Robert Vanstan, executive officer police records; Mick Lydon; Chris Jones; Matthew Tucker; Helen Fielder and the team at the Prison Service Press Office; Alan Hadfield of the Metropolitan Police; Gary Tubman and Jane Murray at Springfield Hospital.

I would like to thank the very talented writer Robin Blake for his continued care and skill in adapting the film of *Trial and Retribution* to the page.

Last, but by no means least, I have to thank Ferdinand Fairfax for his dedication and talent. His input into the scripts was of major importance and his direction and care for the series ensures that we have yet another terrific drama that I, and everyone concerned, am proud to be part of.

CHAPTER ONE

WEDNESDAY, 19 MARCH

It was on a breezy spring morning that Jane Mellor took her daughter Tara, with Tara's best friend Diana, to walk Henry the black Labrador in Binley Wood, about a mile from their home. There had been rain in the night and showers were again threatened. The two nine-year-olds, with a day off school for 'staff training', had been kicking around the house all morning, complaining of nothing to do. After lunch they were going to the cinema, to see the new *Star Wars* film. But Jane told them they must take some fresh air first, while it still held fine.

The woods were probably older than England. These days it took just ten minutes to walk from one side to the other, but this had once been part of a forest that covered most of the land between London and the south coast. Game had abounded among the oaks and beeches. Deer and wild pigs were hunted for miles by the King and his courtiers, and taken, too, by peasants and outlaws at the risk of being summarily hanged. The woodland paths, now the preserve of tracksuited joggers and Barbour-clad dog walkers, had originally been marked out by the tracks of badgers, rabbits, hedgehogs and foxes. You no longer heard the rooting of boars in the blackthorn thickets, or the clash of stags' antlers in the rutting season. But the woods were as dense in places as they had ever been, and still concealed an

1

abundance of squirrels' nests and rabbit warrens, and even a few badger setts.

With the car securely locked, Henry was led, straining and snuffling on his leash, across the road that separated the car park from the woods. Once into the trees, Jane unsnapped the lead and he raced off with a joyous yelp to find a squirrel or a rabbit. A crow flapped croaking from the path up towards the canopy of trees, which were on the edge of coming into leaf.

A man appeared from a lateral path, with a small, silky-coated dog trotting along behind him. He nodded at the woman and children as he passed them on his way back to the car park. Jane called Henry, who reappeared, bounding like a hurdler towards them. She sent a stick wheeling through the air and he instantly changed direction to deal with it.

Meanwhile, she was entertaining the girls with a legend about the woods.

'This wood was once part of a huge forest, and there was an ogre living in the middle of it.'

'What kind of ogre?' asked Tara.

'Just an ordinary, every day kind of ogre, I should think. You know, hairy feet, big teeth, *terrible* breath.'

'What did the ogre do?'

'Preyed on people. Dropped down from the trees on top of them and ate them. And once the King's daughter was passing through the forest riding a milk-white mare. She was on her way to marry the Crown Prince of Brittany, but she was ambushed by the ogre. It dropped down and knocked her off her horse.'

'Did it eat her?'

2

'No. Because the Princess had the longest red hair you've ever seen, all the way down to the ground. And she just swirled herself around so that her hair covered her up completely and hid her from the sight of the ogre. So he looked around for a bit then gave up and made do with eating the milk-white mare. He was a very stupid ogre.'

'Did the Princess run away?'

'No. She couldn't. Because in the earth underneath the tree lived the mother ogre, and she was furious at the trick played by the Princess on her son. So she reached up out of the earth and grabbed the ends of the Princess's hair. Then she pulled them into the earth and tied them around the roots of the tree. The Princess was helpless inside her own hair. Then the ogress grabbed the Princess's dainty white feet and pulled her right down into the ground.'

'And she was Never Seen Again,' sang Di, picking up a stick for Henry to fetch.

'That's right,' said Jane. 'Never Seen Again. What's up with Henry, though? Look!'

She pointed to where the dog had pulled up, about fifty yards away, his hackles raised and his tail down, growling and then barking. He was on the edge of a bushy dip in the ground, beside a wide-girthed oak, and seemed to be disturbed by something in front of him. Unable to see what it was, they called the dog, each of them in turn. Henry took no notice, not even looking round or wagging his tail. Then in mid-bark he seemed to jump or pitch forward out of sight in the dead ground before him. Over the sound of the wind they heard his voice again, giving a single truncated yip.

3

Jane Mellors frowned.

'Stay on the path,' she told the children. 'I'd better go and see what the matter is.'

She strode off, swinging Henry's lead and calling his name, last year's bracken crackling and rustling under her boots. The children watched as Jane reached the tree and stopped for a moment, leaning forward to look down into the dip. She was speaking but at that moment an extra gust of wind rushed through the trees and they couldn't make out the words. Then she went forward again, down into the dip. As she went lower her figure seemed to shorten. Then she went completely out of sight, first her blue shirt, and finally her head with its bell of blonde hair. Almost immediately after that Henry reappeared, galloping away with his tail down into a patch of dense bushes to the children's left.

Di stood rooted to the spot. Tara left her and ran back along the path, to a place where she might see her mother again, or at least catch poor Henry. She changed direction to run along the lateral path and was looking towards the big oak when she saw a dark head bob up from the dead ground beside it. At once it disappeared again. Suddenly there was a cry, at a horrible, despairing pitch.

'RUN! TARA, RUN!'

Tara screamed herself in a long, ululating note of panic and fear. She turned to look for Di, then back again to where her mother had been. Suddenly, Henry tore out of the undergrowth and on to the path between the two girls, his tongue flailing and his tail between his legs. Now Di too had started to run with flapping legs along the path towards her friend. And, from the undergrowth, at

4

some place between Tara and the tree, there came a new sound of bracken rustling, twigs cracking and branches being pushed aside. At this point Di tripped on the path and tumbled.

Di did not stay down. She picked herself up and ran over in terror to Tara. They stopped, looking this way and that, at a loss as to what to do. There was a loud, vigorous rustling of bushes and they saw the burly shape of a man rearing up in the undergrowth about twenty yards away. The man's face was broad and covered in hair, both on top and around the cheeks and chin. As one, they screamed again and turned to sprint back towards the car park. Tara had just a single thought in her mind as she pelted along: *Get help, get help.*

There was a mobile phone in the car. Reaching the road the friends raced across it and into the car park. But the car was locked and Jane had the keys.

'What's happened?' screamed Di, as Tara frantically and uselessly pulled at the car door. 'Where's your mum, Tara? Where's your *mum*?'

Tara was crying now, her features pulled out of shape and crumpled.

'I don't know, I don't know! She's gone. There was someone there.'

'I know. I saw. Has she been *attacked*, Tara?'

Tara looked around wildly. Then she pointed along the road, in the direction of their arrival.

'Quick! There were some houses over there. Come on! We've got to get someone.'

And the two girls were off again. Their wellingtons smacked the Tarmac as they ran with all their strength towards the houses and some sort of help.

There had been a police car on the scene within

fifteen minutes of the 999 call and its two officers had gone immediately to Jane Mellor's car. They found it still locked and apparently undisturbed, with no sign of its owner, either in the car park or the immediate vicinity of the woodland path along which Jane and the children had strolled with Henry less than an hour before. Apart from the silent evidence of her parked car, it was as if Jane Mellor had never been to Binley Wood on that day at all.

Soon after the patrol had radioed back a terse report, a woman police constable arrived to take the girls home, while a more systematic sweep of Binley Wood by a line of uniformed officers was begun. At nightfall, when the wood had been walked over in its entirety, and with no more promising result, the search was suspended. Clearly, a more wide-ranging investigation must be put in place in the morning, and one that could not be orchestrated by the local force. The suspected abduction of a female was the sort of thing that went straight to the in-tray of the Metropolitan Police Serious Crime Group at New Scotland Yard.

The Commander in charge of SCG (West Area) was an urbane, public school type of whom one wit had said that his purr was worse than his bite. He knew that, in the Binley Wood case, it was imperative for all energy, care and available resources to be deployed. It had every ingredient of a proper tabloid media-fest. The victim was an attractive woman, the children were traumatized, the woodland setting was spooky and, above all, they had in all likelihood an unknown, lone-wolf perpetrator, well capable of scaring the shit out of the public while they waited for him to strike again.

After half an hour's thought he decided to give charge of the case to Detective Inspector Pat North. It was true she was still waiting for a Superintendent vacancy, and would be a rookie heading up this level of investigation. But she was one of the Commander's rising stars, and it was time he blooded her. In the evening he picked up the phone and dialed her mobile. Pat North was, of course, surprised and delighted to be appointed Senior Investigating Officer for the first time. It was a chance she had long been waiting for.

CHAPTER TWO

FRIDAY, 21 MARCH

Pat North's appointment to the SCG was still fairly recent, but she'd come to it knowing a great deal about the unit's methods and personalities. This was because she had lived for the past three years with Detective Superintendent Michael Walker, who may have been a maverick but was still one of the Met's most experienced murder investigators. In fact it had been on a murder that she'd met Walker, in Docklands, during her stint on CID at a station there six years ago. That had been just after she'd made Inspector. Walker had seconded her to his team—hotly denying for ever after that he'd only done it because he fancied her.

As a professional role model, Walker left some things to be desired. He was impatient, unconventional and irascible. But he was also incisive and passionately committed, and that more than anything was the reason she'd first respected him, fallen for him and finally loved him. At some point in the future, when his interminable divorce from Lynn at last came through, they were due to be married.

It took most of Thursday to assemble North's team of eight officers for the Binley Wood enquiry, and she was pleased to find a leavening of familiar faces amongst them. Detective Constable Lisa West was well known to her as a reliable girl, and sharp as a pin. North also went way back with DC Doug Collins, a solid officer and a reassuring, experienced presence on what could turn out to be a high-profile case. The one problematic figure might be Dave Satchell, she thought. The Detective Sergeant was Mike Walker's oldest friend in the job, and had been his faithful colleague—'sidekick' was the term she had heard used by malicious tongues—on numerous investigations dating back to before North and Walker had got together. But she at least would be forewarned about Satchell's foibles, not least his belief that no woman could be a better police officer than a man, and that no other man could be a better Senior Investigative Officer than Michael Walker. At the same time North knew Satchell to be honest, bright and capable of long hours of hard work. Looking around the Incident Room, on this second morning following her appointment as SIO, she thought the team assigned to her could have been a lot worse.

The purpose of this morning's briefing was to review all inquiries made so far by the local boys and then, last evening, by Satchell, and to plot the immediate steps they themselves needed to take.

North had lain awake that night, with Walker snoring beside her, thinking things through. It might conceivably be a family thing but it looked at this stage much more like an abduction, with the most likely motive being sexual. In other words, Jane Mellor had probably fallen into the hands of a predatory rapist. If so the most important factor for North to bear in mind was that the victim might still be alive, and that police actions—North's own actions—would therefore affect her chances of staying that way. The second and closely related consideration was the identity of the abductor. And at this point the questions began to multiply. Was he known to Jane? Was he a local man? Did he have a police record? Was his action premeditated? How did he travel to the scene? Did he have accomplices? Did he leave any traces?

There was another possibility, an even darker one, if that were possible. Perhaps this man's real target had not been Jane Mellor at all. Perhaps he'd been trying to get at Tara and Di.

She had kicked off the briefing by asking Dave Satchell to give an account of his interview with Jane Mellor's husband the day before. Both James Mellor and his wife taught music. The routine of work and family life had not recently been disturbed. There was no indication of anything amiss.

As Satchell finished speaking, North took up the thread, reiterating the same questions she had asked herself the night before.

'Both girls gave the same description,' she said, turning to Satchell. 'White male, five foot eight to ten, bearded. Yes?'

Satchell nodded.

'Yes. They both told the same story without putting their heads together. Said the man was hiding in the woods when they got there.'

When Satchell spoke it was not just to North, she noticed, but to the team as a whole. He walked across and tapped a map of Binley Wood, which was pinned to a wall-board at the end of the Incident Room. Beside it were photographs of Jane Mellor, and Polaroids taken of the woods from the path which Jane and the girls had taken.

'It was just about here.'

At the moment his index finger touched the map his mobile phone rang. He was expecting a call from the lab, where various items already found in the woods were being tested. He looked at the LCD display on his phone. It wasn't the lab. It was Mike Walker. He put the mobile to his ear and thumbed the connect button.

'Excuse me,' Satchell mumbled to the company at large, strolling to the side of the room. 'It's the lab.'

Collins cleared his throat, preparing to take up the thread of the briefing. He was detailed to take charge of the crime scene.

'OK,' said Collins, 'it's a huge area to search, so we're going to need dogs . . .'

'Hi,' said Satchell loud enough for everyone to hear. 'You boys got anything for me yet?'

Walker was on a short study leave. In a couple of weeks' time he was up for an interview to be promoted to Commander and was currently at home wrestling with his computer, trying to get up to speed on information technology in the police force. Trying but still, as far as Satchell could see, a long way from succeeding.

He heard Walker's voice, sounding cheerfully frazzled.

'*What* did you say? It's Mike, you plonker. Listen, I need help.'

Walker regarded Satchell as the guru of all glitches and computer foul-ups. In fact, when the Detective Sergeant had recently upgraded his own home computer, Walker had bought Satchell's redundant PC. Since then, hardly a day had gone by that he hadn't been on the blower for a spot of after-sales service. Walker was a baby when it came to computers.

'Satch, you sold me the thing,' he went on. 'I've taken a week off to work on this, and it's bloody useless!'

Satchell turned his back to the meeting and spoke in a murmur, though an urgent one.

'Mike, it's not a good time, I'm in a briefing. What's up, anyway?'

'I've got the date for the big interview,' said Walker. 'If I'm going to be talking about computers and modern policing, I have to at least be able to do more than turn the damn thing on!'

The meeting had gone quiet behind Satchell as the team waited for him to finish the phone call. It might, after all, be important news affecting the investigation. Satchell glanced round and grinned self-consciously. Then he turned back to Walker.

'Look just press "Control-S" for now,' he whispered. 'Make a cup of tea. I'll call you later.'

Satchell clicked the mobile off and turned back to the waiting team.

'Right,' he said, marching back to the wall-map with compensatory assertiveness, 'so for this big an area we're going to need dogs.'

11

'I already told them that!' said Collins.

Lisa West raised a pencil.

'We've also got quite a long list of local pervs from the Sex Offenders Register.'

She handed the list of usual suspects to North. Each name had an address and a brief note of the man's police record. Some of the addresses were as much as twenty miles from Binley Wood.

'Can this list be reorganized,' North asked, 'in the order of their distance from the crime scene? Then we can start with those living nearest—say, five miles from Binley?'

Satchell took the list and scanned it quickly.

'No problem, Pat—er, I mean Gov. Computer'll handle it.'

'And Doug, get on to dog section will you? They'll want an idea of how long we're going to need them. And remember, all of you. If this *is* an abduction, which certainly looks likely, he might very well be holding her alive. So I want you to work quickly yet *very* thoroughly. We've got to find this bastard fast. But it'll be doing Jane Mellor no favours if we simply trawl the SOR and get fixated on the wrong molester. Satch, can you get the pervert patrol going, and be ready to go out at one? You're coming back to the Mellors' place with me.'

* * *

Walker had had a trying morning, sitting for hours in front of the screen, attempting to work out how to use the police database program that Satchell had pre-loaded on to the hard disk. Walker could certainly understand why the bloody system was called Windows. But the cursed Windows kept opening and closing by themselves, apparently at random, and always just after he thought he'd made some kind of breakthrough.

He had just entered a bunch of data for the umpteenth time when he heard the chimes of his Entryphone. He crossed the living room and snatched up the handset. It was Lynn, his wife. He was too preoccupied to wonder why she was here, just buzzed her in at street level and unlatched the door of the flat, before dashing back to check on the computer screen. That last time, what had he pressed, the 'Control' or the 'Option' key? Whichever it was, it must have been the wrong one. His data had vanished again.

He threw down his reading glasses and picked up the cigarette that was smouldering in the ashtray. As he took an exasperated drag, Lynn bustled in. She was still his wife, though he'd been trying to turn her into his ex for longer than he cared to contemplate. She had thrown every conceivable obstacle in the path of their divorce— house, kids, maintenance, access, legal fees, and each of his proposals on these matters were disputed with all the fury of a female scorned. He braced himself for more of the same from this woman, who always claimed she still loved him while doing little else but make his life a misery.

But Walker was surprised. Lynn walked in wearing a friendly smile.

'Hello!' she said in a cooing, placatory tone that he knew from the old days but was surprised to hear now. He rose from the desk, stubbing out his smoke.

'Hi, come on in.'

Lynn had a sheaf of documents tucked under her

13

arm. Without ceremony she presented it to Walker and he glanced at them. My God! It was the divorce papers!

'I know these have been a long time coming,' she said. 'But here they are, signed, sealed and delivered.'

Walker looked at Lynn. He suddenly realized what a big moment this must be for her.

'Thanks, Lynn. You OK about this?'

Lynn nodded. She seemed genuinely pleased to be surprising him this way, as if she had just delivered a birthday card.

'Yes, really, I'm fine. After all, it means we're both young, free and single again!'

Walker beamed at her. He forgot the bloody computer and was full of *bonhomie*. Without warning a compliment escaped from his lips.

'Hey! And you look fabulous. You been dieting?'

As a matter of fact she was probably plumper than he had ever seen her, but he knew she liked to be told she looked slimmer. Throughout their married life he had been driven to distraction by Lynn's obsession with her weight. Yet it was true she looked well, better and prettier than he had seen her for years. The plumpness rather suited her.

Lynn's cheeks developed small pink spots.

'Not really. Just working out, getting fit, looking after number one for a change. As a matter of fact, bringing the divorce papers were a bit of a pretext. I wanted to tell you something.'

Walker raised his eyebrows.

'Oh yes? And what would that be?'

Lynn's blush grew a shade deeper.

'I've met someone.'

14

Walker blinked. *Met* someone? It took him a moment for it to dawn. She meant a *man*!

'Well that's . . . *great*,' he said, searching for the words. 'That's . . . really good news, Lynn. I'm glad.'

Lynn's eyes sparkled.

'He's really lovely. We met at my new gym. I'm sure you'll like him. As a matter of fact he's waiting in the car, with the kids. I was wondering if I could leave them with you for the weekend.'

Walker glanced back at the PC. He'd been planning to get Satch over tomorrow for a session on the accounts package.

'Oh right, yeah. *This* weekend?'

'Actually, today as well. It's a school holiday, staff training or something. Is it a problem?'

In view of the arrival of the long-awaited divorce papers, Walker didn't think he could possibly make it a problem.

'Er, no, no,' he said quickly. 'It'll be fine, absolutely fine!'

'Good. I'll pop down and get them. Um, he's called Eric, by the way . . .'

A couple of minutes later, Lynn was ushering Richard and Amy into their father's flat. Following closely behind was a very tall man of forty-plus. His pate was bald except for a thin frontal fringe of long dark strands which were pulled back to merge with a thick pelmet of hair growing in a semi-circle above the neck and down to the collar: a comb-back rather than a comb-over. He was probably a foot or more taller than Walker.

'It's Eric, right?'

They shook. Eric's giant mitt dealt with Walker's hand as if it was wringing a wet sponge.

'Nice to meet you,' said Walker, suppressing a gasp.

Eric's smile was all good nature.

'Likewise, Mike.'

He took up a proprietary stance behind and between Richard and Amy, with hands resting meatily on their shoulders. The children seemed to accept this without question.

'I'm sorry if this is inconvenient,' he said.

Walker shrugged.

'Hell,' he said, 'they're my kids.'

'It's just I've got an unexpected long weekend off, and we—Lynn and I—wanted to spend some quality time together.'

Quality time. It was a strangely poncy way to talk about a dirty weekend. But the kids were here and Walker let it go.

'Oh right,' he said. 'So, where are you off to?'

'The Peak District,' put in Lynn. 'Eric loves hiking.'

Her boyfriend ruffled Richard's hair in the jocular manner of one who thinks of himself as a favourite uncle.

'I'm going to buy her a good pair of walking boots. We can't wait to get out of London.'

He grinned wolfishly at Lynn, who returned the signal with a flirty little smile of her own. Walker forced himself not to be irritated.

'Well,' he said to Eric, 'take good care of her, then.'

*   *   *

At around one-thirty, North and Satchell walked up to a semi-detached house, with a standard,

16

neatly kept, privet-contained front garden in a pleasant outer-London suburb. North was carrying a cardboard file of statements in the case. She was thinking this was a moderately affluent, middle class home. Nothing flashy, but it was comfortable enough.

The front door was of varnished wood and bottle-end glass. Satchell's long ring of the bell woke the family dog inside and he launched himself at the door with a slavering volley of barks.

After about thirty seconds a man in his early forties opened it, his face pale and strained. As if to belie the stress that obviously afflicted him, he was dressed as casually as possible: frayed jeans, a nondescript baggy T-shirt and deck shoes without socks. He was bending to restrain a stocky black Labrador, with two fingers hooked into his collar.

He looked up at the officers and smiled bleakly.

'Sorry about Henry. He makes a lot of noise, but he's more likely to lick you to death than bite your head off.'

Satchell flicked a glance at North. It was an odd turn of phrase under the circumstances.

'Hello again, Mr Mellor,' he said, indicating North. 'This is Detective Inspector Pat North, who'll be leading the inquiry.'

Mellor extended his hand.

'Do you have any news?'

She shook her head and his hand at the same time.

'I'm sorry, we don't. But I would like to talk to you if I could.'

Mellor stood aside.

'Come in.'

The room into which he led them was decorated

17

with restrained good taste. North noticed an upright piano in one corner with an untidy pile of sheet music lying on top. Beside it stood a music stand with a violin laid carefully on its side along the stand's ledge. Mellor gestured at the two comfortable armchairs and North sat in one of them, opposite the sofa into which Mellor nervously lowered himself. She opened her file. Satchell remained standing.

They went over Jane Mellor's movements during the period before she'd taken the girls out, as Mellor had already described to Satchell. There were no discrepancies. There had been nothing unusual about the previous three or four days, no unexpected change in the normal school holiday pattern. None whatsoever.

'And there was nothing troubling your wife?' asked North, flicking through the file and glancing at a summary of his previous statement. 'I mean, over the last few days?'

Mellor got up from the sofa, unable to keep still.

'Not that I was aware of.'

'So she wasn't anxious or worried about anything at all?'

Mellor crossed to the piano and fidgeted with the pile of sheet music, trying without conviction to tidy it.

'No.'

'You said you were both due at your daughter's concert the evening Jane disappeared?'

'Yes, Jane's been teaching Tara the piano, and it was quite a special thing for us to be there. We're both musicians you see.'

He left the music and tapped the violin lightly, as if to confirm his credentials, then came back to the

18

sofa.

'We both teach up at the school. I mean . . . what I'm saying is, Jane had plans for that evening, so she would hardly . . .'

Mellor's train of thought lost its momentum. He was pacing the floor now, between the piano and his visitors. He turned to Satchell.

'Look, I've already told you this once. This is wasting time. Why are you wasting time here with me when you could be—'

Satchell gently interrupted.

'Why don't you sit down, Mr Mellor.'

Obediently, Mellor perched on the edge of the unoccupied armchair. North closed the file on her knee and looked up. She smiled encouragingly.

'Can you tell me a bit more about what Jane is like as a person?'

Mellor did not seem to hear.

'What?'

North gently repeated herself.

'What is Jane like as a person?'

Mellor's face took on a tortured look.

'She's a very special lady, a very talented pianist, and . . . a wonderful mother.'

'Is there anyone else she was close to who might be able to help us?'

Mellor's voice retained the sullen tone with which he'd just spoken to Satchell.

'Well, I suppose you'd better talk to Crispin, Crispin Yates. He lives with us.'

This piece of information hung in the air between them for a moment. North let it hang. Satchell flipped open his notebook and jotted down the name while Mellor sat picking at one of his fingernails, as if trying to formulate his next

19

remark.

'You should probably know,' he said eventually, 'that Jane and I don't live as man and wife. I mean, we have separate bedrooms.'

This *was* new information. North and Satchell exchanged a glance, which Mellor registered. In a small flurry of nervous defiance, he raised the pitch of his voice a few semitones.

'I know how it must look from the outside. But all I can tell you is, it works for us.'

Satchell was studying the name in his notebook.

'And this Crispin Yates . . .'

Mellor looked at him sharply.

'What about him?'

'Is he here now?'

'No. He teaches piano at the school on a Friday.'

So, thought Satchell, a cosy little threesome of musicians. A *trio*, in fact. He was rather pleased with the conceit.

'And how long has Mr Yates lived here?'

Mellor considered.

'It'll be, what, three years this September. He moved in a few weeks after he started teaching at the school.'

'Why didn't you mention this to me before?'

'What? That Crispin lives here? I don't really see what—'

He was interrupted by the trilling of North's mobile phone. Mellor waited while she fished it from her bag, then went on.

'What's it got to do with Jane going missing?'

North strode to the window and took the call with her back to the two men. In the background she heard Satchell saying,

'Mr Mellor, if we're going to find out what's

20

happened to your wife, we do need to know all the circumstances.'

The call was from Walker.

'Hey, Pat! You're never going to believe what I've got in my hand. The divorce papers! Lynn came round with them. And we've got the kids staying for—'

North interrupted.

'I can't talk right now. Later.'

Walker didn't press it.

'Fine,' he said. 'Just thought you'd like to know.'

'I'll talk to you later,' she repeated, then ended the call. For a moment she gazed out of the window. The divorce papers had come through. She knew she should feel something, some surge of happiness or adrenaline. But, right now, all her feelings were reserved for the case, her first big job as an SIO. Celebrating Mike's divorce would just have to wait.

CHAPTER THREE

FRIDAY, 21 MARCH, AFTERNOON

As North and Satchell walked away from the Mellors' front door, James Mellor began to play the piano. It was a drifting, melancholy piece, a song without words. Hearing classical music, North tended to feel inadequate. She could recognize several of the obvious favourites, like 'Blue Danube' and 'Bolero', but was much less sure of the difference between the 'Apassionata' and the 'Moonlight', or a Mozart and a Chopin concerto.

21

And yet, when she heard these pieces, she would have flashbacks to school music lessons with Mrs McAllister, who used to have them lying on the floor to listen with eyes closed. She remembered then the secret depths of feeling the music could sometimes release, like bubbles rising up towards the air through deep green water.

Satchell, on the other hand, seemed not to hear Mellor's piano at all.

'You want me to interview this lodger bloke, Crispin Yates?' he asked.

The car was parked on the other side of the road, nearly opposite the house. As Satchell worked the electronic key and the locks clunked, North turned and looked back over the privet towards Mellor's sitting room window. The piano could still be heard, mixing itself up with the wind.

'No,' she replied after a moment. 'I'll go. You organize a reconstruction with the girls.'

'Right.'

'But keep the two of them apart, if you can. Is that Chopin or Mozart?'

Satchell shrugged. How the hell would he know? If he wanted a Bohemian Rhapsody he put on Queen.

It was the end of the school day when North, now accompanied by Lisa West, arrived at St Radegund's. It was a mixed, independent, Church of England school housed in a hotch-potch of buildings that were flanked on one side by Tarmac playgrounds and on the other by a spread of rugby and hockey fields.

That inevitable smell of all schools—seemingly a compound of body odours, chalk-dust, boiled cabbage and carbolic—permeated the place. Pupils were moving along the corridors, or lingering in groups outside the exits, laughing and tussling with each other. Staff steered their way between them, weighed down by steepling piles of weekend marking. Everywhere was a hubbub of young voices, scuffling feet and banging doors.

Unnoticed by the police officers, a dark-haired lad of ten, pale and small for his age, passed them *en route* to the junior boys' locker room. He lugged a chunky, rexine-covered guitar case, plastered with Oasis and Radiohead stickers, which seemed almost as big as he was himself.

As the two officers approached the Junior School Assembly Hall, where they had been directed by the school secretary, they heard the sound of a pianist working on scales. They rippled fluidly up and down the keyboard, then transformed with an elegantly managed change of gear into a Chopin Mazurka. North stood for a moment at the door of the hall, listening.

'Ah,' she said, looking pleased with herself. This had been one of Mrs McAllister's favourite pieces. 'Now that's definitely Chopin!'

As they pushed in through a squeaky pair of double doors, West shot a sideways glance, wondering what the DI was on about. West had no more clue about the classics than Satchell.

Big curtains were drawn across the room's high windows and the hall was shadowed and gloomy, apart from a lamp casting a pool of light across the stage. At one side of this stood a grand piano. It was obvious, even to the tin ear of Lisa West, that the player hidden behind the piano's raised lid was a performer of the highest class.

'Mr Yates?' called North.

With the suddenness of a power failure the music stopped. The feet of the piano stool scraped the boards of the stage as it was pushed back. The pianist stood up. His astonishingly handsome face was creased with annoyance.

'*What?* I'm sick to death of constant bloody interruptions here!'

Crispin Yates was in his early twenties. His appearance was that of a Fulham Broadway bohemian, with dark, collar-length hair swept sleekly back, jeans, a T-shirt and an old green cord jacket. But he was not as cool as a true bohemian. There was an intense, bristling urgency about him.

North advanced to the edge of the stage where she showed him her warrant card.

'I am Detective Inspector Pat North. I'm investigating the disappearance of Jane Mellor.'

Yates's expression went from truculence to contrition in a moment.

'Oh! Is she all right? Have you found her?'

He was so eager for good news that North hated to disappoint him.

'I'm afraid not. Can we talk here or would you prefer . . .'

Yates seemed not to hear her.

'How can she be snatched in broad daylight, and just disappear?' he demanded.

'That's what we're trying to find out,' said North.

Yates strode around the piano and down the steps from stage to floor. He slumped into one of the front row of chairs, which North took to mean he was happy to talk where they were. She sat a couple of seats away from him.

'You live with Mr and Mrs Mellor?'

'That's right.'

'Were you at home the night she disappeared?'

Yates shook his head slowly.

'No. I was in Paris for a concert. I only got back yesterday.'

'And when did you leave?'

'Wednesday morning.'

He was leaning forward with bowed head, his elbows resting on his knees. He had the long elegant fingers of his profession, and was now clenching and unclenching them spasmodically.

'Please God, don't let her be dead,' he moaned. 'Don't let her be dead. I couldn't bear it.'

There was an extended squeak followed a thud from the double doors at the back of the hall. Two teenage girl pupils pushed in.

'Mr Yates!'

Yates sprang up, waving them away.

'Not NOW, Janine. Get out, go on! I'll see you later.'

The girls looked at each other and pouted. Then they swung out again. North said, in a low voice,

'When was the last time you saw Jane?'

'The night before I left.'

'And did you notice anything unusual about her? Was she anxious in any way?'

'No, no. She was fine.'

'We understand that Mr and Mrs Mellor lead separate lives. I mean as, er, man and wife. Did this ever cause any friction in the home?'

Yates reacted sharply, snapping back his head and looking directly into her eyes.

'You mean with *me* living there as well? Why are you asking that?'

It was a powerful, intense, perhaps mesmeric gaze that he had. God, thought North, this guy must have some effect on his female pupils.

Yates looked down and shook his head again, as if over a matter of the utmost desolation.

'No, no. There wasn't any . . . friction as you put it.'

'Were you having a relationship with Jane Mellor?'

This time Yates did not snap back. It was difficult to see on his lowered face, but perhaps he was even smiling. But the tone of his voice in reply was not humorous. Just sad.

'No. No, I was not.'

He coughed once into his fist and North realized he was on the verge of tears.

'Please,' he said, choking back his pain, 'just find her. This is unbearable. Please, *please*, find her safe.'

Walking back to the main foyer, they found the school was already practically deserted. The two officers could hear the sound of Yates's resumed piano playing pursuing them in echoes along the corridor.

'Yates is dead sexy,' said West. 'Do you think he and Jane really have been having an affair?

North smiled, thinking of Yates's compelling eyes.

'Anything's possible.'

She snapped a look at her watch. They were almost due at Binley Wood for the reconstruction.

'We should get a move on to the woods.'

North led the DC through the foyer and out into the Visitors' Car Park.

'If they are an item, she's got to have something going for her,' mused West. 'I mean, he can't be much more than twenty and Jane Mellor is

26

forty-two.'

North gave a tired sigh. Her sleepless night was catching up with her.

'I don't think she has anything going for her, Lisa, not now. I think she's dead.'

*   *   *

Walker's children were in residence at the flat, Lynn and Eric had left for their weekend of fun and frolics, and Walker had gone back to the cybernetic purgatory of his PC. But concentration was becoming increasingly close to impossible. For the past hour Richard had been playing his Gameboy, which made an intermittent and (to his father) extremely irritating beeping noise. With his own, rather more cumbersome, computer, Walker had run into another virtual blind alley and was cursing loudly. He snatched up a heavy paperback volume and began riffling angrily through the pages.

Amy wandered in from the kitchen area carrying a glass of orange squash.

'What're you reading, Dad?'

He snorted.

'A book not very tactfully entitled *Computing for Idiots*.'

He slapped the book down on the desk.

'And I don't understand a word of it.'

'I suppose that means you're not an idiot, then,' she told him, most seriously.

Walker laughed. Thank God for children. He put his arm around his daughter and hugged her.

'I'm grateful for the vote of confidence, Princess.'

'Anyway, Eric's good at computer stuff. He could teach you.'

Walker sighed.

'Yes, well, I'm doing fine by myself thank you.'

Wishing it was true, he released his daughter, lit a cigarette and sat back in his chair.

'How long's Eric been coming round?'

'Oh, for weeks. AND he bought me a Britney Spears CD.'

'That's nice.'

He studied the screen and the keyboard again and gingerly pressed a key. As if by cause and effect, the entry phone chimed just as he did so. Startled, Walker called out,

'Can you answer the door Richard?'

Amy had herself started towards the entry-phone but Richard beat her to it.

'Hello? . . . Hey, it's Satch, Dad.'

'Well press the buzzer and let him IN!' barked Walker.

'Dumbo!' shouted Amy, trying to reach the button first. Richard barged her aside. But in the end they both pressed the buzzer.

'Will the pair of you just sit down,' shouted Walker. 'I SAID SIT! Daddy's trying to sort this program out.'

'Eric's been showing me how to use the Internet,' announced Amy, collapsing on to the sofa and picking up a comic.

Walker glared at her and looked again at his screen. It was different. Not all the windows he'd had up before were still there.

'Shit! Now what's happened?'

Satchell walked in and Richard hurled himself at him.

28

'Satch!'

Satchell adopted a prizefighter's posture.

'Put your fists up, Rickie Dickie. Come on, gimme a right hook.'

Richard swung, but Satchell danced back, then used the flat of his hand to fetch the boy a featherweight tap behind the ear.

'Gotcha!'

Satchell looked around for Walker.

'Hi,' he said. 'How're you doing? I can't stop. I've just got a few minutes. You know Pat's heading up this case I'm on?'

But Walker wasn't listening. His head was in his hands, trying to remember the exact sequence of keys he'd just pressed. This was made more difficult by the fact that the children were scrapping again, this time over Amy's comic.

'Mi-ike, hel-lo!' said Satchell. 'Did you hear what I said?'

Walker looked at his friend beseechingly.

'Will you have a look at this, Satch? The screen keeps changing, or else seizing up . . . Hey, kids, that's enough!'

Walker surrendered his chair to Satchell, who studied the screen.

'Let's see. You pressed "Save", did you?'

Walker couldn't remember. Satchell tapped two keys simultaneously, then a third, before positioning the mouse and clicking. Two windows closed, revealing a third entitled 'Mike's Database'. It was the lost folder.

'Hey, what did you just do?' demanded Walker.

'Just did "Control, Alt, Delete". And then I clicked on "end task".'

Walker proffered a pencil.

'Write that down, will you?'

Satchell scribbled on a note pad next to the computer and then tapped again briefly on the keyboard. He sat back, the computer's hard disk whirred and a tiny spinning disk appeared on screen.

'What's it doing now?'

'Searching.'

Satchell stretched his arms and gave way to a yawn.

'If only it was as easy to search a wood. We've got bloody miles of it! I thought Pat might be a bit funny with me, this being her first case as SIO. Wondered if it'd be a problem working with someone of my high intellect and prowess!'

But Walker did not take Satchell's bait. He seemed perversely determined to avoid all discussion of the Mellor case. To take the most charitable view of this, he was too busy concentrating on the upcoming interview. His next remark, at least, bore that out.

'Do me a favour will you, Satch? Keep your nose to the ground for me. I've got to know who my competition is. The big interview's in only a couple of days. It's what I've always wanted—you know that, don't you? "Commander Walker". It's got a nice ring to it, eh?'

But Satchell had by now quit the chair and was on his way out.

'You'll make it,' he said. 'Because you deserve it. See you later and in the meantime, take it easy, *Commander.*'

*　　　*　　　*

Barbara Mackenzie was the Child Protection Officer assigned to accompany and assist any child witnesses in the case. She arrived at Binley Wood with the Mellors, father and daughter, while North was looking over the woodland footpath, from which the children had seen the ogre in the undergrowth. As North returned to the car park, Lisa West hurried across to meet her.

'Tara Mellor's here, but the parents of the other little girl say she's still in shock. Having nightmares, poor thing.'

North nodded. She didn't mind. She had wanted to take the two girls through this thing separately in any case. As she'd once heard on a CID training course, two witness statements of the same event are more than twice the worth of one. 'It's like a stereoscopic viewer,' the lecturer had explained. 'You put both pictures together and you suddenly get depth of field. *But only if there's no possibility of collusion.*'

Barbara Mackenzie brought Tara across to greet North, who had not met the child. She knew Barbara, though. Five or six years ago, before Walker and North had met, Barbara had been Walker's—what? 'Girlfriend' didn't quite fit the case because he'd not yet split with Lynn at that time. 'Mistress' was too formalized and settled for a man like Walker. In the clonking canteen jargon of Satchell and his chums, Barbara had been Walker's 'bit of spare'. North could not think of a better term.

'Tara, this is Pat,' said Barbara, presenting the child.

North smiled and bent forward, to be level with Tara's face.

31

'Hello, Tara.'

The child said nothing. She was looking nervously towards the entrance to the woods, from which North had just emerged.

'Now,' said North, 'we want you to walk the same route that you took with your Mummy. All right?'

Tara compressed her lips. There was a hint of a quiver in them. Barbara touched her arm.

'You know your Daddy and I are here, so you don't need to feel frightened in any way. If you do, you can just hold on to my hand. Look! Here's Henry.'

Doug Collins had appeared leading Henry. Tara ran to the dog and threw her arms around his neck.

'A word of warning,' murmured Barbara, turning North slightly aside. 'She's in denial. Won't admit that anything bad's happened to her mother. She keeps saying she's coming home. Thinks she's just lost.'

Tara had taken Henry's lead from Collins and was walking him around in circles. She did not seem distressed, now that she had to play a part.

'So has Mike got his divorce through yet?'

Barbara's murmured question had come out of nowhere.

'Yes, he has, as a matter of fact,' said North crisply, almost adding *not that it's any business of yours*.

'So, when's the wedding day?'

Barbara's voice had that bright, brittle edge to it, a sure sign of underlying anxiety. She was not a stupid woman. But she had once made a fool of herself over Mike Walker, and even now had not completely got over him.

'I'm sure Mike will let you know,' said North stiffly. 'Shall we start?'

Barbara took hold of Tara's hand and they set off towards the woods. North crossed to walk with Mellor.

'We went to talk to Mr Yates this afternoon,' she told him.

'Oh yes?'

'He was very upset about your wife's disappearance. They must have been very close.'

'Yes, they were. I mean, they *are*.'

'When Jane was abducted, you were at the school?'

'That's right. I was working.'

'So were you planning to meet Jane later?'

Mellor seemed surprised by the question.

'What?'

'For the concert?'

'Oh, I see. Yes. Yes, I was.'

They were on the woodland path by now. North was going to ask where Jane and James Mellor had intended to join up with each other that night, but she heard running footsteps behind and turned. It was Satchell. By the time the Detective Sergeant had caught up with her, Mellor had pressed on to walk with Tara and Barbara.

'Nice of you to show up,' commented North.

Satchell was breathing heavily.

'Sorry, just called in on the Governor. Wanted me to help him out with his computer.'

North bristled, tapping her breastbone emphatically.

'*I'm* the Governor on this case, Satch. And if I ask my team to be at a certain place at a certain time . . .'

33

Satchell nodded submissively.

'Sorry.'

To punish him, North whipped round and strode ahead to rejoin the group around Tara. Looking behind him, Satchell caught a mocking glance from Lisa West and answered with a defiantly raised eyebrow.

Up ahead, Tara had stopped. She turned to the others.

'Mummy threw the stick for Henry and he ran off into those bushes. He was gone for a bit, and he was barking, so Mummy went after him.'

Tara pointed in the direction of the big oak.

'Are you sure it was exactly there?' asked Barbara.

Tara nodded firmly.

'Yes.'

'And what happened next?'

'Henry was barking and barking. Then he ran out. He was going over that way. So I went to try and get him.'

She had started back along the path until she reached the lateral path which headed deep into the wood. The group followed Tara along it.

'And what did you see when you went to find Henry?' asked Barbara.

'This man was in the trees and got Mummy. She shouted at me to run away.'

Her voice was trembling violently now.

'So I ran back to the path that way, and Diana fell over.'

They followed the child back along the pathway, past the junction of the lateral path and towards the entrance to the woods, opposite the car park. Suddenly Tara broke away from them and began to

34

run, with Henry leaping in pursuit. She was crying. Barbara and the others hurried after her but Tara was already some way ahead, around a bend in the track. For a moment they lost sight of her. But they could hear her voice, and it was calling out heartbreakingly for her mother.

With mournful, echoing barks, Henry seemed to be doing the same.

CHAPTER FOUR

SATURDAY, 22 MARCH

There was mostly disappointing news to kick off the next day's work. Visitors to Binley Wood at the relevant time on Wednesday had been hard to find. Only the dog walker who passed Jane Mellor and the children on the path near the car park had come forward. But he had seen nothing.

On top of this, there were just four men on the Sexual Offenders' Register living within five miles of Binley Wood, and they were all clean-shaven. Never mind. They would have to be questioned anyway and North decided to pick them up in a coordinated, simultaneous operation. Jane Mellor's disappearance had featured that morning in the national press, having already been covered by yesterday's edition of the local weekly. She had no complaints about the coverage, which confined itself almost entirely to the facts provided by the Yard's Directorate of Public Affairs. The point was that she knew she was under scrutiny now and must shine in all that she did.

North herself interviewed the two SOR suspects whom she privately considered the most likely. The first of these was Jason Loctor, a man in his forties who had recently served time for having sex, at different times, with both of his teenage daughters. His file contained psychological reports suggesting he might pose a danger to other children, and Loctor was certainly an unsavoury character. Still, Doug Collins's remark, as he and North made their way to interview him, was hardly the most helpful.

'Gov, this has got to be our man. Takes after his Uncle Hannibal.'

But Loctor quickly ruled himself out. He was making bread at the time, he said. He was a master baker and had fifteen bakery workmates able to vouch for him.

David Ori was an even nastier piece of work. After a career as a teen rapist—two charges of rape had been proved against him, with further assault attempts on file—he'd served twelve years. Ori never admitted his guilt or showed remorse. He had started his bird maintaining he'd been stitched up, and finished it in the same state of mind. Under questioning he was sullen and uncooperative but he, too, claimed an alibi. Ori said he had been in the outpatient's department at the St Cross Hospital in Penge, having veruccas removed from his foot.

Meanwhile, Satchell had taken on the other two, less promising suspects. Norman Drayton proved a tiny, weasel-faced man in his thirties, wearing a leather jerkin and a permanently hangdog expression. Drayton had been prosecuted twice for having paedophile porn, and Satchell's snap assessment on seeing the man was that he was unfit

36

physically or psychologically to abduct Jane Mellor. Satchell was right. At the time of the victim's disappearance Drayton had been plying his trade on a street market six miles away, where he had a bookstall with a sideline in murky mags and dodgy videos. Hundreds of people must have seen him.

The last of the suspects was Robert Brickman. He provided every kind of contrast to Drayton. Brickman stood six foot four, with an added two inches of wild curly black hair on top, and the general physique of an all-in wrestler. He lived nearer to Binley Wood than the other three men but his form, like Drayton's, was unconvincing. He'd been picked up twice for shoplifting women's underwear and had been arrested, though not charged, on suspicion of indecently assaulting a sixteen-year-old girl. It wasn't what you might call indicative of a psychopath or a slasher and Satchell had sat down at the table opposite Brickman without much hope of a result. He was about to be very much surprised.

North was in the corridor, enjoying a break in her interview with the repulsive Ori. She had sent Collins down to the Incident Room to see if anyone had yet contacted the verucca doctor, to confirm or deny the man's alibi. When the DC returned, it was with some different, but very interesting, news.

'Gov! This just came in. The concert in Paris—Crispin Yates, right? Well, it was cancelled. Never happened at all.'

'Really?' said North. She was intrigued. She visualized Crispin Yates's face as he begged her to find Jane Mellor. Why wouldn't he have mentioned the cancellation? And what had he been doing instead of tickling the ivories in Paris?

'Well,' she added, 'we'll need to clarify that.'

'Oh yes!' said Collins eagerly. 'I'll do it. I fancy a trip on Eurostar.'

'You'll be lucky. I meant with Yates.'

At that moment Satchell emerged from his interview room. The smile on his face was a mixture of smugness and bewilderment. He strode quickly across to join North and Collins.

'Bob Brickman's just confessed,' he said, without preamble.

North swung round, taking a moment to grasp the import of this.

'*What?*'

'I'd not even got my bum on the seat and he says, "Listen, I know what this is about and I want you to know I done it".'

'Done what, exactly?'

'He says he killed her.'

North took a deep breath. A confession, already! It was too good to be true. Or, from the point of view of the Mellor family, too bad.

'So what does he say he did with the body?'

'I don't know. Haven't got that far yet. He's being booked on suspicion now.'

North thought for a moment, then nodded.

'OK,' she said. 'I'll be with you when I've finished with David Ori.'

'Why wait?' Satchell wanted to know. 'We got him, haven't we?'

'*No*, Satch!'

North was annoyed. It was Satchell's presumption that riled her. By taking two of the four suspects each, they'd both, if you like, put money in the fruit machine. Now Satchell was crowing like a man who'd got three plums. But he

38

was a highly experienced officer. He should know better than to take Brickman at face value, she thought.

'Remember, this is *front page* news. We could have every nutter from here to Watford confessing. So why don't you go and get me all the data we have on Brickman? I'll be with you when I'm done. Excuse me.'

North crossed to the interview room door, opened it crisply and stepped inside. The Detective Sergeant was aggrieved.

'I just tell her that we got a suspect that's confessed,' he complained to Collins. 'And she goes straight back in to interview that nonce Ori. He's obviously got nothing to do with it!'

Another five minutes in Ori's company and North found herself wishing his alibi would collapse and she could charge him with abduction, rape, murder, treason or any damn thing. But the story had checked out and Ori was released. It was time to have a look at Robert Brickman.

First, she went over his file with Satchell. The indecent assault on the teenager had been eleven years ago, an incident after a pub drinking session. According to the girl's statement he'd got her into his car and tried to force her to have sex but after a struggle she got away. The case didn't get to court for lack of evidence. But the more recent underwear incidents were in both cases prosecuted. As a woman, it was these offences more than the other that puzzled her.

'Why did he do that, Satch?' she asked. 'You're a bloke. What's with the ladies' lingerie? I don't see the point of it.'

Satchell shrugged.

'Don't ask me Gov. Not my scene . . .'

'But it's got to be kinky, right?'

'Oh yes. Or a present for his wife.'

'He's not married.'

Satchell snuffled.

'Well, his mother then.'

North gave him a pitying look.

'Well I grant you she's living with him, but she's sixty-something and an invalid. So what I want to know is, what turns a thirty-six-year-old feller with a fetish for underwear—he did it *twice* don't forget—into a killer?'

'But he's admitted it. Do we need to know more?'

'Yes, Satch,' said North firmly. 'We need to know everything. What about his family, his job?'

'His younger brother's quite a big noise in the building trade. Owns a sawmill up near Chadham. Seems Bob is kept by his family. He's a real loser. Unemployed and draws benefit.'

'Has he got a solicitor?'

'Yes, Edwin Shawlcross, the last of the walking dead. He's used him before.'

She turned the pages of the file slowly, trying to memorize the details.

'If you want my advice—' began Satchell.

'When I do, I will most certainly ask for it, thank you, Satch.'

She continued studying the file, making Satchell wait.

In the Interview Room North made the usual preliminary statement for the benefit of the recording equipment then took a searching look at Robert Brickman across the table. He was certainly huge, spilling over his chair in every direction, giant

40

shoulders fully revealed under the sleeveless, sweaty vest. His lawyer, the skinny and cadaverous Shawlcross, sat beside him. She was reminded of some end-of-the-pier comedy duo, with the poker-faced Shawlcross as the feed and Brickman the funny man.

'So, Mr Brickman,' she began. 'I understand you have something to tell me.'

Brickman indicated Satchell, who sat on North's left.

'I've already told *him*.'

'Well, now tell me.'

Brickman glanced at the lawyer who minutely inclined his head.

'I killed her, didn't I?' said Brickman. 'The woman in the woods.'

'How did you kill her, Mr Brickman?'

'I hit her over the head with a big piece of wood and then suffocated her.'

Brickman's words were matter-of-fact but his manner was edgy. Sitting at the table he bounced his right leg up and down on the ball of his foot, making the table vibrate.

'Where did you put the body?'

'I buried it in the woods.'

'Can you take us to the body?'

'Yes, if you want me to.' Brickman seemed almost eager at this point. 'I'll show you.'

North looked to Satchell, then informed the tape she was suspending the interview. She took the DS outside.

'I don't want to waste time, Satch. If there's a body to find let's go and find it.'

'Now, Gov? It's raining?'

'So get your wellies.'

Over the last twenty-four hours Walker had not had much time to dwell on his up-coming job interview. Richard and Amy were at their most quarrelsome and demanding. There was an hour's blessed relief while they watched cartoons on television but after that the bickering and complaining had redoubled. Now rain was sheeting down and there was no question of getting out to the park, or the zoo, as Walker had planned. He thought of promising them a film in the afternoon, but they'd been to the cinema the night before and good parents didn't take their children to two crap comedies—one about talking dogs and the other time-travelling robots—in less than twenty-four hours.

By lunchtime he was frazzled. Richard had pestered him to be allowed to use the PC to play a computer game he had with him. Amy wanted to go out and get a Disney video. Attempts to persuade them to do some of their school work had been met with flat refusal. Then a game of Monopoly had degenerated into fiasco. As a father, Walker felt an abject failure. As a potential Commander in the Metropolitan Police he desperately wanted more time on the computer. Some hope.

Before she'd left early that morning, North had opened the fridge and showed Walker the child-friendly food she'd picked up from the late-night supermarket on her way home. But Walker didn't feel up to cooking. So at twelve-thirty he went out to the High Street for cheeseburgers. When he

42

returned, Richard was seated in front of the computer screen, leaping around on his seat as he stabbed buttons on his father's keyboard. Blood-curdling noises were issuing from the computer's speaker system.

'What the hell's that?' he demanded, crossing to the kitchen area, which was separated from the main living room by a counter for eating snacks and breakfast. His arms were full of the bagged lunch.

'A game.'

'Where did you get it?'

'It's Eric's. He lent me the CD ROM.'

Walker began unpacking the food on to a serving dish.

'Shall I get out some plates, Dad?' asked Amy.

'Good girl,' he said and then, to Richard, 'You haven't been messing with Daddy's files have you?'

'I told him,' said Amy, with a stack of plates in her hands. 'I told him not to touch it till you got home.'

'Richard, I'll wring your neck if you've lost my files.'

Richard was absorbed in the game. His father said,

'Richard!'

'I never touched them,' yelled the boy. 'She's always telling tales.'

'I am NOT!' screamed Amy.

She tried to stamp her foot but ended by letting go of the plates. They dropped and shattered noisily on the floor.

Walker grimaced but forced his anger down.

'All right, all right. Look what's happened now. Just calm down the pair of you. Let's eat.'

'She did that on *purpose*,' crowed Richard.

But Amy stood looking down at the shards of china around her feet. To ward off her imminent tears, Walker fetched the burgers. He ruffled Amy's hair to show he didn't blame her.

'Just get the dustpan and brush, why don't you, Princess. Hey, I got cheeseburgers as per your request. We don't need plates for those anyway.'

Later, when they'd filled up with the junk food, Amy announced she wanted to wash her hair.

'There's a shower attachment on the bath,' Walker told her. 'Do it there.'

Amy ran up the flight of three stairs to the passage which led to the bedrooms and bathroom while Walker asked Richard to show him the game Eric had lent Richard. It was called 'Mutilation Highway'. Richard showed him how to select a victim and then choose from a series of options how to send him (or her) to a very bloody death.

'See, there's different options, Dad. Burn, shoot, decapitate, disembowel and hang.'

He selected 'Shoot' and Walker watched in dismay as the head of the figure on the screen was blown bloodily from his shoulders, with a mess of blood and brain tissue spattering across the wall behind him.

'Wow!' shouted Richard. 'Look at that Dad! Cool!'

'You're not playing that,' said Walker with icy calm. He lent across to the mouse and clicked on 'Quit': his week's computer study hadn't been entirely wasted. 'Eric lent you this, did he?'

'Yes. He's got lots like this. Nothing wrong with a bit of blood and guts, he says.'

'Has your Mum seen it?'

44

'No. You know Mum. She's not interested in computer games. She only does Internet stuff.'

'Right. Give me the disk.'

'Aw, Dad, come on. Let me play it.'

'No way, son. It's X-certificate as far as you're concerned. *And* its garbage.'

'But there's nothing to *do* here.'

'Can't you go and read a book? Daddy's got work he wants to do . . . Yes, Princess?'

Amy came into the sitting room wrapped in a towel, her hair dripping. She held the detached shower head.

'Dad, look, it just came off in my hand!'

Walker stood there with closed eyes. He exhaled slowly, fighting to stay calm. He crossed to the window. It was still raining powerfully and steadily.

'Well, look,' he said in despair. 'There's that film on at the Odeon, the one with Arnold Schwarzenegger that we nearly went to last night instead of the other one. How about we go to that this afternoon?'

*   *   *

The group searching Binley Wood, directed by the handcuffed Brickman, was not a happy one. Several officers from the Territorial Support Group, dressed in blue coveralls and rubber boots, had been brought in with spades and picks. Although normally deployed at big football matches and political demos, they were also called in to assist in missing-person searches. With them were three dog handlers with their bloodhounds, a breed which the police had recently readopted as their primary search dogs. With North, Satchell and Collins they had all tramped around the woods, churning up a lot of mud, rain-sodden and cold. Brickman, on the other hand, seemed peculiarly in his element. He kept saying,

'I'm sure it was over there . . . or here . . . or there, near that tree . . .'

But when they all got to the places he'd indicated, he'd find himself less sure.

'Mr Brickman, we've crossed this area already,' said North, trying to control her temper. She had not been able to find any boots to fit and her shoes were ruined. 'Please try to remember, did you go to the right or to the left from here?'

Brickman sighed theatrically, looking around, then pointing away to his right.

'Over that way, I'm sure of it. Keep on walking. I'll recognize it when I get there! I'm sure it was by the ponds.'

They reached the ponds, which lay towards the middle of the wood and were wired off. Attached to the mesh were notices warning of danger and forbidding fishing. Running along the top of the fence was a line of barbed wire. Two dog handlers brought their bloodhounds up to the wire and set them sniffing around.

'It was just here,' said Brickman. 'I know it. I know I'm right because look . . . you see this?'

He held up his hand to show a scratch on the lower edge of the palm.

'I cut myself on the barbed wire fence. You see the cut I got. This is where I did it. Just here.'

North motioned for the TSG men to dig where Brickman had indicated. The prisoner watched them for a few moments, then suddenly shook his head.

46

'No, hang about. You know what? I think I got it wrong. It was further along that way . . .'

He led the diggers along the fence for about ten yards and pointed to another patch of boggy ground.

'He's lying,' murmured North to Satchell. 'I know it. He's wasting our time. Let's get forensics to check that barbed wire and a medic to look at the cut on his hand. It looks too fresh if you ask me. Come on, lads. We're getting nowhere. We're going back!'

Forty-five minutes later, in the Incident Room, Satchell was strolling around enjoying a sandwich when he found North sodden, bedraggled and cross, standing by a radiator. She was shoeless, trying to dry and warm her feet.

'He's in interview room one,' the DS told her, his mouth full.

'He'd better have a bloody good reason for that wild goose chase he just led us on,' she remarked darkly.

Lisa West came up.

'You want me to find you some shoes?'

North shook her head

'No thanks. Let's just get on with it. Come on, Satch. Forget that. You can eat later.'

Satchell looked with regret at his uneaten portion of lunch and dropped it in a bin, then followed North towards the interview room. She was still in her stockinged feet.

'Now, Mr Brickman,' began North. 'We are going to go back to last Wednesday and go through your movements in detail. What time did you go to the woods?'

Brickman's mood was oddly cheerful. He smiled

47

wanly at Shawlcross.

'About four. I was taking pot shots at the squirrels. Not with a gun, nothing like that. I got a sling I made, never really get to hit 'em, but I like fooling around. You know, get a stone, fix it and *prang!*'

His mouth widened in a rueful smile.

'Usually miss, but sometimes I don't. *Prang!*'

'Tell me what happened when you got there,' North continued briskly.

Brickman scratched his head and, as he raised his arm, she took proper notice of the tattoo, just below his right shoulder. It looked like some kind of heraldic animal, with a rodent head. A squirrel, perhaps.

'Yeah, well, I wandered around, then I saw her and the two kids.'

He was agitating his leg again.

'Their dog ran towards me and she followed it.'

'Had you ever met Jane Mellor before that afternoon? Did you recognize her?'

Brickman was looking down at the table. He shook his head slowly.

'No.'

'Had you ever seen her in the woods before? Walking her dog perhaps?'

'No, I didn't know her before.'

'So why did you approach her?'

Brickman shrugged.

'I liked the way she looked.'

'And what did she look like to you?'

Brickman considered. He lowered his head into his hands and spoke in a muffled voice.

'She was very pretty. Blonde. She had this nice flowered blouse on, blue and pink.'

48

'What else was she wearing?'

'Dark jeans, boots.'

'What kind of boots?'

Brickman looked up and met North's steady gaze.

'You know, *boots*. Because it was muddy . . . I, er, didn't think about it, you know? It just happened.'

'What happened?'

'I wanted her, see? So I just sort of lunged at her and got hold of her like, you know.'

North fixed him with her steeliest look.

'No, I don't know, Mr Brickman. Can you explain a bit more? I mean, you say you lunged at her.'

With a sudden convulsive movement, Brickman reached across the table and grabbed at North's throat, trapping it for a moment between fingers and thumb. His hand was so huge they almost met at the nape of her neck and she rocked back in shock. The uniformed escort standing beside the door jerked into action but Satchell pre-empted him, leaping up and pushing Brickman backwards. The suspect yielded and withdrew his hand, almost delicately. He gave a brief, half-triumphant laugh.

North took a deep breath and touched the place where the bridge of his hand had briefly compressed her throat.

'Note for the tape,' she said, 'the suspect moved forward to grab me and was restrained.'

Brickman looked at Shawlcross, wide-eyed.

'She wanted me to explain. That's what I did. I got her by the throat, dragged her close to me. The girls ran off screaming. I put my hand over her mouth to stop her, but she was screaming. She kept on trying to scream, so I—'

He was studying the ends of his fingers, as if still relishing their contact with North's neck.

'I hit her over the head and she went limp. Like a doll, it was.'

'Then what did you do?'

'I wanted to play around with her for a bit, didn't I? So I tied her up.'

'What did you tie her up with?'

'A bit of rope.'

'Where did you get the rope from?'

'My pocket. I always carry bits and bobs with me.'

'Was Jane still alive after you hit her?'

Brickman smirked.

'*Jane?* Yeah, she was still warm. I took her home. Carried her there in a sack. She wasn't heavy.'

It was his matter-of-fact tone that made her suddenly want to grind his nose into the table.

'Where did you get the sack from?'

Brickman tapped the table.

'You're not listening. I told you, I had a sack with me, for the squirrels.'

'Why did you take her home?'

'So I could have sex with her in my barn.'

'Mr Brickman, weren't you worried that she could have been seen?'

'No. She couldn't. She was in the sack.'

'What happened when you got back to your barn?'

'I had sex with her.'

'Was she still unconscious?'

'Yeah, for some of it, but then she screamed so I stopped her.'

'How?'

'I stuffed something into her mouth, an old sock

I think.'

'Did you ejaculate inside her?'

His meaty face suddenly acquired a cunning look.

'Yeah. I used a condom, of course. I'm not stupid.'

'And what did you do with this condom?'

'Threw it away.'

'Where?'

'Some bin on the way back.'

'Way back to where?'

'The woods. Where I buried her.'

'Was she still alive?'

Brickman paused, thinking.

'Not sure.'

'You said earlier that you suffocated her.'

'Yeah I did, with a blanket from my barn.'

'So *was* she dead?'

'Yeah.'

'Why do you think you're having so much trouble remembering where you buried her?'

'Well it was dark. But it must be near where we were earlier because I cut myself lifting her over the barbed wire. I showed you. Got a handkerchief and wrapped it round it.'

'What were you wearing that night?'

'A pair of jeans and an old shirt.'

'What about shoes?'

'My wellies.' He leaned sideways and peered under the table at North's unshod feet. 'Like *you* should've worn.'

He looked around, taking in Satchell and the uniformed officer posted by the door.

'Are you getting all this down?' he asked self-importantly. 'It'll be evidence.'

North inclined her head and closed her eyes for a moment.

'Thank you, we are.'

Brickman looked to his solicitor, tapping his arm.

'Can we have a break now Mr Shawlcross? I'm tired. I want a cup of tea.'

CHAPTER FIVE

SUNDAY, 23 MARCH, MORNING

North passed the night in exhausted, dreamless sleep. She had come home late and the flat appeared like a war zone to her tired eyes. Walker was asleep on the sofa with a glass of Scotch resting on his chest, rising and falling with his breathing. She had clattered around in the kitchen, repairing the worst of the battle damage. He hadn't woken and she'd left him there. Later she was aware of him creeping into bed.

In the morning, as it was Sunday, she allowed herself a couple of hours' lie-in. Walker wasn't so lucky. The children were up at seven and ravenously hungry by eight, so North had woken to the sound of clattering pans and the smell of bacon. When North finally emerged from the bedroom, it was clear that kitchen hostilities had been resumed in a serious way. The area was a bomb-site.

'God, Mike! It took me ages to clean the kitchen last night.'

But Walker was back sitting at his PC, his brow corrugated with the effort to concentrate. He said, wearily,

'Now I can't get the files up. I don't know what he's done.'

He stretched his arms upwards and peered into the coffee mug on the desk by his elbow. It needed a refill.

'And I'm sick of cleaning up,' he went on. 'It's a waste of time. I've only got to cook again. They're always hungry.'

As he carried the mug into the kitchen, Richard protested his innocence.

'Anyway, I didn't bloody touch the files!'

Walker turned and pointed at his son.

'Hey! Don't speak to me like that! You were on it last night, and I couldn't get them back, and you were on it again this morning.'

'Well, there's nothing else to do.'

Amy had got hold of North's make-up bag and was experimenting with lipstick, rouge and eye-shadow. Now she took up her brother's theme, chanting,

'Bored-bored, bored-bored, bored-*bored*!'

Meanwhile, Richard was appealing to North.

'I didn't even go into Word. I was on the Net. I never went into his stupid files.'

With a sigh, North leaned over the computer and tapped the keys. In a moment she had accessed the errant files while, from the kitchen, Walker called out, banging the greasy saucepan into the sink.

'Do you want coffee, Pat?'

She retrieved her make-up from Amy, who had left the table and sashayed across to the television, switching on and filling the room with loud cartoon sound-effects, *Whizz! Crash! Slurp!* North grimaced.

'No, I'll get some breakfast in the canteen. I'll see you later.'

'It's Sunday,' said Amy. 'Are you working today?'

'Yes, I'm working on an important case, Amy. Mike! See you tonight. Bye, kids.'

Amy turned towards the door as it closed behind North, making a lipsticky *moue* of disapproval.

North was still sceptical about the Brickman confession. There was something too damn *eager* about it, which, in her experience, was the tone generally found in false confessions made by nutters. These usually fell into two categories: one, nutters who were under the impression that to be a murderer was glamorous, but who didn't have the nerve to commit one of their own; and two, nutters with some deep need for self-punishment, people who *believed* they were murderers even though they weren't. She thought about Brickman. He certainly didn't seem to know the whereabouts of the body he claimed to have buried. But if he was a lunatic, which kind was he? In the meantime she found herself in the slightly unusual position, for a police officer, of trying to disprove a suspect's confession to murder. One urgent step to take in this direction would be to show the children an identity parade. If they picked Robert Brickman, that would probably be enough to charge him, but there was no clear path ahead of her in any event. ID parades involving kids were always tricky to handle and often misleading.

The search of Brickman's barn, where he claimed to have taken his victim, would have begun early, long before she herself arrived for work. Forensic officers in blue overalls were at

54

this moment combing the building and its surroundings, with crime scene specialists taking photographs and bagging possible exhibits. Priority was to find proof that Jane Mellor had been there at all, dead or alive. Next came the uncovering of any evidence (such as the discarded condom and the squirrel sack) to support the details of Brickman's story.

The Incident Room was already busy with shrill phones and whirring photocopiers. She called the team together for a briefing.

'OK, everyone, can I have your attention? I've applied for an extension to hold Brickman since we're still looking for the body. But that doesn't mean we stop looking for other suspects. To be honest, I have my doubts about Brickman. Tara Mellor and her friend described a much shorter man of around five feet eight or nine. Brickman is six foot four. He also told us he'd cut his hand on barbed wire on the night. But the cut he showed us didn't look four days old and we have no blood from the wire.'

'But there are lots of things he did get right,' objected Satchell. 'He knew what she was wearing, where it happened, what time. We should charge him with abduction for now at least.'

North fixed him with a stony look.

'I'm afraid I don't agree. I'm just not happy with his evidence. So I've arranged for the Forensic Medical Examiner to take a look at the cut on his hand.'

'So are you saying we have the wrong man?' asked Collins.

'I'm saying we need to keep an open mind. We do not, as yet, have a body, OK?'

'But Dave's right,' chimed in Collins. 'He knows too much not to have been involved in some way.'

'Like covering for someone else,' added Satchell.

'Yes,' said North. 'Which is why I need to talk to Brickman's family. You want to say something, Satch?'

'I'd charge him, if I were you.'

'But you're not me are you?'

Satchell smiled uncomfortably. He leaned towards North and said, quietly,

'Come on, Pat. I know that this is your first time out but there's no need to go by the book all the time.'

North did not like the patronizing implication that a more experienced officer (like Michael Walker?) would certainly do it Satchell's way, but she chose to ignore it. Turning away from him, she spoke to the room at large.

'Has anyone talked to Crispin Yates yet about his concert being cancelled?'

No one answered. Collins, whose job it had been, reddened but North turned back to Satchell. Just for now she wanted to give him something to do out of her sight.

'Well, I suggest you get on it, Satch. And have you organized an ID parade with Tara Mellor and her friend?'

Satchell shook his head.

'Not yet. Both of the girls are still very upset and their parents don't want to put them through the ordeal when the guy's already admitted he's done it.'

North did not hide her annoyance.

'Oh, that's great!'

'Never mind,' said Satchell sweetly. 'Forensics

are over at Brickman's place now. If he did take Jane back to his barn they'll find something.'

She had to admit he was almost certainly right. On cases like this the finest forensic techniques were applied. If Jane Mellor had been at this barn, they'd surely know about it in a matter of hours.

She beckoned Lisa West to follow her into the SIO's glass-partitioned office.

'You're coming with me to see the Brickman place and talk to his family,' she said. 'I'm not saying our Robert has told a completely cock and bull story. But I reckon for everything he's said that's true, there's something else that is pure bull.'

'Or pure cock,' said West, dryly.

The barn was a free-standing structure of creosote-painted weather-boarding and a corrugated iron roof. It had once formed part of a substantial farm, whose other outbuildings had been given over to Brickman's Sawmill Ltd, an apparently thriving wholesale business. The air smelt of spicy timber resins mixed with machine oil and, here and there, a whiff of wood smoke from where sawdust and bark was being burned in an oil drum brazier. Hardwoods and softwoods lay in giant stacks around the yard, some of them protected from the elements by tarpaulin or corrugated iron, others left to the weather. To one side was a large shed, the sawmill itself, its floor thick with sawdust and woodchip between the big circular saws and planing machines. At the end was the barn. They made their way towards it.

The search had revealed some surprising items. There were a large number of lacy brassieres, suspender belts and thong knickers, as well as a cornucopia of pornographic magazines and videos.

They had also found a bed, sleeping bag and shaving materials. So the barn appeared to be Brickman's living-quarters, as well as what might be called his hobby-room.

'He could have opened his very own sex shop with all that porn,' remarked West as they left the white-suited searchers and made their way between wood stacks towards the former farmhouse—the home of Robert Brickman's mother and his brother Alan.

As they neared the house the back door opened and the figure of a man emerged. He acknowledged them with a wave and walked down the path towards them. North nudged her companion.

'See that, Lisa?' she murmured. 'Whoever it is, he's the exact description the two girls gave. He's even got the beard.'

'All right?' the man called out. 'I'm Alan Brickman, Bob's brother.'

He was a short, dark man in his early thirties, who looked like a scaled-down version of his older brother, except that Alan wore a full beard. He was at least ten inches shorter than Bob but had a similar mass of untidy curls crammed under his dirty baseball cap.

'Come back to the house,' he said. His manner was perfectly equable as he led them through a passage which gave on to a large, untidy kitchen dominated by a scrubbed pine table. A dog crept in behind them and lay in front of the old-style and now redundant cast-iron kitchen range.

'Mum's very distressed,' Brickman warned, as he shifted a few dirty plates from the table. 'I've had our local GP in with her. She's not slept all night and she's not very strong. Had a stroke a while back.'

'Is it just you and your mother who live in the house?' asked North.

Before he could answer, a series of loud chiming electric guitar chords came from upstairs. Brickman jerked his head towards the ceiling.

'And Donny.'

They heard a female voice, also upstairs, screeching for the music to stop. It didn't.

Exasperated, Brickman crossed to the foot of the stairs and shouted up.

'Donny! Stop playing that guitar NOW!'

The guitar music did not stop. With an exasperated click of his tongue Alan Brickman turned back to his visitors.

'I'm sorry about that. That's Donny playing.'

He pointed to a framed photograph on the wall. It showed a small, incredibly skinny waif in a voluminous T-shirt. He was holding a white electric guitar almost as big as himself.

'Picture was taken five years ago. I dunno how this is going to affect him. I haven't told him anything yet. He's a bit sensitive.'

The guitar music suddenly changed as Donny switched to fuzz, and played a series of rapid riffs. He was impressively good.

'Hey! Donny, stop it!' yelled Alan Brickman again. And again, his command had no effect.

Brickman picked up a used mug from the table and crossed to the sink. He rinsed it and filled it with water, which he drank thirstily.

'He's your son?' asked North.

Brickman shook his head.

'No, no. He's Bob's.'

'I see. And is Bob's wife in touch?'

'They were never actually married, you know? She sort of lived with him for a while, then upped and left. She let us have custody.'

North noted the 'us'. The Brickman family, she thought, were keen to show they all sang from the same hymn sheet.

There was a large mounted stag's head on the wall which Lisa West found fascinating, with its glassy stare and branching antlers.

North sat at the table but Brickman remained standing. His earlier easy manner had tightened up and he seemed nervous now that the questioning was about to begin. He did not join her at the table.

'Now,' began North, 'as you know, we are interviewing your brother in connection with the disappearance of Jane Mellor.'

Brickman was contemplating his dog, which lay apparently asleep on the floor. He nodded. North took a deep breath.

'Well, your brother has made a number of admissions. He says he abducted Mrs Mellor and brought her back to his barn, where he raped and then killed her.'

Brickman stared at her for a moment, then looked down at his feet. Suddenly he grabbed the peak of his cap, wrenched it from his head and hurled it into a corner of the room.

'Oh, Christ! I knew it was bad when they wouldn't release him last night. He called us here.'

'A few questions about yourself, if you don't mind, Mr Brickman . . . Were you at home last Wednesday afternoon?'

'Wednesday?'

He thought for a moment, scratching his neck.

'I usually pick Donny up from school about four—Bob don't drive, you see. I come home, had a cuppa with Mum, then went back to work until around seven. That's my usual routine.'

'Did you see your brother at all that day?'

'No. As far as I can remember I didn't. To be honest, I don't really see that much of him.'

'Why doesn't he live in the house here with you?'

'It's the way he wanted it. Bob don't work, right? He couldn't afford to get a flat, or look after Donny, so we came to an arrangement.'

'So he doesn't work? What does he do?'

Brickman shrugged.

'Just maintains the house and the garden. As you can see, he doesn't make that good a job of it. But he looks after Mum, well, he's around if she needs him.'

'Does your brother usually have a beard?'

The question brought Brickman up short.

'What? A *beard*? Er, yes, yes. He does, sometimes.'

'Did he have a beard the last time you saw him?'

Brickman took a step towards his dog and crouched to fondle its ears.

'Erm, yes. I think so.'

'You said Donny's mother lived here for a while. What was her name?'

'Sharon, Sharon Fearnley.'

It was odd the way he said the name, as if it were a foreign phrase whose meaning he didn't quite understand.

'Why did she leave?'

'Well she was a complete tart, a real tough woman that he insisted on bringing into the house. Mum had heart failure. She's as common as muck,

61

you know? We only put up with her because she was pregnant. Then, when she couldn't squeeze any more cash out of us, she ran off.'

Brickman stood up so suddenly that North thought she heard the crack of his knees.

'Oh God, I can't believe this is happening.'

North found it hard to read the undertone of this remark. Brickman spoke almost automatically, as if trotting out the expected thing. Or was it that he was dulled by shock and anxiety?

'How long ago was it when she ran off?'

'Well, er, Donny was five at the time so it must have been about 1998. I have no idea where she is now. We haven't heard from her since she left.'

Again he scratched his neck.

'I can't get this to sink in. He's my brother.'

The electric guitar music, which had continued more quietly, now burst into a series of loud, aggressive chords. North raised her voice to compensate.

'Have you ever met Jane Mellor?'

'Er, no. No, I haven't. Jesus, this noise!'

He strode quickly to the kitchen door.

'I'm sorry. I'll go and shut him up. He doesn't understand what's happened . . .'

At the door he swivelled to face them.

'And nor do I. I can't take it in.'

He went into the passage and peered up the stairs. North got up and the two women followed him.

'Mr Brickman,' said North. 'I'd like to speak to your mother now.'

Brickman was surprised, expecting to have more questions to answer.

'OK,' he said. 'She's upstairs. I'll take you up.'

62

At the top of the stairs, North located the guitar music coming from a bedroom halfway along the straight landing which faced them.

'She's just down there,' said Brickman, pointing down the landing. 'In the room at the end.'

The women left Brickman and walked along the landing towards Mrs Brickman's bedroom. As they passed the open door of the room where the guitar music was coming from, North glanced in. Donny was playing his guitar in front of a full-length mirror, a small, expressionless boy of ten or eleven. He could not have heard them, but he immediately sensed strangers passing his doorway and looked up, without ceasing to play. North smiled at him but his expression did not change as the chords pulsed and churned from his amplifier.

She continued along the passage to speak to old Mrs Brickman. There was no doubt about Donny's extraordinary virtuosity on the instrument, she thought. He played with dizzyingly rapid finger-work and expert timing. But he did not play with any love or lyricism. If it could be said to express anything, Donny Brickman's guitar music was all about anger and pain.

CHAPTER SIX

SUNDAY, 23 MARCH, AFTERNOON

Walker managed to get some more time on his computer during the morning, after allowing Richard and Amy to go down to the video library. Two feature-length cartoons would keep them happy for a good three hours, and meanwhile he was beginning to get the hang of things, feeling more adept and fluent on his keyboard, gaining in confidence by the minute. Then the phone rang. It was a man's voice and at first he didn't recognize it.

'Hello?' said the voice. 'Mike, hello. Listen, it's Eric, Eric Fowler, Lynn's friend.'

'Oh . . . yeah.'

'I need to speak to you about something. Have you got a minute?'

From the acoustic of his voice, it sounded like he was in a call-box.

'Go on.'

'It's just I wanted to explain it to you before she did because it wasn't right, I know that.'

What was he talking about?

'Eric? What are you talking about?'

'I'm distraught about what happened and I want to set the record straight, you understand?'

'What's happened?'

'We got into an argument and she started yelling at me and . . . I have never hit a woman before in my life. I swear to you, it just happened. May God forgive me. I'm so ashamed.'

'Where did this happen?'

'Here, on our holiday.'

'Where is Lynn now?'

'I don't know. She left me here but I want to make sure you know that it was nothing. I hardly touched her. I swear on my life.'

'Is she at home?'

'I don't know. I've been calling and calling. That's why I've rung you. I want to sort this out. I don't want you to think badly of me. I'm a good guy, I really care about her. I want *you* to know

64

that. I want you to approve of me.'

Walker closed his eyes.

'OK, Eric. I hear what you say. Now hang up and let me call her. Just hang *up*.'

Walker dialled Lynn's number but she did not reply. He walked through into the living area, collecting his coat as he did.

'Kids, I've got to go out. You all right watching that?'

They were. In fact, they didn't even reply. With a sigh he left them to their film and knocked on the door of the widowed Mrs Jeevons, his neighbour across the hall. She agreed to keep an eye on the children while he went to see if their mother was all right.

He found Lynn in a dressing gown. She'd showered and her hair was wet, but there was nothing she could do to wash away the nasty contusion around the right eye and swelling cheekbone which by morning would be blotched red and yellow. Now she was sitting at the kitchen table, snuffling and blowing her nose, while Walker made tea.

'We'd been walking all Saturday afternoon,' she explained. 'Until dark. God, he could walk! He was like someone in a race. I just couldn't keep up. Got a hell of a blister. Anyway it was all OK until this morning, really. We'd had quite a few laughs and lots of fun and, well, you know . . .'

'Just tell me about the shiner,' said Walker quickly, in case she was tempted to dwell on Eric's bedroom prowess.

'Well, actually, it was all my fault. I goaded him and he just went into a temper.'

She gave him a wan smile as he poured her a cup

65

of tea. He added two sugars, for the shock.

'He didn't mean to hit me. You see, I wanted to call you, to find out if the kids were all right and he said it wasn't necessary, just leave it. Well I said it *was*, you know the way I can get. He said it was our weekend and I was worrying too much to enjoy it. But I wasn't, Mike. I just wanted to make sure they were OK, that's all. So I went to a phone box and he followed. He was trying to get the receiver out of my hand when it happened. It was an accident. He didn't mean it.'

Walker shook his head.

'Why are you making excuses for him, Lynn?'

'I'm not. I just don't want you to jump to conclusions.'

But Walker felt it wasn't a very long leap to the obvious truth.

'Lynn, he obviously scared you enough for you to run off.'

Lynn made no reply, but simply looked blankly ahead of her. Walker sighed and let it go. He drained his cup of tea.

'You know, I didn't like him calling me at home. I think I'd better get back to the kids. I left them with the neighbour.'

Lynn pushed back her chair and stood up.

'Oh! I'll order you a cab then. Eric's got my car, else I could drive you.'

Walker frowned.

'He's got your car?'

'Yes, I caught a train back. It's all right, he'll return it.'

'You're not still going to see him are you?'

Lynn shook her head.

'No, of course not. Though I will have to see him

66

to get my car back. I'll need it because your mother's coming to stay for a few days.'

This information took Walker completely by surprise.

'*What?* She never told me. What's she coming for?'

'To see her grandchildren. I was going to ask you and Pat over for dinner.'

Walker frowned darkly. His mother and his lover had never liked each other.

'Hmm. Pat's pretty busy right now and so am I. You know I'm short-listed for Commander and—'

But Lynn had suddenly started to cry again. He came to her and wrapped his arms around her.

'Shh, Lynn. There's no need for this. You're all right. I'll make you another cup of tea.'

Lynn sniffed and said ruefully,

'I'd prefer a brandy.'

'OK,' said Walker, striding to the drinks cupboard with sudden alacrity. 'I'll join you.'

*   *   *

Old Mrs Brickman had little to say beyond 'Yes', 'No' and 'I don't know'. She was a weary old woman with a hoarse voice, who lay in bed wearing a shawl and chain-smoking cigarettes. She refused to speak about her son Bob's criminal convictions and appeared to know next to nothing about her family's movements during the previous week. After fifteen minutes, in which no new information whatsoever had been elicited, North gave up and decided to resume the interview with Alan Brickman.

Back on the ground floor she was surprised to

67

hear music coming from the sitting room that was very different to Donny's guitar playing. This was romantic piano music, a slow, meditative piece that North knew she knew, but couldn't put a name to. It was so beautifully performed that she expected to find a CD playing when she entered the room. Instead, she saw the pianist was Donny Brickman. Listening from a position near the fireplace was his uncle Alan.

Donny lifted his hands from the keyboard in mid-phrase.

'That's great, Donny,' said Brickman. 'I have to talk to the police ladies now. Why don't you go and watch TV?'

Donny did not move.

'So you play the piano too!' exclaimed North. She approached and squinted at the sheet music he'd been playing from. It was the 'Moonlight Sonata' by . . . She scanned the line below the title, just to make sure. Yes! She was right. Beethoven.

'Hello, Donny,' she went on. 'I'm Pat North and this is Lisa.'

Brickman cleared his throat in warning.

'You're not going to ask him about this are you?'

'No, don't worry,' North assured him. 'If we do need to talk to Donny he'll have a Child Protection Officer with him.'

Brickman waved his hand at Donny.

'Hey, Donny, go and watch TV!'

The young musician slid off the piano stool but, instead of leaving the room, slouched down in a chair in the corner of the room, staring at the three adults, each of them in turn. His uncle gave up trying to eject him as North resumed her questions.

'Does Donny have lessons?'

Alan Brickman nodded.

'He used to.'

'Who taught him?'

Uncle and nephew exchanged looks.

'Someone up at the local school,' said the uncle.

'Do you know the teacher's name?'

'I think it's a Mr Yates. Funny first name. *Crispin*, that's it! Crispin Yates.'

'Didn't Jane Mellor also teach Donny?'

She glanced at Donny. He was staring intently at his uncle, who was shaking his head.

'No, no, she didn't,' he said.

Donny suddenly jumped up and ran from the room. The adults watched him go out before North continued.

'Are you sure you have never met Jane Mellor? Jane Mellor is a close friend of Crispin Yates.'

But Alan Brickman was adamant.

'No,' he said firmly. 'I've never met her.'

Back in the Incident Room, North brought the team together for a further briefing. She gave them a summary of Alan Brickman's evidence, and of the Brickman family's unusual domestic set-up.

'I'd like a check on Alan Brickman's whereabouts on the day and night of the murder, OK? And, before you ask, he closely fits the description the girls gave of the attacker.'

Satchell wanted clarification.

'Gov, are you now saying they did it together?'

'Very possibly, Satch. How I see it is, we've got a good brother and we've got a very bad one. Either they did it together or the bad one's covering up for the good one. Bob Brickman is suspiciously keen to get himself arrested for this, and that makes me nervous.'

69

She looked around. No one wanted to challenge her theory.

'OK, what else have we got?'

'The FME says the cut on Brickman's hand is definitely not from barbed wire,' contributed Satchell. 'It was more likely done with a serrated edge. And you were right, it's relatively fresh—too fresh to have been done as long ago as Wednesday. So he's lying about that for sure.'

Collins raised his hand.

'Forensics found items of female underwear and an old pair of wellington boots at the barn, but no clothes matching the ones he claims to have worn on Wednesday. The boots are being tested to see if the mud matches samples taken from the Binley Wood.'

'And,' Satchell added, 'I tried to talk to Crispin Yates but James Mellor put me off. He said Crispin had a bad migraine and couldn't talk to anyone.'

North smiled tightly.

'Well then, we'll go back when he doesn't have one. And Lisa, check out whether James was at the school the day Jane disappeared, like he said he was.'

'Hang on,' interrupted Satchell. 'Are we also putting Mellor and Yates in the frame now?'

North spoke patiently and clearly, as if to someone marginally deaf.

'Yates taught Donny Brickman the piano and he also failed to mention that his concert in Paris was cancelled. I'm just saying there are links there that need to be checked out. And inconsistencies. So let's get on with it, please.'

She left them to return to her SIO's cubby-hole. Satchell looked around the faces of the team.

'How many more suspects does she need?' he asked.

Acting on Bob Brickman's admissions, Territorial Support Group were still combing Binley Wood for traces of Jane Mellor. Yet the prisoner had not been able to point out the location of the body. North now brought him back to the Interview Room, with his solicitor, for further clarification.

Bob sat where he had before, still nervously bouncing his right leg, while twisting a small piece of tissue paper in his fingers.

'We've been to the barn, Bob. Do you live there all the time?'

'Reckon I do.'

'Well, we have not been able to find the clothes you said you were wearing on the day of Jane Mellor's abduction.'

'That's because I got rid of them.'

'Where?'

'Burnt 'em.'

'Where did you burn them?'

'Had a bonfire in the woods.'

'What about the wellington boots? Did you burn them too?'

'Yeah, *and* they were brand new!'

He laughed mirthlessly as North looked down at her notes. She changed tack.

'Did Jane Mellor ever teach Donny the piano?'

Bob aimed a dark frown in her direction.

'No, I never seen her before, I *told* you.'

'What about Crispin Yates?'

For the first time his knee stopped juddering.

'Who?'

'Crispin Yates,' she repeated patiently. 'Don't

you recognize the name?'

'No.'

'You see, the reason I mention the name is that your son Donny takes music lessons from him.'

Bob shrugged evasively. He was rocking slightly, forward and backward, over the table.

'Maybe, I don't know. That side's taken care of by my brother. Al looks after him more than me.'

'Your brother seems to take care of everything in your family.'

'Yeah, that's right, he's a good man, my brother.'

'Your brother runs the family business, owns the house, provides for you and your son. You might even say that you owe your brother a lot, don't you?'

Bob sat there, carefully inspecting his hands. His leg was still bouncing.

'Mr Brickman?'

Bob's face creased, as if he was tasting sour milk.

'YES!' he almost shouted. 'I'd be in the shit without him, all right?'

'Was your brother at home that afternoon?'

'I don't know. And I don't like the way you are asking these questions about Al.'

He shaped a fist and thumped the table.

'*I* done it! I've admitted to what I have done. Now I'm not saying any more. I'm tired. You hear me? I'm tired.'

'Very well,' said North, looking at her watch. 'We'll take a break, Mr Brickman.'

In the corridor outside the Interview Room, North met Satchell.

'I want Brickman's sawmill searched. Not just the barn—all of it.'

'We've got everyone still searching the woods!'

72

Satchell spread his arms out wide. Surely she didn't want to spend a great wodge of the budget on a second TSG team.

'Split them into two teams.'

'But we—'

'Do it, Satch!'

North spun round and strode away, leaving a frustrated Satchell to get on with it.

*   *   *

All had been well at Walker's flat and, shortly after he arrived back, Lynn was on the phone to say Eric had returned her car.

'I'll come over and get them, shall I?'

At the last minute Walker decided to travel back to the house with Lynn and the children, in case Eric was lurking around in the dark. But there was no sign of him. After dropping the car keys through the letter slot and ringing the bell, Eric had apparently made himself scarce.

'Well, at least the bastard brought your car back,' said Walker to Lynn, standing at the front door. He had declined her invitation to come in for another brandy. 'Just make sure that's the last time you see him.'

Lynn nodded resolutely.

'It will be. It's over.'

He reached out to touch her temple, just beside the injured eye. The contusion had already started to colour up violently. Suddenly he had a memory of her when they'd first been introduced, sixteen years ago: such a pretty girl in her summery print dress.

'It's fine,' she said now, taking a step back and

73

into the hallway. 'I put some ice on it.'

Walker gave her a crinkled, sentimental smile.

'You'll call me if you need anything, won't you, sweetheart?'

He hadn't called her that for many a year. Lynn's cheeks dimpled, though it hurt to smile.

'I will, Mike. Just don't worry. We'll be fine. Your mother will be here tomorrow, so why don't I cook us all a nice casserole? Your favourite? Say about seven?'

'OK, you're on.'

Walker called through the door.

'Night kids. Be good!'

*   *   *

Eric enjoyed the feeling of exhilaration at the trick he had planned as he lay quietly in the boy's bed. He managed to lie there without a sound, without movement, completely concealed by the quilt, for a long time, for as long as it took. His face felt hot and itchy in the mask, the hideous latex goblin mask that he'd bought at a market stall some weeks ago. He'd known it would come in useful some day. Anyway, his discomfort would be worth it, just to see young Richard's face when the kid pulled back the bedclothes and found a nasty grinning goblin in his bed. How they would laugh afterwards, the two of them! It was so clever of him to make Lynn give him a key to the house, so he could come and go just as he pleased.

He heard Lynn at the front door getting rid of that shit-faced Jock policeman. Then there was clattering in the kitchen as she made the children something to eat. He thought he smelled toast and felt a pang of hunger. Never mind that. Playing the trick on Richard came first. Then he'd tell Lynn to cook him something. She was a good cook, though you couldn't say she was much use at anything else. Her walking stamina had been pathetic. She'd made squealing noises all through the business in bed, which revolted him. And the bitch couldn't even take a firm slap around the head. Never mind. She was certainly a gem in the kitchen, a proper little stock cube.

The door creaked and he tensed. Richard was coming into the room on his way to bed, closing the door, opening a cupboard, then a drawer. Soon, soon, he would cross the room and pull back the duvet . . .

When the moment came Richard's face, glimpsed through the eyeholes of the mask, was a perfect picture of shock and horror. He cried out, almost a scream, then choked back a second cry. So, just to scare the boy a little more, Eric let out a frightful cackle, said 'Boo!' and removed the mask. By now the boy was blatantly weeping.

'It's just Eric's little joke, Richard,' he'd whispered. 'Don't be such a fucking wimp.'

He was disappointed in Richard, really he was. Oh, well. He rolled out of bed and left the kid snivelling and pasty-faced. He headed for the landing and the stairs. Suddenly Eric felt utterly ravenous.

CHAPTER SEVEN

MONDAY, 24 MARCH

North spent most of the morning on the kind of paperwork which some SIOs use as an excuse never to leave their Incident Room: budgets, rosters, performance sheets, progress reports, resource allocations, staff assessments, equipment maintenance. After three hours, during which she'd shifted a large stack of paper, there came a tap on her door. It was Child Protection Officer Barbara Mackenzie.

'Hi there,' Mackenzie said. 'I've just come from seeing Donny Brickman. You want to look at the tape?'

North tried to forget that Mackenzie was in love with Walker, and had been for six years. She was a highly competent officer in her own right. They were women together, in a world still often run by men for men. There didn't have to be friendship, but there should be solidarity.

'Oh, yes please,' she said, pointing out the video monitor and player. 'Did you get much out of him?'

Mackenzie shook her head.

'Not a lot, but he certainly likes to play the guitar. If you ask me he almost talks through the thing. He's very monosyllabic. It's hard to keep his attention.'

'Has he any idea what's going on?'

'More than he did when you last saw him. He's been kept off school so he has to know something's up by now.'

She fished a standard VHS cassette from her shoulder bag and posted it into the slot of North's video player. She switched on the monitor and pressed 'Play'. The screen showed a clock counting down from thirty seconds to the beginning of the recording proper.

'OK,' Mackenzie went on in a businesslike tone. She drew up a chair and sat. 'We've got a bit of his Jimi Hendrix first. It takes a long while before he stops playing and agrees to talk. But eventually he does.'

North crossed to the door, closed it and perched on the edge of her desk to watch Mackenzie's interview with her prime suspect's ten-year-old son. Something told her Donny was one of the keys to the case, if only she knew which lock it was that he fitted.

The interview was in Donny's room, where North had met him yesterday. Donny was standing with the guitar slung on a strap from his neck. It looked at least three sizes too big for him. Mackenzie was sitting to one side and listening to the music, which was just as raucous as before. When Donny came to a stop she applauded, but her praise for his playing was drowned by an immediate resumption of jangling chords and rough fuzz-riffs. Mackenzie took the handset and pressed 'Fast Forward'.

The sound went off and the screen blurred as the figure of Donny began to dance like a puppet crazily jerking on it strings.

'How's Mike?' asked Mackenzie after a moment.

North's face showed no reaction. But she might have known Barbara Mackenzie wouldn't be able to leave the subject of Mike Walker alone for long.

'Fine,' she said, keeping her voice under control.

'I expect he's under a bit of pressure, you know, being up for Commander. Everyone's hoping he gets it.'

They watched the screen for another fifteen seconds before Mackenzie came back to the subject, like a dog to a bone.

'How are his kids?'

North again kept her voice level.

'Fine.'

She couldn't just keep saying 'Fine' so she added,

'They've been staying over a bit more, actually.'

Mackenzie smiled that sad, suffering smile of one disappointed in love.

'That's nice,' she said.

Another few seconds went by before Mackenzie again circled round to the subject that obsessed her.

'Do you know where you're going for your honeymoon then?'

God, thought North. This was torture.

'No. Not yet.'

After another period of silently staring at the screen, the business end of the video was reached at last.

'OK, here's where I really got started,' said Mackenzie. 'Watch what he does with the guitar.'

She pressed 'Play' on the handset. On screen, Mackenzie was showing Donny a photograph of Jane Mellor.

'Do you recognize this lady, Donny?' she asked.

Donny glanced at the photograph briefly and looked away. He played a rapid scale on the guitar, then stopped. The sound reverberated for several seconds.

'Yeah,' he said. 'That's Crispin's friend.'

'And who's Crispin?'

Donny played another scale, going on to do so before each one of his answers.

'My teacher.'

'And does Crispin come to your house to teach you?'

Donny shook his head.

'No. I go in school—after school.'

'So when did you meet Crispin's friend, Donny?'

'She was at the school sometimes when I had my lessons.'

'And who takes you there?'

'Uncle Alan did.'

'Did? Don't you go any more?'

'No.'

'Why not?'

Donny's fingers ran nimbly around the fretboard, this time playing rapid arpeggios.

'They had a fight.'

'Who?'

Mackenzie waited a moment, then prompted again, her voice raised above the arpeggios.

'Who had a fight, Donny?'

'Uncle Alan and Crispin.'

'Where did they have this fight? At school?'

'No. Here.'

'Was anyone else there when they had this fight?'

Donny did not reply. He was looking at the guitar strings, merely strumming rhythmically now. Mackenzie showed him the picture of Jane once again.

'Was Crispin's friend there? Look at the

photograph, Donny. Was this lady with your uncle when they had their fight?'

But Donny would not look at the photograph. His mouth clamped shut as he once more started to strike loud, menacing chords. The sheer power and authority that this weedy child could command with a guitar in his hands was incredible.

'Stop playing, please, Donny,' begged Mackenzie. 'Answer the question.'

But Donny was back in his own private world. His arms began to windmill, rising above his shoulder before descending on the strings to strike a series of furious, discordant sounds.

'Donny . . . Donny! Stop playing. Look at the photograph. Donny!'

But Mackenzie was helpless now, as Donny completely shut himself off from her. He sounded half a dozen more ear-shattering clusters of notes and then, as the last of them reverberated, he slipped the guitar strap from his shoulder, reversed the instrument until he was holding it axe-wise, and heaved it in an arc so that it struck the floor with force. The strings jangled on impact. Donny's face was distorted in a grimace of fury and disgust. He raised the instrument above his head once more and Mackenzie took avoiding action, half-jumping, half-sliding sideways off her chair. The tape's sound-track recorded a splintering sound as the joint between body of the guitar and the arm cracked on impact.

Mackenzie fingered the 'Pause' button on the handset and the mayhem on screen froze.

'He eventually stopped smashing his guitar, but he still wouldn't talk. I couldn't get another word out of him. Plus . . .'

She raised her foot, displaying an Elastoplast on the ankle.

'He caught me a hell of a whack. I think he knows a lot more than he's saying.'

'Let me see it all again.'

North nodded at the monitor, then added hurriedly,

'The part where he talks, I mean.'

The suspicion that Donny was concealing material evidence strengthened North's feeling of the boy being the key to the case, but it got her no nearer to knowing why. At the same time she had learned one important new fact: Alan Brickman and Crispin Yates had had a row. As soon as Mackenzie had gone, mercifully without mentioning Walker again, she had collected Lisa West and set off to speak once more to the handsome musician. The young man might look like a Greek god, but he was stingy with the truth. She meant to find out why.

They drove to Mellor's place and found Yates at home. Mellor was somewhere about but North said it didn't matter. She only wanted to speak with Yates.

'I have just a few follow-up questions for you. I hope you don't mind?'

Yates did not greet the officers with a smile of welcome, but there was also no hostility.

'If it helps find Jane, of course I don't mind.'

Yates was certainly edgy, though no longer either angry or distraught, as when they'd last seen him. North plunged straight into the deep end of her concern.

'We know your concert in Paris was cancelled. Why didn't you tell us about this when we talked to

81

you before?'

Yates was momentarily wrong-footed. He took a step back, stammering.

'I-I-I don't know. I guess I didn't think it was important.'

He led them through the hall and into the kitchen, a light, brightly painted room with stainless steel fittings and a good deal of ethnic pottery.

'I *was* still in Paris at the time I said I was. Surely it doesn't make any difference to you what I was doing there?'

North watched Yates as he pottered about, filling the kettle and removing a mug from the dishwasher. She could see his point on this, though it didn't show Yates as much of a brain. A more intelligent witness would have realized the police must check on his story. North sat down at the table and changed her line of questioning.

'Now, I understand you taught a Donny Brickman?'

Yates took a moment to register this new interest of North's. Either he'd not been expecting it or he was a great actor.

'Yes, Donny Brickman, I did. What's that got to do with Jane?'

North did not explain.

'Why did you stop teaching him?'

'You'll have to ask his uncle that. Why are you asking me about Donny?

Again, North decided against a detour into explanations.

'Donny tells us you had a fight with his uncle, Alan Brickman. What was it about?'

Yates frowned, still apparently baffled by

mention of the Brickmans. He spooned instant coffee into his mug while the kettle approached boiling point.

'OK, I'll tell you about Donny. He is *incredibly* talented, easily good enough to get a scholarship to a really good music school, provided he puts in the work. But I felt it would be better for him to live away from home for a bit and concentrate on that. Why have you been speaking to Donny? What about?'

Still North ignored his questions and pressed on with her own.

'Did Jane ever meet either of the Brickman brothers?'

Yates nodded his head as he poured water into the coffee. He did not offer a mug to the police officers.

'Erm . . . yes, yes, she did. I took Jane with me to talk to the uncle, Alan Brickman, because she's on the board of the music school I wanted Donny to apply for. She knows a bit more about it than me.'

Suddenly struck by a thought, he swung round to face North.

'Oh my God! He's not involved with Jane's disappearance? Is that what you're saying?'

He almost ran to the door and called out, with a note of hysteria in his voice.

'James! James! Come in here.'

He hung by the door as they heard James Mellor's feet on the stairs.

'What is it?' Mellor asked, coming into the kitchen where he acknowledged North's presence with a nod.

'They're asking me about that time I went to Brickman's place.'

Mellor seemed as surprised about this as Yates had been.

'The Brickmans? Why do you want to know about that?'

Yates hammered his breastbone with a fist.

'I'm the one who took her there!'

North briefly touched James Mellor's shoulder.

'I'm sorry Mr Mellor, but we do need to speak to Mr Yates alone. So if you don't mind . . .'

Mellor hesitated, contemplating defiance. Instead he turned to Yates and grasped his upper arm in a comforting grip.

'I'll be here when you're done, Crispin. Everything's going to be OK.'

When he'd left the room, North continued.

'So you and Jane both went to the Brickmans' house?'

Yates returned to the counter and picked up his mug.

'Yes, just the once. Some weeks ago.'

'And how did Alan react to your suggestion about the scholarship?'

Yates held his mug of untasted coffee and stared intently at the wall, as if trying to visualize the answer to the question.

'Mr Yates?' North prompted.

'He refused to even listen. I tried to explain what a chance it would be for Donny. He became very angry and then when Jane tried to explain to him that she felt it would be beneficial for Donny to be removed from the pressures at home he went crazy.'

'Please, go on.'

'Well, he hurled abuse at us, then he head-butted me in the face. Jane tried to get him off me

84

and he grabbed her by the hair. She shouted at him, she shouted she'd call the Social Services. It was horrible. Worse, because Donny was actually there. Brickman was like a mad man.'

'Just let me be sure, Mr Yates,' said North in measured tones. 'This was *Alan* Brickman who attacked you and Jane, not his brother? Not Bob Brickman?'

'Yes. Alan. The two of them are both nuts, of course. Why do you think we wanted to get Donny away from there? It's tragic, because the boy is so talented, but his environment . . . He's pulled in two by it. His dad says only guitar, his uncle says only piano . . . The result is Donny smashes up the music room.'

'I'm sorry?'

'We left him alone in the music room at the school once and he just went crazy. He started smashing up every instrument in sight. His so-called family has turned him into this confused, monosyllabic animal instead of a fine musician.'

'Did you report this incident to the Social Services?'

Yates shook his head.

'No. The school kept it all quiet. Alan paid for the damage and made a huge donation to the school fund. But please, what has this got to do with Jane?'

Yates pulled himself up. Suddenly he saw, as if in a revelation.

'Oh my God,' he said, almost whispering to himself. 'It's Alan. It's Alan Brickman!'

He could see all the implications, all the possible conclusions.

'He did it, didn't he? Oh my God!'

Yates was deeply agitated and North felt unwilling to push the man further, as his distress seemed so utterly genuine. And he'd probably already contributed as much as he could at this stage. She signalled to West with a motion of the hand and stood up, ready to leave.

'We don't know that, Mr Yates. Thank you for your time today. There may be one or two other matters but why don't we leave those for another time?'

*   *   *

Bob Brickman was back in the woods, handcuffed to Collins. He was in manic mood, pulling the Detective Constable around like an over-excited dog on a lead, as he charged through undergrowth and across clearings. They were nowhere near the ponds now, and much closer to the spot where Jane Mellor had last been seen.

'Mr Brickman,' said Collins, panting. 'Why have you brought us here? We've asked you to show us where you put Jane's body, not where you abducted her.'

'Right, and I am doing. It's just over there.'

He set off again, yanking Collins after him.

'Oi!' shouted Collins. 'Don't do that!'

Satchell was half running beside them.

'But you said that you buried her near the pond,' he said. 'Are you saying now that you brought her back here?'

'It was further up,' insisted Brickman. 'Behind the bush. Look, I'll show you.'

Sharply, he jerked the handcuffs again. Both men's wrists were raw from the chafing of the cuffs,

86

though Brickman didn't seem to mind half as much as Collins, who roared,

'I bloody well warned you! Leave off!'

'Show us where you left her body, Mr Brickman,' said Satchell. 'We're getting sick of your games.'

Brickman suddenly veered off towards a different clump of bushes, inevitably pulling his minder with him. But Collins resisted, using all his strength to pull Brickman up again.

'I've had enough of this,' said the Detective Constable to Satchell. 'Look at my wrist.'

Satchell looked, then rolled his eyes towards the sky, still heavy with leaden rain-clouds, and let out an exaggerated sigh.

'Fine, give him to me,' he said.

He released Collins's wrist and attached the cuff to his own. Then he raised his hand to show Brickman who he was now cuffed to.

'Right, chum, try any funny business with me and I'll bloody deck you.'

Collins and the others exchanged grins behind Satchell's back. The Detective Sergeant was probably ten inches shorter and ten stone lighter than Brickman.

The prisoner surged forward again, dragging Satchell through a patch of brambles and then across a depression in the ground.

'This looks familiar,' he said.

He stepped back for a moment into the depression leaving Satchell above him. Satchell swivelled, wondering what bloody caper Brickman was up to now. Meanwhile Collins, who had skirted the brambles and was approaching from another direction, saw something else.

'Satch,' he called out, waving his arms. 'Wait

there! Look at the height difference!'

Then Satchell saw it too. He and Bob Brickman were at eye-level for the first time since he'd put on the cuffs. And from Collins's point of view, with bracken obscuring the unevenness of the terrain and the position of their feet, they might have been two men of exactly the same height.

*   *   *

'Mmm! Beautiful,' exclaimed Walker, lifting the lid of the casserole simmering on Lynn's hob. 'Smells just perfect.'

He turned back dutifully to his mother, who was more interested in talking than in listening to him. This was how it had always been between the two of them.

'I got the train,' Violet Walker was saying. 'I think it would have been quicker to walk. Took twice the time it should. There was no restaurant car and it was freezing cold.'

She pointed to one of the bottles of wine that he'd brought with him. They were standing on the counter.

'Open the wine, then,' she said. 'I've got something to celebrate.'

Walker stopped in mid-movement. *What* did she say? His Ma with something to celebrate? His Ma, who suffered Christmas like an illness, and defined birthdays as the stepping-stones of death?

'You have? And what would that be? Don't tell me, you've won the Lottery and you're splitting it with me and I can retire?'

Walker opened a drawer and rummaged for a corkscrew.

'No, Michael. Jimmy's coming home, at the end of the week.'

As he heard the name 'Jimmy', Walker's fingers had just closed around the corkscrew. They froze in place. His whole body felt chill. Oh no! Not Jimmy, in London. Not after all this time.

'All right,' he said wearily. 'What's he done now? Come on, tell me Ma. Did they throw him out of New Zealand or what?'

Violet wagged a finger at him.

'Don't start. Your brother's got a big job in Florida, and he's rearranged his journey to come through London so he can see me.'

Walker slapped his forehead in a parody of self-punishment.

'I knew it. I knew there was something behind you coming down to London. Oh my God. Jimmy!'

Violet was indignant.

'It's been ten years and I'd like to see him before I die.'

'Ma!'

'And I'd like it even more if you two made up.'

Walker picked up the bottle and began savagely to drive the screw into the cork.

'There's nothing to make up, Ma. You know the way I feel about him—he's no good, he never was and ten years without him has been ten years without aggravation. If he puts one foot over my doorstep, I guarantee he'll cause trouble big time.'

'Och, why don't you give him the benefit of the doubt? He's been a good lad. He's even written to me every few months.'

Savagely, Walker yanked the cork from the bottle.

'And how much did he tap you for when he did?

89

Ma you can't make me see him. He's bad news and if he hadn't taken that plane ticket—that *I* paid for—he'd be behind bars right now.'

Walker carried the bottle through to the sitting room where he found three stem glasses waiting on the low table. He poured.

'Where's Lynn?'

'Putting the kids to bed. She's a wonderful mother.'

'Hey!' warned Walker. 'Don't start! She's not my wife any more and she's got this house all to herself, which is bankrupting me.'

'So when are you getting married to Pat then?'

'When we've got a second to arrange it. She's in the middle of a big case and I'm up for Commander.'

He proffered a glass of wine.

'I'm going be top of the tree!'

Utterly ignoring his offer of a drink, Violet sniffed and set off towards the door.

'So you should be big enough to see your brother!'

And she started climbing the stairs to say good night to her grandchildren. She was always one to have the last word.

CHAPTER EIGHT

MONDAY, 24 MARCH, EVENING

'She's a wonderful mother,' Violet Walker had said. Walker himself wouldn't for a moment disagree— Lynn had hardly put a foot wrong with the kids. It was Violet's none-too-subtle criticism of his own performance that made him smart. What kind of father is too busy to be at birthday parties and school concerts? Too busy even for the simple things like taking his children to a match or the park on Saturdays? But even these were minor issues compared with the big questions. What kind of a father abandons his home, his wife and his children? What kind of a father shacks up with another woman?

Walker knew full well what kind of father. His own father's kind, Harry Walker's kind, who had upped and left when his son Michael was ten. It hurt him deeply to know that his own mother sided with Lynn over the breakdown of their marriage, but he understood why. Violet knew what it was to be left, and the wound was still as raw thirty years later as it had been on the morning she'd found Harry's note weighted down by a toast-rack on the kitchen table.

It didn't have to be that way. Men left home and still managed to be good fathers. And anyway there was no such thing as a perfect father. That type of perfection didn't exist. So what place did he have in the general scale of fatherhood? He thought about this as he climbed the stairs to kiss Amy and Richard good night. He may be good and he may be bad, but he didn't think he was indifferent. He loved his children so much it made him cry, sometimes, and he cried over nothing else. But was it enough?

Amy, his Princess, was asleep. As he looked down fondly on her, the head half-buried in the pillow, surrounded by fine-spun hair, his eyes prickled. He leaned over, kissed her on the

91

forehead, hiked up the quilt and went through to Richard's room. His son was sitting by the Scalextric circuit, which Walker had got for him the previous Christmas. Walker sat down beside his son on the floor and for a while they watched the cars hurtling round in what seemed to him companionable silence.

The news that his brother was about to arrive in London made him think of the bond between Amy and Richard. On the whole it was a good bond and he didn't want it broken, the way his own relationship with Jimmy had fallen apart which, as far as Walker was concerned, had come about exclusively because of Jimmy's selfishness and disregard for decency. And because of their mother's obvious favouritism. As a father, Walker didn't want to have to take sides over his kids. He couldn't bear the thought of having to choose between them as his mother had chosen to cherish only Jimmy, her baby, despite his appalling behaviour year after year. No, Walker resolved, this would never happen between Richard, Amy and him.

Walker jerked out of this reverie, which the circling cars had induced. He struggled to his feet stiffly.

'Time you were in bed, son,' he said. 'Just a few more laps and then lights out.'

But Richard looked up at him in obvious alarm.

'No, Dad,' he said. 'Don't put the lights out. I don't want the lights out.'

Walker was puzzled. What was this? Was Richard afraid of the dark? He couldn't remember, but then there were lots of things about the children he couldn't remember, as Lynn so scathingly pointed out from time to time.

'All right, no lights out,' he said. 'Hey, are you feeling OK, Richard?'

The boy said nothing. He had turned back to the race-track.

'Nothing wrong at school is there? You'd tell me if something was up? If there was anything worrying you?'

'But you're not here any more,' mumbled his son.

Walker squatted down on his haunches.

'That doesn't mean I'm not around for you. If you ever need me, all you have to do is ask Mummy to call me. Better still, you can call me yourself. Richard? You've got Daddy's phone number, haven't you?'

Richard nodded, without removing his gaze from the cars. Walker ruffled his son's hair and stood up.

'I've got to go talk to Mummy now. I'll come in and see you before I leave, OK?'

With a nagging sense of his own inadequacy, Walker quietly let himself out. Whatever was bugging Richard, he hadn't been able to tell his Dad about it. But perhaps if Walker *was* here all the time, he would have . . . Walker sighed and went quickly down the stairs.

Richard had switched the cars off and was standing nervously by his bed. He was trying to pluck up the courage to pull back the bedclothes when he heard the long, whining creak of his bedroom door. He stood there, not daring to look round. But it was only Amy.

'I was asleep but Dad woke me when he came in to say good night,' she whispered. 'Did you tell him about Eric?'

Richard shook his head.

Amy came forward and touched him consolingly on the arm.

'Don't worry, Richard. Eric's not coming back. Mummy promised. She's got the key she gave him.'

'Yes, but Eric took my keys.' Richard's voice was squeaky with fear. 'The ones with the monster on the key-ring. And it's got the key of Dad's flat on it too. Dad'll kill me if he finds out.'

'Don't cry, Richard! Eric's not coming back.'

But now there was uncertainty in Amy's voice, too.

*   *   *

When it was dark, Donny crept into his Dad's barn, like he used to when Bob was there. It was where the two of them played, swapping guitar phrases and trying to outwit each other, as if they were on opposite sides of a tennis net. Battling banjoes, Bob called it, although Donny didn't know why. He'd never even picked up a banjo.

The barn still showed the signs of the TSG's intensive search. All potential evidence had been spirited away. Samples had been cut from every piece of fabric. The bed linen was gone, with the mattress, so that only the bare bed-frame remained. The big old wardrobe in which Bob had kept his guitar, his porn magazines and most of his clothes, including the unusual collection of lingerie, stood with its door hanging open.

The clothes and pornography had gone. But the guitar, amp and speakers were still there, stacked on the floor of the wardrobe. Donny pulled them out and plugged them up. He performed a quick sound-check and found everything OK. Then he pulled a mobile phone from his pocket, placing it carefully on top of one of the speakers. Then he sat down on the edge of the stripped bed and began to play, a slow, quiet, moody and wandering improvisation which ran on seamlessly and endlessly. He did not stop until he heard the telephone's ringing tone, half an hour later. He picked up the phone. It was his father.

'Hi, Dad.'

'You in the barn, Donny?'

'Yes, Dad.'

'You set up the amp and speakers?'

'Yes.'

'OK, just play me something, son. I got no guitar here so I can't play to you. I just want to hear you play.'

And Donny played. It was different from the dreamy stuff he'd been doing before. That was a kind of musical doodling. This was performance. It was loud and raucous. It was rock music: Black Sabbath, Led Zeppelin, Meatloaf, all his Dad's favourites, specially served up in a kind of medley. From time to time Bob interrupted him, suggesting ways to improve his use of the fretboard. Other times, he could hear his father yelling down the phone

'Good, good, yeah! Go, Donny! That's rock 'n' roll, baby. Fantastic!'

*   *   *

Eric held his breath as Shitface stood on the doorstep and kissed Lynn on the cheek. From his observation post, behind the hedge of an empty property almost opposite Lynn Walker's home, he watched as the copper said good night and walked smartly through the gate and away down the road. Eric eased the breath from his lungs.

Now, who was in the house? Lynn, of course; the kids, who'd be no trouble because of course they were crazy about him; and the crabbed old grandma who'd arrived during the afternoon. Granny was an unknown quantity but he didn't think she'd be difficult to deal with, given reasonable exposure to Eric's famous charm and forceful good looks.

He glanced at his watch. There was no time like the present. He felt in the pockets of his zipper jacket, his fingers sifting the assorted detritus that always accumulated there. Finally, they closed on the object he sought, and he drew it out: the set of keys, attached to a fob in the shape of a monster's head, which he'd borrowed from Richard. With extreme care, not wanting the keys to jingle in any way, he selected the one which he knew to be that of Lynn's front door. Then, mindful not to crunch gravel or break a twig, he emerged from his hiding place and purposefully, silently, crossed the road.

He inserted the key in the lock, turned it, released the catch, pushed. The door gave and he eased it open a crack, listening intently. He could hear the sound of the television leaking into the hall from the sitting room, through the closed door. Gales of laughter and a male voice cracking jokes. He gently pushed the door, meaning to step smartly inside and click the door shut before anybody knew he was there. He loved to surprise.

But the door had opened no more than three

inches before it crunched gently against the safety chain, which Lynn must have slid into place after waving Shitface Walker away. Under his breath, Eric cursed. He inserted his left hand and pulled the door painfully on to his wrist hoping vainly to get enough slack to enable him to unhook the chain. But he soon gave up. Silently, Eric withdrew his hand, re-closed the door and retreated down the path.

Walking away along the pavement, he looked again at the bunch of keys Richard had 'lent' him. A couple of them had nothing to do with Lynn Walker's house. They weren't keys either to its front door or its back. They weren't Richard's bicycle keys or the keys of his money-box. Eric rubbed his chin. He wasn't a fool. He knew what they must be the keys to.

CHAPTER NINE

TUESDAY, 25 MARCH, DAY

'So you're feeling positive about the job interview?'

It was seven-fifteen, and Walker and North were getting dressed. She sat at the dressing table, deciding whether to wear the plain silver chain with the St Christopher, the blue beads, or both. He was about to start shaving but at the moment was walking around in his vest, with a towel draped over his shoulder. This was a habit of his that had only lately begun to get on her nerves. It was what men did at campsites, she thought, walking to the communal showers. Where was the need for it in

97

your own home?

'More than positive,' he said. 'I'm getting this computer jargon under my belt. They're going to ask me about IT, I'm certain.'

He tapped his nose to indicate he was second-guessing with instinctive skill.

'I'm ready for anything they fire at me.'

He entered the bathroom and began running hot water into the basin.

'And another thing, the rest of the applicants haven't got my twenty-five years experience behind them. Some of them are just out of training school.'

North followed Walker into the bathroom and opened the wall-mounted cabinet. The cabinet's doors were faced with mirrors and Walker needed them for his shave. He waited patiently while she pulled out one item of make-up after another.

'I want this job, Pat. I never thought I would, you know, but now . . . well, it makes everything I've been through worthwhile.'

He looked at her as she balanced the claims of one lipstick against another and felt a sudden twinge of tenderness.

'Anyway, that's enough about me. How's the case going, sweetheart?'

North shut the door of the cabinet and wiped a small hole in the now steamed-up mirror. Walker's face appeared, with its crinkle-cut smile. She met it with a quick smile of her own.

'Slowly,' she said. 'I've got two dysfunctional families, one more so than the other.'

Walker soaped his cheeks and chin and picked up his safety razor.

'This day and age, hey? What family isn't fucked up?'

With the first sweep of his razor, he frowned. With the second, pressing deeper, he cut himself. A thin trickle of blood ran into the white lather on his cheek, staining it with a pink blot.

'Shit, this razor's blunt. Have you been shaving your legs with it?'

North was indignant.

'No, certainly not! I've got my own.'

Walker ejected the offending blade, tossed it into the bin and fitted another. There was a silence between them.

'What's bothering you?' asked Walker. 'You worried about the case? Bloke's confessed hasn't he?'

'Yes, but . . . It's just that I'd feel a whole lot better if we could find a body.'

Walker ploughed a furrow in the lather on his cheek.

'You want some advice from an almost Commander?' he asked. 'Arrest the bastard now!'

North's car was parked in the driveway outside their block. At eight-fifteen she bleeped it open, tossed her briefcase inside and settled behind the wheel. Then she ignited the engine and drove sharply down to the road, where she signalled right, saw there were no vehicles coming, and accelerated.

'Oh my God!' she gasped.

A shadow, resolving itself into the more solid shape of a human body, seemed to launch itself at her car bonnet. It hit with a loud, dull thump, sliding up and reaching as high as her windscreen before sliding away. She jammed on the brakes and, disentangling herself from the seatbelt, climbed out. A balding man of about forty, in a beige zipper jacket, was picking himself up from the pavement.

'Oh! I'm sorry,' she said. 'Are you all right?'

The stranger was smiling as he dusted down his jacket.

'No harm done,' said Eric, leaning towards her. 'Just an accident. My fault.'

His voice was confiding, familiar, though she was certain she'd never seen him before. She flicked out a smile.

'Well, as long as you're sure . . .'

North checked that the bonnet wasn't dented, returned to the driver's seat and drove away to work. Eric stood and watched her go, his face a smiling mask turning to a scowl. He spat out a single word in her wake.

'Bitch!'

Eric had slept on the Common. Eric had not washed or shaved, and had not breakfasted. But now Eric intended to do all three. He waited at various points up and down the road, without staying anywhere long enough to attract notice, and half an hour later he was rewarded by the sight of Walker leaving the block and driving away.

Letting himself into the flat with Richard's key presented no more problems than it had yesterday. Once inside, Eric began to saunter from room to room, looking around him in an assessing way.

'Well, this is very nice . . . yes, very nice indeedy. Comfortable, tasteful, dee-light-ful.'

Picking up a couple of party invitations propped on a shelf, he read the handwriting on the first of them.

'Mike and Pat.'

He looked at the other.

'Pat and Mike. Hmm. Interest-ing!'

He circled round the living area, then darted into the kitchen where he opened the fridge and studied its contents. Finally he took out a bottle of milk.

'Now what have we here, hmmm? Milk.'

Picking off the foil cap and dropping it on the floor, he jammed the bottle against his lips and gulped, splashing milk down his shirt. He grimaced, wiped his hand across his mouth and then wiped the same hand on a cupboard door.

'Yeuch! I hate milk.'

He splashed milk into the sink until the bottle was all but empty.

'Chocolate!' he muttered. 'Eat chocolate!'

He slammed the milk bottle down on the drainer, scattering more of its contents, and delved into the pocket of his jacket. He took out a half-melted chocolate bar, ripping the wrapper and pushing the bar into his mouth, chewing greedily. But the chocolate bar had a toffee centre, which oozed out over his upper lip and chin.

'Dirty boy,' he muttered. He wiped the toffee away with his fingers as he moved around the kitchen, then out into the living room and the hall and up the stairs. As he went he opened drawers and cupboards, poking around and leaving toffee smears on the objects and surfaces, like an animal marking his territory.

In the bathroom he spotted the laundry basket and pounced on it. Lifting the lid, he sifted through the clothes, selecting, touching, smelling. But after a few moments he slammed the lid back down.

'Dirty boy! Get a smack! Dirty boy needs a bath . . .'

101

Eric turned the bath taps and, as the water ran, he picked up a razor and examined it.

'Don't let it near your neck,' he whispered. 'Don't let it rip your fucking neck!'

Instead he drew the razor violently along the wall beside the mirror.

*   *   *

Collins had memorized a round-the-houses, rat-running route from the offices of SCG West to Alan Brickman's sawmill, which could be done in a maximum of twenty-three minutes, even without the use of a siren. North was impressed when, today, he did it in less than twenty. As they drove into the yard, where TSG searchers were still to be seen, she congratulated him.

'I got lucky with the lights, Gov,' said the modest Detective Constable.

'I'm lucky to have such a good driver. Now, we're here to talk to Alan Brickman about this disagreement with Crispin Yates, right?'

She looked at Collins.

'But it's not the barney itself I'm particularly concerned about. It's the fact that Jane Mellor was there when it happened.'

Collins looked confused.

'But Brickman said he'd never met Jane Mellor!'

North nodded.

'Precisely.'

In his living room, Alan Brickman had not seemed particularly concerned when North broached the subject of Donny's music lessons with Yates. She asked if he had been worried about the lessons in any way—in how the teacher and pupil were getting on, for instance.

'I was worried that he—Yates, I mean—might be pushing Donny too hard. You see, he's a very sensitive kid. Bob doesn't help. He wants him to play Muddy Waters and Yates has him doing Chopin. Trying to please them both only confuses him.'

'As well as being expensive,' commented North. 'We've been told how Donny vandalized the school music room.'

Brickman's face showed concern at the Detective Inspector's use of the word 'vandalized'. He waved a hand dismissively.

'Oh, just a couple of instruments, and I paid for them.'

'Did Mr Yates ever come to your house for any reason?'

'Yes, yes, he did. Not too long ago as a matter of fact. We had a few terse words.'

'And when you had these "terse words", who else was there?'

For the first time Brickman looked uncomfortable. He frowned, recalling. He said,

'Well, Donny was.'

'No one else?'

'No.'

He looked up, checking North's facial reaction. He raised his hand.

'Oh, wait, yeah. There was someone, someone with him . . .'

North ostentatiously consulted her notes.

'I see. "Someone with him", you say. You see my problem is that the someone who was with Crispin Yates was Jane Mellor, and both he and Donny seem to think that it was much more than just a few

103

"terse words".'

Brickman blinked rapidly.

'Look, I know where this is headed. I am not saying another word. I want my solicitor . . . that's it.'

*   *   *

Eric, carefully washed and purified, stood at Lynn Walker's front door, holding a bunch of flowers and straightening his clothes, as though ready for a date. He rang the bell.

He saw a shadow flit across the door glass as Lynn approached.

'All right, all right,' she called. 'I'm coming.'

He heard her slide the safety chain into its groove. Then she opened the door a crack and saw Eric's great moon face smiling sweetly at her.

'Hi, Lynn.'

With a sudden reflex action, she slammed the door shut, rattling the chain and the letter flap.

'Go away, Eric.'

But Eric stayed to plead his case.

'Lynn,' he wheedled, 'let me in. We have to talk. We *can* work it all out.'

'No, I told you last night, it's over.'

But Eric detected the tremble in Lynn's voice. His own climbed a few notes up the register of emotion.

'If it's over,' he declaimed, 'I'm going to kill myself.'

She did not reply. Eric held the silence for a moment, but could not risk her going out of earshot, out of contact, so he began again.

'Lynn, my key won't work. You've changed the

104

locks. How could you, Lynn? Please don't lock me out. Don't do this to me Lynn. You know how much you mean to me. I do love you, Lynn. You must know that. Please. Open the door and let me in. Let me explain. Please don't finish with me. Look what I brought you . . . I brought you *flowers*!'

He was openly sobbing now, like the little boy he'd told her about, whose mother had beaten him and made him lie in cold baths as a punishment.

'Please, Eric,' she said, pleading herself now. 'Don't be like this.'

'Lynn, I just want to talk, that's all.'

'Don't . . . Oh, Eric.'

But he had intuitively sensed her hesitation, just a fractional one, but it told him all he needed to know. Now he was sure she would open the door and he prepared himself. After a moment, through the sound of his own artificial sobs, he heard the chain being slowly drawn back. A little bit more . . . a bit more . . . and he heard it drop from Lynn's fingers and swing free. He threw himself at the door with all of his weight, smashing it open. Lynn took the full force of it in the shoulder and side and, with a yelp of pain, she ricocheted backwards into the hall and fell, groaning. He strode in, shut the door and stood over her. Good. Very good. Now he was lord and master again.

'I brought you flowers,' he said, dangling the bouquet above Lynn's face. 'A floral tribute for the woman I love more than any other.'

*   *   *

Barbara Mackenzie sat in one of the waiting-rooms at the Identification Suite, with Tara and James

Mellor. When North arrived from her inconclusive interview with Alan Brickman, Mackenzie had just finished spelling out for the child the exact procedure of an identification parade.

'Tara knows what's expected of her,' said Mackenzie to North, 'and she's not scared, are you Tara?'

Tara compressed her lips and shook her head.

'No.'

'Remember,' said North, crouching to be at Tara's level, 'if the man's not there then you mustn't worry.'

'I've explained it all to her,' repeated Mackenzie. 'She knows that he won't definitely be there.'

'Good girl,' said North. 'Do you want to take her through, Barbara? Thanks.'

Mellor got up from his chair, nodded and smiled encouragement at his daughter. After she'd gone out, his smile faded to grey.

'I don't really approve of this, Detective Inspector. I don't see why it's necessary. He's admitted it, hasn't he?'

She stood up.

'People do lie, Mr Mellor.'

Mellor looked incredulous.

'Surely not about something as horrendous as this!'

'I'm afraid they do.'

And on the subject of lies, thought North . . .

'Mr Mellor,' she continued smoothly, 'we've interviewed the school caretaker, and he is very sure you were not in the building on the day your wife disappeared.'

Mellor's face suddenly set hard.

'Then he is MISTAKEN! Look, has this man—

this Brickman fellow—told you where Jane is?'

Before North could reply there was a tap on the door. It was Satchell.

'You want to come into the anteroom now, Pat? She's going in. You can come in as well, if you like Mr Mellor.'

Despite her promise that she did not feel afraid, Tara was shaking violently as she and Mackenzie walked hand in hand the length of the long, acoustically sealed, one-way window, to inspect the line of men seated within. Each of them held a number, and all looked gloomy and oppressed. As Mackenzie had asked, Tara tried to picture in her mind the face of the man she'd seen in the bushes. But the face of her mother kept coming up instead, and the memory of her mother's voice too, so gaily telling them the story of the ogre of Binley Wood. Before Tara had even reached the end of the window she was weeping and couldn't distinctly see the men any more. The nice policewoman wiped her eyes and held the tissue to her nose. She said to her,

'Are any of these men the one you and Di saw in the woods, Tara? Would you like to have another look?'

Snuffling and shivering, Tara just wanted to get out of there. As far as she was concerned, they were all ogres.

North and Satchell stood together by the window of the identification building. They looked across the parking area as James Mellor and Tara walked hand in hand away from them, towards their hatchback car.

'So,' said North. 'We must hope for a better result with the other little girl, Diana.'

'You sure you want to put her through it?' asked Satchell. 'Tara Mellor was very upset.'

'We've got to. I need a positive ID or else the CPS will make us let the bastard go.'

Lawyers of the Crown Prosecution Service take over the running of criminal cases in England once a suspect has been charged. They apply two tests before finally deciding on a court prosecution. First, they want to know if there is, on balance, enough clean evidence to secure a conviction and, second, whether such a prosecution is in the public interest. With no dead body, and no credible forensic or identification evidence about her suspect, North's case hung by the single thread of Bob Brickman's uncorroborated confession. It did not even begin to pass the first of CPS tests. And unless she could swing things around it did not, in view of a trial's huge cost, look like passing the second.

'Here, Gov,' said Satchell. 'Look who I see.'

The door of the Mellor car had been flung open and Crispin Yates was hurrying across the asphalt towards Mellor and Tara. The child broke into a run and threw herself into Yates's arms. He swung her round, kissing her on the cheek as her father joined them. Soon all three were caught up in a three-way hug. When the embrace broke up, the two men walked, with Tara between them, towards the hatchback. They exchanged a few words. No doubt Mellor was letting Yates know that Tara had not picked anyone out. But what else, North wondered, was being said? She noticed Mellor shaking his head in almost a despairing way, while Yates attempted to reassure his friend by repeatedly patting him on the shoulder. Had

Mellor by any chance just told Yates about the school caretaker's statement? And was Yates trying to embolden him, trying to keep him on side?

'Do you think James Mellor's bisexual?' mused North aloud.

'*What?*' exclaimed Satchell. 'Mellor, a shirt-lifter?'

It seemed to strike him for the first time.

'Well, now you mention it, Gov, he could be. I mean, *they* could be—don't you think?'

But North shook her head with a sigh. Even if Satch was right, what would it mean? How would it help? These were matters falling under the heading of 'lifestyle' choices, the same kind of thing that had led North herself to throw in her lot with the married Walker, or Lynn to throw herself at this Eric chap that Walker had been talking about. Such choices didn't carry the old moral burden any more. And they didn't lead to the old kind of 'foul play' either. They were easy-squeeze choices, with no scary social consequences, no tragic undertones and no criminal fallout.

'I don't know,' she said. 'It's just them being so friendly. Possibly they really are the pair of ordinary buddies who go to the pub and play squash every Tuesday, like they make out. But to me it doesn't ring true.'

There was a knock on the door and West appeared carrying a fresh fax.

'Forensic reports just came in on the wellington boots found in Bob Brickman's barn,' she announced. 'They examined the layers of soil caught in the treads and none of them support the idea that the wearer was in the woods. There were several different types of timber shavings and sawdust, though.'

'Of course there were,' said North, scanning the fax. 'He lived in a sawmill. So let's not waste any more time. Satch, you have organized a warrant to search Brickman's sawmill?'

Satchell raised his eyebrows. He'd done it yesterday.

'They're already there, Pat!'

'Oh, right,' said North limply.

At this point, Collins put his head round the door to tell them Diana was about to face the same identification line-up as her friend Tara. She took the whole thing in a much more confident spirit, though and it took her just forty seconds to point to one of the men.

'It was him,' she said in a clear voice. 'Number seven.'

They all looked. Number seven was Bob Brickman.

*   *   *

After Donny had been playing guitar for an hour and a half in the darkened barn, his uncle decided enough was enough. He had always taken it on himself to be the child's disciplinarian. Bob had been useless about matters like limiting Donny's intake of junk food or, as in this case, sending him to bed. So now Alan took a torch and walked firmly across the former farm-yard. The sounds from Donny's guitar, floating on the night breeze, veered between lyricism and raw anger: sometimes a guitar gently weeping, sometimes an electric storm. Alan had not thought a ten-year-old capable of such feeling and such expression.

110

Alan pushed open the barn door and shone his torch around. Donny was sitting on the edge of the bare bed-frame, hunched over the instrument. A lead connected it to the amplifier and speakers. A single desk lamp on the floor provided a little dim light. Next to Donny was the battered guitar case with its multiple rock band stickers.

'Bedtime, Donny, there's a good chap,' he called. 'Unplug your guitar. Come on now it's late. You take the torch and go back into the house and say good night to Granny.'

Donny dealt with this, as usual with adults who tried to control him, by pretending he hadn't heard. His uncle approached and touched Donny's shoulder. Donny flinched away and played on, more loudly than before.

'Hey, what's the matter with you? Donny?'

'Dad said I could play in here.'

'I know, but you've got school tomorrow and—'

'I want my Dad.'

Alan sighed.

'I told you, he's not coming home. He's got to go to court. I told you this.'

Donny played a minor scale, rapidly once, then a second time more slowly.

'I want my Dad,' he said.

Alan adopted a threatening tone.

'If I wanted to I could take that guitar off you, Donny. I bought it—me, not your Dad—and I can take it away from you. Now go on, go to BED!'

He bent over the desk lamp and switched it off. His torchlight swept the room.

'Put your guitar away, Donny.'

'No, I want my Dad.'

'I'm the only Dad you've got now. So let's pack

111

the guitar away, OK?'

He bent and flicked the catches of Donny's guitar case, lifting the lid. Donny watched him, his pale face expressionless. Alan flashed the torch at the interior of the case, blinked, then trained the beam on the object he'd seen there. He sank to his haunches in front of the case.

'Sweet Jesus!'

He jerked the beam of his torch back at Donny, then reached and slammed the lid of the case down again.

'Take your guitar and get out, Donny. GET OUT!'

At once, Donny stood up and pulled out the jack plug connecting his guitar to the amp. He carried the instrument to the door where he turned and glared at his uncle.

'You're not my Dad.'

Alan said nothing. He crouched by the guitar case, his eyes shut, waiting for Donny to get clear. Once he heard the barn door slam, he eased open the lid of the guitar case and shone the torch again. There, lying snugly in the place normally reserved for Donny's acoustic Gibson guitar was a baseball bat. For most of its length it was relatively clean and new looking. But at the business end, the end that struck, it was crusted with some red-brown matter. That, to Alan's eye, could have been anything. It was the embedded golden hairs, glinting in the torch light, that told him what the encrustation really was.

CHAPTER TEN

TUESDAY, 25 MARCH, EVENING

Walker had taken the phone call from his mother at five-thirty. She told him she was coming round in half an hour, but did not explain. On the doorstep she seemed flustered, unusually apologetic, and even a little chastened.

'I packed my suitcase,' she said. 'I need you to put me up, Michael. It's just for a day or two.'

Walker took her suitcase.

'Sure, Ma. Why this all of a sudden?'

She stared at him and rolled her eyes to the side, to indicate she was not going to discuss a delicate matter on the doorstep. Walker ushered his mother into the hallway of the flat and shut the door.

'Right,' he said. 'No problem. I'll make up the bed in the spare room.'

'I don't want to put you to any trouble. I've got to stay in London to see my Jimmy and I couldn't think where else to go. I'd had enough of being at Lynn's.'

'It's no trouble. You go and put the kettle on and we'll have a cup of tea.'

'I could do with one. My nerves are in shreds.'

Wondering what had happened at Lynn's place, Walker took the suitcase into the spare bedroom. His mother went straight to the kitchen, checked the water in the kettle and switched it on. She opened the fridge.

'You've hardly any milk,' she called up to him.

She had found a bottle with about an inch of

milk inside. She sniffed it for freshness.

'There should be a whole pint there,' called Walker.

'Well, there's not.'

He was still busy in the spare room with sheets and pillow-slips, but he could tell she was already recovering her self-possession.

'I'll be right with you,' he called.

'You know,' Violet went on. 'Lynn's getting herself into trouble if you ask me. That's why I left. I couldn't stand being under the same roof a minute longer.'

'As Lynn?' said Walker, puzzled at his mother's sudden change of opinion.

'No, that new boyfriend of hers. He's moved in.'

She heard his feet thumping down the short flight of stairs between the bedroom corridor and the living area.

'What?' he said coming right into the kitchen. 'Did you say he's *moved in*?'

She frowned disapprovingly.

'He has, and he doesn't appear to have a job. The kids say he stays in bed most of the day.'

Walker clenched his fist.

'The stupid girl! She promised me she wouldn't see him any more. Why didn't you call me before?'

'Don't put me in the middle of it all, Michael.'

She had made the tea by now and was pouring from the teapot.

'I just wish Jimmy could have made it up to Scotland to see me. I fixed his old room up specially for him.'

'You think he'd notice?' said Walker.

'Yes, he would,' she maintained indignantly. 'He's not like you. Jimmy was always the artistic

114

one.'

'Oh yeah?' He laughed, but without enjoyment. 'Is that what you call being a lazy bum? *Artistic?*'

'Yes, he was. Look, he took it badly when your Dad left. Not like you. You never cared one way or the other, but Jimmy . . . Jimmy cried his heart out. That's why he started skiving off school, and getting in trouble. That's when it started.'

Walker decided not to contradict his mother about his own feelings *vis-à-vis* his father's exit from the family. It was far and away too late.

'You're still at it, aren't you?' he observed instead. 'Always making excuses for him.'

Violet sipped her tea.

'He's my son and I know he's not been the best but when your Dad left he was younger than you.'

'Put another record on, Ma. I'm tired of hearing the same old refrain.'

'You had every girl after you. There was no need to go after Jimmy's.'

Walker couldn't at first follow his mother's train of thought. Then he remembered. Jennifer McTaggart.

'But I didn't! It was *her* who . . . Ma, I'm not getting into this. It takes two to tango, and two to quarrel.'

'That's what I always say,' she announced, jabbing the air with her finger in her son's direction. 'It takes two to tangle.'

He drained his cup of tea and stood up.

'Anyway, if you don't mind, I'll get over to Lynn's and see what's going on.'

He went to the door and was immediately face-to-face with North, who'd just let herself in. After the day's work, she looked tired—and even more so when she saw that Violet Walker had come round for tea.

'Pat!' said Walker, wrapping his arms around North and placing a very deliberate kiss on her mouth. 'Look, I'm sorry sweetheart, I've got to go round to see Lynn and, well, as you see, Ma's here . . .'

'Oh, right, fine . . .'

She waved her hand at Walker's mother.

'Hello, Violet.'

Walker revolved North back towards the front door and murmured in her ear.

'I'm sorry to do this to you, but she's staying over . . . I know, I know! But it's just the one night. Lynn's got that sicko round at her place again, so Ma's left.'

Without further explanation he gave her a rapid smile and hurried across to kiss his mother on the cheek.

'See you later.'

Then he had gone.

'Well, it's nice to see you again Violet,' said North, attempting a bright tone as she slipped out of her coat and hung it in the hall. She came back through to the living area. 'It's been quite a while.'

She spotted the teapot on the kitchen counter.

'Oh good, a cup of tea.'

'You've no milk.'

North frowned, put down her briefcase and crossed to the kitchen.

'But there was a fresh pint this morning.'

'Well there's none left now!'

On examination of the fridge, North found this to be the case. Then, closing the door, she noticed the wrapper of a chocolate bar lying on the floor.

116

She could have sworn it had not been there in the morning. She bent, picked it up and crumpled it before tossing it in the bin.

*   *   *

Lynn's sitting room was in an untypical state of disorder. In fact, it reminded Walker of his own place after he'd had his children for the weekend. He looked around.

'Where are the kids?'

Lynn pointed to the ceiling.

'They're in bed, asleep. Having an early night. They're exhausted after the weekend's late nights.'

She looked accusingly at her ex-husband but Walker ignored the implication.

'This Eric bloke's moved in, according to Mum. Is that true?'

He examined her face. In addition to the yellow and brown bruise, half disguised by make-up, she looked drawn and exhausted herself.

'No, he just stayed one night. But I don't see that it's any business of yours.'

He noticed how hurriedly, and anxiously, she had shaken her head at his question. In her dressing gown she looked pathetic and vulnerable. He said,

'Ma told me he was living here.'

'Well, he's not. What are you interrogating me for?'

Walker sighed.

'Look, right now I've got a lot on my plate and all I am doing is looking out for you and for my kids.'

'Bit late for you to start doing that, isn't it?'

117

This was said with undisguised bitterness.

'Hey!' he protested. 'What's that supposed to mean?'

'You left *us*, remember? You've no right barging in here telling me who I can have to stay, and who I can't.'

Walker held up a hand.

'Fine, right, have it your way. But in my opinion any man that slaps a woman around is a worthless bastard with no balls and—'

'It was my fault, I told you.'

He was circling the room, looking for traces of Eric. He could see none.

'How do the kids get on with this Eric then?'

'Fine. They like him.'

'Well you tell him from me. If he touches a hair on their heads I'll come after him and there'll be no place to hide. No place! You tell that to Eric. By the way, what *is* his last name?'

'Why? So you can check up on him? Just go away, Mike. I don't want you intruding into my life. Leave us alone.'

'Fine, Lynn. I'll go. But don't . . . No, all right, all right. I'm going.'

She stood still, waiting to hear the front door slam behind him. Then she started tidying up, picking up used mugs and scattered cushions, reassembling dismantled newspapers. As she did so, she heard the light patter of feet coming down the stairs. It was Eric.

' "You tell him," ' he quoted loudly, wagging his finger satirically, ' "if he touches a hair on their heads, I'll come after him and there'll be no place to hide." Ha-bloody-ha! Are you going to tell me that, Lynn? *Are* you?'

'Please, Eric. Don't start. I don't want to argue with you.'

Her tone was pathetic and exhausted. Eric's mouth curled in disdain.

'He's a wanker, and he should learn to show me some respect. Who does he think he's talking about? So he says I've got no balls! I'll show him who's got balls! And why didn't you tell him I was living here?'

Lynn shrugged hopelessly.

'I didn't want to get into an argument. I don't now. Don't frighten the kids, Eric, please.'

Eric threw himself on to the sofa.

'You put them before everything, before yourself. It's the kids, kids, kids, until I am sick of hearing about the kids, your kids, *his* kids. They're spoiled rotten. They have no respect for you, or for me. But let me tell you: when I've finished with them, they *will* respect me.'

He got up and moved close to her, enfolding her in his arms. He smiled now, and gently kissed her neck as his hands smoothed her hair.

'I love you, Lynn,' he whispered. 'Doesn't that mean anything to you? I am *in* love with you. And all I'm doing is proving to you how very much I love you.'

Lynn lowered her head and let her eyelids fall shut.

'So no more threats, eh?' he continued, soothingly. 'You and me make a good team together. You do love me, don't you?'

Lynn stood still, rigid in his embrace.

'DON'T YOU?'

She moved her head, perhaps in a nod of agreement.

119

'Then SAY it! Go on! Tell me how much you love me.'

'I love you,' she murmured, with the dreary enunciation of a robot.

Sensually, he drew down the collar of her dressing gown and kissed her shoulder, her purple, bruised shoulder.

'And you need me . . . don't you?'

'Yes' she said in the same flat monotone. 'I need you.'

But Eric stepped back and in the same movement raised his hand.

'Liar!'

In one fist he seized the collar of her robe and used the other viciously to punch her face. He followed up with a swinging backhand slap. The concussion of his blows caused her head to snap sharply back, first this way and then that.

'Bitch!' he said. 'If you so much as—'

At that moment the front doorbell rang.

'Lynn! Lynn, it's me.'

It was Walker's voice, calling through the letterbox. 'I forgot to ask. Have you got any milk I can borrow? You've changed the locks. Lynn . . . open the door!'

Eric dragged Lynn to the sofa and forcing her down, pressed her face into the cushions. It was the ideal position, Eric thought with satisfaction. She couldn't cry out to alert Walker, while at the same time presenting herself for some really hard blows in the small of the back and the kidneys, where it really hurt.

'Bitch!' he mouthed as he punched her again and again.

Out on the doorstep, Walker was puzzled. He

heard knocking and someone's voice calling. He took a couple of steps backwards down the path and glanced up. The window on the right was the room he had once shared with her. There was no one there so he scanned the left-hand window, Richard's room.

His son was standing at the window, with his pale and tearful face pressed against the glass, and his small fist hammering it. Walker's hesitation disappeared and he shoulder-charged the front door, cannoning into it with a thump but making no other impression. He drew back to make another assault when the door swung open with a click. Behind the door was Amy.

'Hello, Princess,' he gasped. 'Where's Mummy?'

Amy tossed her head backwards.

'In there. With Eric.'

'Right!'

He stepped past Amy and into the living room. Lynn lay on the sofa, a pathetic sobbing figure. She looked up at her husband, seeming surprised to see him again so soon.

'Where is the bastard?' shouted Walker.

Lynn tried to control her tears. Her face was blotched red and already showed new swellings on top of her existing bruises.

'I fell down the stairs, Mike!'

Walker stared at her, shaking his head.

'No, she didn't! She didn't!' cried Amy, standing in the doorway. Next to her was Richard, trembling violently.

'Where is he?' Walker asked his children.

Richard pointed back into the rear of the hall.

'He ran out the back.'

From the back door there was a path leading

around the side of the house. Eric must have used it because, at that moment, they heard the ignition of a car, followed by a furiously revved engine. Walker went to the window and pulled the curtain aside. He was in time to see Lynn's car being driven away at speed.

Walker left the window.

'Get your night things, kids.'

Lynn winced as she tried to sit up.

'I told you, I fell—'

But Walker wasn't listening.

'I'm calling a taxi. The children are going back to my place. No, don't worry—I'll stay here with you. But this has gone on long enough and it's time it stopped.'

'It's all right, Mike. You can go home.'

'Bollocks to that. We've not heard the last of that fruitcake, I can guarantee it.'

*　　　*　　　*

Violet Walker had retired early and North had been about to do the same when the children arrived. She gave them hot chocolate, put them to sleep in her own bed and phoned Walker. As they talked, Amy reappeared behind her, dressed in one of North's nightshirts. It enveloped her, trailing along the carpet and making the child look even more forlorn.

'Yes, Mike,' North was saying, 'they're here and they're fine. I've put them in our bed for now . . . How's Lynn? . . . No, don't worry, we'll be fine. You stay at the house with her.'

Amy tugged at North's sleeve.

'Pat, Richard's done a wee in the bed and it's all

122

wet.'

Without letting Amy see, she closed her eyes in an effort of self-control.

'Mike, I've got to go. Talk to you later. Bye.'

Amy was close to tears. North took her by the hand and led her to the spare room.

'Hey, come on now, cheer up. Why don't you share with Granny tonight? You'd like that, wouldn't you?'

She didn't give Violet the choice.

Later, stripping the double bed, she tried to reassure Richard, miserably awake and wearing one of Walker's pyjama tops, that he had done nothing wrong.

'Don't you worry about it Richard. Accidents happen and you've been through a scare.'

She went and crouched beside him.

'That's all it is Richard, isn't it? Eric hasn't hurt you has he?'

Richard's face puckered and she took him into her arms, feeling his tears leaking through her shirt. For a few moments she rocked him in her arms. Downstairs she thought she heard the front door click open. She held him still.

'Did you hear something?' she asked.

They listened. It was definitely the front door.

'Maybe it's Daddy and I've put the chain on. Just wait here, all right?'

She ran down to the door. The door had been opened by means of a key—had to be Walker, right? At the moment a man's hand was feeling through the gap between door and jamb, trying vainly to release the chain.

'Mike? Is that you? Just wait a second.'

The hand withdrew as she approached the door

123

and reached for the chain. But first she peered through the gap. She gasped. Eric was there, leering at her ingratiatingly.

'What is it?'

The voice came from behind her. It was Violet, in her dressing gown and hair in rollers. 'Pat, what's going on?'

'Open the door,' pleaded Eric. 'Let me in. I have to collect the kids, for Lynn . . .'

He pushed the door to the extcnt of the safety chain and thrust his arm inside. For a moment his fingers brushed her shirt and, in horror, she rammed the door as hard as she could. Violet gave a gasp. Eric, whose hand was momentarily trapped, roared in agony.

'Get OUT of here!' yelled North. 'Do you hear me? GET OUT!'

Eric's hand, maimed (she hoped) by the force of the door, withdrew. North slammed the door and reached for the secondary security bolt, which she shot home. There were thuds and shouts from Eric as he kicked and hammered to be let in.

'I want to explain about me and Lynn. I have to explain that it isn't my fault. OPEN THE DOOR!'

North put her mouth close to the door's lock.

'Listen to me, you! I am a police officer. Leave these premises immediately—IMMEDIATELY— or I will have you arrested.'

There was silence. She and Violet listened and, from the top of the stairs, Amy and Richard listened too. Collectively, they held their breath. It seemed that Eric had gone away. Cautiously, North eased up the flap of the letter slot and bent to peer through. She could see nothing until, with a shriek she leapt back as Eric's hand thrust through and tried once again to grab her. Then the hand was gone and they heard the flap of footsteps running away down the stairs.

*   *   *

Walker was asleep on the sofa with half a mug of cold tea beside him when North called again. He had not meant to sleep, but that was how it often was with Walker. When he wanted to sleep he couldn't; when he meant to stay awake, his eyelids drooped.

'Hello?' he said after grabbing the phone.

'It's me.'

'Pat! Sorry sweetheart, I was asleep. Something wrong?'

She told him.

'Christ!' he said. 'Are you OK?'

'Oh yes, I'm fine.'

'What about the kids and Mum?'

'They're upset, naturally. He had a key, Mike. Richard told me it must be his key, the one you gave him.'

'Did you call the local station?'

He looked round and saw Lynn coming down in her dressing gown, rubbing her eyes. She yawned and then winced, hurt by her facial bruises and swellings.

'Not yet,' said North. 'I wanted to talk to you first.'

'You want me to come home?'

'No, but I think we should ID this guy. I think he's dangerous, Mike. Doesn't Lynn know more about him?'

Mike was still looking at Lynn. He smiled at her.

'OK, OK, I'll have a word with her. Something's got to be done about this lunatic.'

'You can say that again. I'll call the neighbourhood cavalry now, shall I?'

'Yeah, and call me after they've been there. Love you, Pat.'

Walker mimed a kiss into the mouthpiece and hung up. He turned to Lynn.

'No more games, Lynn. That maniac's been round to my place, trying to smash his way in.'

Lynn put a hand to her mouth.

'Oh my God, are the kids OK?'

Walker nodded.

'They're fine. And Pat and my mother are fine too, thanks for asking. The local police are on their way over there. What's his last name, Lynn? I'm not messing around any more!'

Lynn's eyes filled with tears.

'Knowles,' she said. 'It's Eric Knowles.'

'You got an address for him?'

Lynn looked around.

'No. He's been living here. I don't know where else he stays.'

Walker picked up his mug and made towards the kitchen.

'What about the gym where you met him? They must have an address if he was a member.'

Lynn cast her eyes down.

'I didn't meet him at the gym, Mike.'

Walker stopped and swung round.

'What? But you said—'

'I lied. I just didn't want you interrogating me.'

'So where did you meet him, then?'

'On the Internet. I went into one of those chat rooms. That's how we met. I've never been to

126

where he lives. I've no idea where it is.'

Walker suppressed the bubble of rage threatening to pop inside him.

'Well, start thinking where he might be,' he said, patiently. 'Because that nutcase is not going near my kids again.'

Lynn sank into a chair. She looked utterly drained and only half able to understand what was going on.

'Take a look at yourself,' said Walker. 'He's beaten you up and now he's taking it out on us.'

'Do the police really have to be involved? It'll only make things worse . . .'

'Worse! He bloody nearly killed you, Lynn!'

Lynn sighed with a deep, rasping exhale of breath.

'Did you never think that maybe I'm terrified of him?' she asked suddenly. 'You think I don't know what'll happen? If you arrest him, he just gets bail. And if he goes to court what'll he get? A few hours community service and then he's released. I don't want any trouble, Mike. I know he'll make me pay for it.'

Walker spread his arms wide.

'Lynn, for God's sake, I am a police officer, a senior one. I can get that piece of shit off the streets, no problem. I can get a court order that'll mean he's arrested if he sets foot within fifty yards of you.'

'And I'll feel safe with that, will I? You know better than anybody that court orders get broken. All you're doing is making him more and more and *more* angry.'

She rocked forward and covered her face with her hands.

'I'm so tired . . . I can't think straight.'

Walker rolled his eyes upwards and thought,

'You said it.'

Out loud he said,

'Go on, go to bed. Take a Valium. I'll stick around here in case he comes back.'

Slowly Lynn complied, trudging away towards the hall.

'You should come to bed,' she said, automatically. Walker felt the irony. She must have used this phrase hundreds of times during their married life.

'No, thanks anyway.'

Lynn was at the door.

'I wasn't inviting you into mine, you know.'

Walker just smiled grimly as he reached for the phone. He had to call North back with the news of Eric's surname—if it *was* his name.

'Oh, Lynn,' he added before she left the room, 'one more thing. What's your car's registration number? Let's not forget he's a car thief as well as an animal.'

*   *   *

North saw the two uniformed constables out, after giving them all the facts as far as she and Walker knew them.

'Will the police sort him out then?' asked Violet, who came down after checking on the children.

North nodded.

'Yes, I hope so. Are the kids asleep?'

'Out like lights. They're exhausted, the wee bairns.'

'Good. Mike's going to stay with Lynn tonight,

128

just in case he goes back there.'

Violet had gone through to the kitchen to fill a hot water bottle. For her, normality needed reasserting.

'He's used to that kind of thing you know. His Da knocked me around like a punch bag. Mind you, I gave as good as I got but it's the children that suffer most. They never forget the fear. That's what does all the damage.'

It was perhaps the longest and most confiding speech Violet Walker had ever volunteered to her. North was impressed. She went across and put her hands on Violet's shoulders.

'Come on,' she said, looking into Violet's eyes. 'There's whisky somewhere. Let's have a hot toddy!'

CHAPTER ELEVEN

WEDNESDAY, 26 MARCH, MORNING

The search of Brickman's Sawmill was a large and complicated operation. The lifting of huge piles of logs and tree trunks would involve heavy machinery and many officers but, as North had known since Sunday when she'd first visited the place, they would all have to be eliminated as possible concealment sites. So, as a pledge to their continued efforts, SCG had installed Tea Pot One—the mobile canteen—on the site, and it was here that a dozen officers were gathered around it for cups of tea and an informal briefing from Satchell. He directed their attention to two huge piles of tree-trunks arranged lengthways which filled one end of the yard. They were the biggest obstacles the searchers faced.

After a few minutes the Detective Sergeant broke away from the group and walked across to the barn, where Alan Brickman stood in the open doorway. He, too, was drinking a mug of tea. Behind him, nailed to the back of the barn door, was a selection of dead rabbits and birds.

'You want to shift that lot?' asked Brickman, nodding towards the two stacks of wood. 'It'll take for ever. I've got a fork lift you can use, but even so . . .'

'When was that wood last shifted, Mr Brickman?'

'We had a new delivery last week. Before that it hadn't been touched for a couple of months.'

He scanned the great log piles appraisingly and shook his head.

'I know what you're looking for but no way could it be under that lot, no way,' he said. 'And if you start shifting it, where are you going to put it? There's no room anywhere.'

Satchell was standing with hands on hips, also looking across at the log pile.

'We reckon there might be room to the left there.'

'You better watch out, then, or you'll knock down my Portakabin. And you can't leave them there. You'll have to put them back exactly where you found them.'

Satchell's eyes narrowed.

'Yeah, I see what you mean. It's kind of time-consuming.'

He left Brickman and rejoined his men. He told

them to begin on some smaller log piles, ranged along the dirt lane leading from the road into the yard. As his grandmother used to tell him, you don't climb Everest just to see over the garden fence.

*   *   *

Pat North turned off the highway and drove along that same rutted lane a few minutes later. She had got the children to school by eight-fifty-five. Violet had made it clear she was less than keen on having Amy and Richard on her hands and, anyway, she'd decided to move to a bed and breakfast that same morning. North didn't mind at all that Violet was retreating to a place of relative safety. And it seemed best to let routine reassert itself in the children's minds as soon as possible. So now, despite the previous evening's events, and the consequent shortage of sleep, she was glad to be working again.

The search of the logs along the lane was in full swing as she drove into the yard. It had not prevented commercial operations from continuing in parallel and she heard the shrill rasp of a three-foot circular saw as one of Brickman's men, wearing a face mask and ear protectors, began to convert a tree trunk into three-quarter-inch planks. Walking towards the canteen truck, she passed the open doors of the covered sawmill, where another masked employee was feeding the same rough-sawn planks into a planing machine. Curls of wood were being flung upwards and a haze of dust filled the building.

She found Satchell with Collins, drinking tea and

eating a sandwich. Collins's already large hands were encased in huge protective gloves.

'Sorry I'm late, Satch. Problems at home.'

Satchell raised his eyebrows.

'Oh yeah? What's up?'

North made a quick wiping gesture.

'It's dealt with. How's it going here?'

'We've done the barn, the garage and the offices, and the little copse round the back. We've just started having a look at some of the timber piles down the lane.'

North nodded at the two big log piles in the yard itself.

'What about that? Have you searched those?'

As one, Satchell and Collins swung round towards the massive stacks of wood.

'You don't want that lot shifted now, do you?' asked Collins.

'Why not?'

'Well, we talked to Alan Brickman,' said Satchell, 'and he said it would probably take days.'

'You'd better get on with it then. What about the fork-lift? Can't you use that?'

'There's hundreds of tree trunks there,' said Satchell.

'How would you know?' put in Collins, yanking up his gauntlets as if preparing to do battle. 'All you've done is hang out at Tea Pot One.'

North pointed out the further of the two piles.

'That one looks newer than the other. Move it first.'

Satchell sighed meaningfully.

'If that's what you want.'

'It is, Satch.'

They worked for three hours while North sat in

her car, making calls and doing paperwork. She was on tenterhooks and wanted to be on hand in case something was found. But the job was laborious and only half done by two o'clock, when Lisa West and Satchell took a quick meal break.

'Wow, this is some manoeuvre,' said West.

Satchell had been tireless. One thing you could say about him, once he knew he had to do something, he gave it his all. But now he was tired.

'Tell me about it,' he said. 'First we shift this pile, then put all the fuckers back, and *then* start on the next pile.'

'But surely if the body is under tons of wood, wouldn't someone have seen him doing it? He'd have been at it all bloody night!'

'Not if he buried it before the delivery last week. Maybe the Gov's been right all along. They killed her together and then hid the body together. If so, we—'

The air was split by a long, searing scream from the big circular saw behind them. As it drowned Satchell's last few words, West turned to look. The operator stood next to his machine, watching the great circular blade cut through a thick pine log that he'd clamped to the cutting table. The table itself was divided so that, from her angle, the saw looked like it was cutting right through the table and into the ground itself. Evidently there was some kind of trench below it.

Having finished his cut, the sawyer hit the cut-off button and walked back to the shed with the two lengths of wood under his arm.

West was still looking at the saw. As the revolving blade slowed to a halt, she seemed to see something fluttering down through the machinery,

133

some sort of fabric perhaps. Satchell went back to Tea Pot One to refill his mug, while she strolled across to the saw to look more closely.

Above the machine was a roughly constructed corrugated roof to protect it from the weather; below, as she'd predicted, was a deep trench, filled with a bed of sawdust, its level almost high enough to be grazed by the wicked teeth of the saw blade. Peering into the trench West spotted a fragment of blue cotton fabric, with a hint of pink in it. She immediately realized the significance of this combination of colours. She crouched and tried to reach down, but couldn't stretch far enough to grasp the scrap of cotton. There was nothing for it but to climb down beneath the cutting table.

As West dropped into the trench she went up to her knees in sawdust. Now she was near enough to secure the scrap of material with her finger and thumb. It was hardly larger than a postage stamp but when she held it to the light she could quite clearly see its pattern: tiny pink flowers over a cornflower blue ground. Feverishly West began gouging into the sawdust in front of her. Something solid was lying under it. She scraped again and gasped. It was a human hand, just beside her own hand in the wet sawdust.

At this moment, directly above her, a log crashed down on the cutting table, the electric motor of the saw kicked in with a roar and the circular blade spun. With a deafening screech it bit into the log. West looked up and realized, in horror, that the blade was only a few feet from her, its lower edge moving down the sawdust trench as it ripped through the log above. It was spewing sawdust as it came. West shrank back but her legs

134

were planted in a bog of damp sawdust and she could hardly move them. She looked again at the advancing saw and screamed with all her strength. The spinning teeth were edging inescapably towards her.

It was lucky Satchell had such highly tuned hearing. He was strolling back with his tea when he heard the scream of the saw but also, right afterwards and from the same direction, another kind of scream, a human one. He dropped the tea and ran towards the obliviously ear-protected operator of the saw. As he reached the machine, the edge of Satchell's eye registered the sight of West craning back in the sawdust trench, as the saw blade cut its way towards her. It would be too late if he politely asked the sawyer to kindly cut the motor. Instead, Satchell launched his body forward and punched the cut-off button himself. The saw blade stopped three inches from West's face.

North had been standing in the door of the barn, watching operations on the big stack. She noticed Satchell drop his tea and sprint forward, so she ran across herself to investigate, reaching the circular saw only a few seconds after him.

'Lisa, are you all right?' she called out. 'What happened?'

West was profoundly shaken, but shock did not completely blot out her sense of triumph.

'I think we found her,' she said.

*   *   *

Walker spent much of the morning pacing around Lynn's house, working himself up to fever-pitch. He'd phoned the local stations both here and near

135

his own flat. He'd phoned Satchell. He'd phoned Records at the Yard. He'd phoned Vehicle Section. No one had a lead on who Eric Knowles was, or where he'd come from. Nor had Lynn's car turned up.

'Did he never drop any hints to you about his background?' he asked Lynn, as she came into the living room with a tray and two steaming mugs of coffee.

She shook her head.

'No, hardly a word. Just that his parents were dead and he had no family. Look, why don't you sit down and drink your coffee? Relax for a moment.'

'Oh, yeah, thanks.'

Walker sat at the dining table and took two heaped teaspoons of sugar from the bowl on the tray.

'Knowles can't be his real name,' he said, stirring vigorously. 'Guy like that's got to have a record, somewhere. And there ain't one for Eric Knowles.'

There was a silence as they both sipped their coffee.

'The only location we've got for him is in bloody cyberspace,' continued Walker gloomily. 'That kissy-kissy chat room of yours.'

'It's not mine!' she protested. But Walker had had a thought. He held up his hand.

'No, wait a minute, that's it! Suppose he's still using it, looking for other women maybe. If we log on to the site, maybe we can find him that way.'

He sprang to his feet.

'I'm going to try it now. But I'll need your help. I've not a clue how to do it.'

Lynn smiled.

'And there was I thinking you were the new Bill

Gates, with all that computer time you've been putting in for the interview.'

Walker swung round and looked at her in horror. He smote his forehead.

'Oh my God, the interview. It's today! It's this afternoon! Oh Jesus! I'm not ready.'

'What time do you have to be there?'

'Five o'clock, at the Yard.'

'It's not twelve yet. You've got lots of time.'

Walker checked his watch. He forced himself to calm down.

'Right, OK. Plenty of time. Let's do the chat room thing first, and then I'll think about the interview.'

He stood by her chair as she booted up the PC and logged on to the Net. She selected an address from her 'Favourites' file and a few moments later they were looking at an invitation to log in to the chat room.

'Move over,' said Walker. 'I'll take it from here.'

He sat at the terminal and scanned the screen.

'OK, so I just type your name in here, right?'

'I didn't use my real name.'

'What did you log on as then?'

'It was "Bubbly Divorcee". Oh no, er, "Lonely Bubbly Divorcee".'

Walker looked sideways at her with a screwed-up, disbelieving face, but made no comment. He typed in the name and hit 'Return'.

The screen displayed a message: *Welcome, Lonely Bubbly Divorcee, to sensualsingles! Warning. This site is live and filtered. Do not use sexually explicit language or your message will be rejected. If there's anyone in particular you wish to contact through sensualsingles, enter the username and your message in the box.*

'Right,' said Walker. 'What did he come on as?'

'Freeman.'

Walker snorted.

'He's not going to be a free man if I get my hands on him. You think he'll be online at this time of the day?'

'Oh yes, he might be. He spent hours logged on to this. It's where we would always talk.'

'Well, let's hope he's on the prowl now.'

He rubbed his hands together and flexed the fingers, like a concert pianist preparing to play.

'Why don't you go put dinner on or something, and leave me to it?' he suggested confidently. 'I think I can take it from here.'

'But you don't know what I said in our chats.'

Walker smiled mischievously.

'I think I've got a pretty good idea.'

Twenty minutes later Walker stood up and stretched, as Lynn came in with his sandwich on a plate.

'I've tried every come-on I can think of,' he moaned. 'Nothing.'

She handed him the plate and sat herself down in front of the screen. Walker bit off a large mouthful.

'Let's try another one,' he said after swallowing. 'Type "Eric, if you are online, answer me. I have to see you".'

Lynn typed and hit 'Return'. They waited. Walker chewed. Then without warning a message flashed up on the screen: *Freeman has joined the chat room.*

'It's him!' whispered Lynn. 'He's online!'

Eric needed only a few moments to pick up the

bait, and then a personal message, a 'Whisper', came through from Freeman for Lonely Bubbly Divorcee, flashed up on the screen addressed to Lynn's online persona: *Hi, Lynn. Let me hear your voice.*

Walker was puzzled.

'What's he on about? You can talk to him through the computer?'

Lynn pointed to the computer's built-in microphone.

'Yes, but we only did it a few times. I'm not sure if I remember how to do it. Computers aren't really my thing.'

Walker smiled and looked at his watch.

'Well, that makes two of us.'

'Eric used to explain it. I think we go to the "Options" menu and . . .'

She moved the pointer and clicked on 'Options'. Walker scanned the items on the drop-down menu.

'Ah, I see!' cried Walker. 'You must have to click "Audio conferencing".'

Lynn hesitated.

'Click on here,' urged Walker, pointing to the screen.

But she was too slow and he reached across and seized the mouse.

'Let me do it. Aha! Got it!'

He lowered his voice.

'OK, now speak into the mike.'

But Lynn had suddenly lost the power of speech. She looked up at Walker beseechingly.

'Come on, Lynn,' Walker hissed. 'Start talking, get him to answer.'

She shut her eyes and when she opened them she was still looking at Walker. Without taking her eyes off him, she at last started to speak.

'I am alone. I need company. I forgive you. I love you. I never stopped loving you. I want you back.'

When Walker heard these words he knew they carried meaning beyond this particular moment, beyond the mere entrapment of Eric. He felt an unwanted flush of shame.

Something new was flashing on the screen.

'What do we do?' said Walker 'I can't hear him.'

'I don't know,' Lynn stuttered. 'Oh wait, are the speakers turned on?'

'What speakers? Where are they?'

She pointed to the box which stood alongside the PC and Walker fumbled with the control buttons mounted on top. A small indicator light came on.

'Nothing,' said Walker after a few more seconds. 'There's still nothing coming through.'

As he spoke, the speaker crackled and a voice was heard. It was low and breathy but unmistakably Eric's.

Hi, Mike, this is Eric, Lynn's boyfriend Eric. And guess what, Mike? I have it all planned out. I'm going to make your life a living hell.

CHAPTER TWELVE

WEDNESDAY 26 MARCH, AFTERNOON

The younger Brickman sat at the table in his kitchen, clenching his hands as if exercising the muscles. He looked bemusedly at North, who sat opposite him with Satchell. It was Satchell who had broken the news to him. They had found Jane Mellor entombed in his sawdust pit.

'Mr Brickman,' Satchell was saying, 'we know your brother abducted Jane Mellor. We know he held her captive. What we don't know—'

'Why do *you* think he killed her?' butted in North.

Brickman looked up at the wall, then down again.

'Why are you asking me? I don't know why he did it.'

He scrubbed his tangled hair with the fingers of his right hand.

'He's had a lot of mental problems since he was a kid. That's why it's all such a mess, such a waste.'

'Waste?'

Brickman seemed to weigh something up for a moment, and then decided. He got up, went to a side table and pulled open a drawer. He returned with a cardboard folder from which he took a fistful of newspaper cuttings, prize certificates and snapshots.

'As a boy Bob was just as talented as Donny. He won contests. Child prodigy, they called him.'

He fanned out the papers from the file, selected a photograph of his brother as a very small boy and showed it to North and Satchell. A full-sized guitar was slung from Bob's skinny shoulders, hanging so low that you couldn't see his knees. It reminded North of the snapshot of Donny that hung on the wall just outside the door.

'Go on, Mr Brickman,' she said.

'And then around . . . I don't know, twelve, thirteen, he was up for this important scholarship

141

and he was offered a recording contract. It meant there was enough money for Dad to buy the sawmill, all paid up front. They reckoned Bob could be the next John Williams or something. So Dad started dragging Bob around to pubs and clubs, showing him off like some circus freak.'

He tucked the sheaf of memorabilia back into the file.

'And then it all went wrong, see? It was the pressure. Bob went into the recording studio and couldn't play a note. He never went up for the scholarship. He got violent, angry, like something had snapped in his head. I remember him and Dad punching the hell out of each other. He never picked up a guitar again, at least not until Donny started showing interest.'

North frowned, concentrating on the details of what she had just learned.

'So you encouraged Donny, even after what Bob had been through?'

'I arranged for the lessons, same as I arrange for everything else.'

'Did your father have to pay back the record company?'

Alan seemed momentarily surprised, wondering what was behind North's question.

'Oh, I think they tried to get the money back, but Dad told them to piss off.'

'So who exactly owns the mill?'

'Bob.'

North's eyes narrowed.

'It's always been in his name. So he had every right to be there that night. This is Bob's business, not mine.'

His eyes met North's steadily now.

142

'I work for him,' he said.

Bob Brickman's story was a sad one, even tragic, but through Donny the family had been given a chance to put things right, a shot at redemption. Just how spectacularly they'd blown it was up to her to prove.

'Just help me with something here,' she asked. 'You encourage Donny. Your brother encourages Donny. So why did you become so angry when Jane Mellor called round?'

'It's obvious, isn't it? They were putting pressure on Donny, just like Dad did with Bob.'

'But why did you become so violent?'

He lowered his voice almost to a mumble.

'Because of something she said.'

'Jane Mellor?'

'Yes.'

'What did she say, Mr Brickman?'

'That Donny would be better off away from us. When I told them to get out, she said she'd report us to the Social Services.'

'Was Bob privy to this meeting you had with Jane Mellor and Crispin Yates?'

Brickman rubbed his hair again.

'He wasn't in the room but he could have been in the house. He was always in and out . . . You know, he lives for his boy.'

'So if the Social Services had been brought in . . .'

Alan shook his head.

'We'd have had no chance. With the way Bob is, they'd have taken him away, wouldn't they?'

*   *   *

When the body of a murder victim is found, it gives a jolt of energy and purpose to everyone involved, from the Metropolitan Police Commissioner to the driver of Tea Pot One. On the other hand, such a moment is sombre, in ways that go beyond the fact that a death has occurred. Murder uniquely confronts the fragility of life and the dark side of the human psyche. It cruelly degrades our dearest pleasures and comforts: sex, love, money, friendship, politics, ambition, religious belief. It shows these are also the constantly recurring elements of bloody violence, hatred and obscene cruelty.

Pat North's feelings on the subject were no different. She had accustomed herself to violent deaths and decaying corpses, but she always veered between the elation of a high-profile case and a lingering depression at the way murder soiled and spoiled all the best things in life.

Returning at speed from the sawmill to pay another visit to her prisoner Bob Brickman, she tried to clear her head of these troubling thoughts. Jane Mellor was dead and there was nothing to be done about it—except find the perpetrator and bring him to justice. Only justice could minimize the suffering of those nearest to Jane. Only justice mattered now.

With the body already under forensic examination North did not waste time before confronting Brickman again. She and Satchell went straight to the police cell where he was being held. They found him sitting on his bunk rolling a cigarette. Seeing him again made North feel something else. Anger. She remembered Brickman's matter-of-fact admissions to abduction,

144

battery, rape and murder. There had been not a jot of regret in the man's giant frame, but a sickeningly cheerful admission that he'd done the deed not for any weighty reason, but merely on a whim. Merely because he'd happened to feel like it.

'Mr Brickman,' she said crisply. 'I know you lied to us. I know you deliberately misled us. I know you have wasted our time. And I know you are still doing it. Why? To cover up your brother's crime? To cover up the fact that your brother is a murderer?'

Brickman was not goaded by her angry tone. Carefully and calmly he worked on his roll-up.

'You don't know nothing!' he crowed. 'I came clean because I don't want no more trouble for my brother.'

'Jane Mellor's body was found at your brother's sawmill. You conned us into looking elsewhere. Why are you protecting him?'

'I'm not. Why you got this thing about him is making me get angry, really angry. You ever think that maybe, just maybe, I'm not as dumb as you think I am?'

'No one is inferring that you are dumb,' said North through tight lips.

Brickman's lips curled into a cunning smile.

'All right, look at it this way. I said I buried her in the woods, then I said I dumped her in the pond right? Why? Because I didn't want you lot to find her. I wanted to give you buggers the runaround, have a bit of fun.'

He was jeering now, enjoying himself.

'And if you hadn't have nosed around the mill, you'd never have found her for years. In fact if I hadn't turned myself in, you would never have got

145

me for years neither.'

He clamped his roll-up between his lips and applied his lighter. He drew in the acrid smoke and, flinging himself back on the bunk, exhaled as if lying in luxury.

'Am I right?' he said.

As they stepped out into the corridor, North's mobile rang. It was the pathologist with a preliminary report on the state of the body. She ended the call with a sigh and she and Satchell began to retrace their steps through security and out of the cell block.

'Did Bob Brickman really do it, Satch? Something tells me he didn't. He says he raped her, but the autopsy can't confirm or deny that. She had severe bruising to her throat consistent with his statements, but she actually died from a blow to the side of her skull, not suffocation as he claimed. The weapon is described as a rounded wooden object three inches across.'

But Satchell was unimpressed.

'Well, I've already talked to the lab. They've found sacking fibres on the body, plus a blanket from Brickman's barn wrapped around her, both as per his story. Plus we already got his confession. He did it, Pat. We've got no evidence that Alan Brickman was involved.'

They handed in their visitor-tags and took the stairs down to the car park.

'It's just a gut feeling, Satch. Indulge me.'

'All right,' sighed Satchell. 'You're the boss.'

*   *   *

With five minutes to spare, Walker arrived for his

interview at the Metropolitan Police Authority, the governing body of the force. In the taxi, he tried to focus on how he should present himself. He'd talked it over with North several days ago and she'd told him it wouldn't do to act the old-style copper, the human bloodhound with the nose for a criminal and unafraid to get his paws dirty in pursuit of an arrest.

'But that's what I am!' Walker protested. 'That's me.'

'No. You're more than that, Mike. You have years of experience, but you've headed up the most modern investigative teams using the most up-to-date scientific techniques. Remember those computer-aided reconstructed clay heads in the Hallerton Road case?'

He'd nodded, remembering.

'Yes, and the forensic work we did in the Mint Murder?'

'You've worked with some of the best forensic men and pathologists in the world, guys like Arnold Mallory.'

'And guys like Deirdre Smith!'

She'd laughed.

'Exactly. The MPA love to hear about that stuff. So let them! You've got to emphasise your willingness to use all the latest investigative tools. HOLMES 2 and simulations in the Hydrasuite—all that.'

Walker had tapped his temple with a forefinger.

'That, merged with cunning and intuition of a native Glaswegian: an irresistible combination.'

'Let's hope they don't resist you, then.'

As the taxi approached the building, Walker had scrawled some words on the palm of his hand to remind him of that conversation. He wrote: *HOLMES 2, HYDRASUITE, INVESTIGATIVE TOOLS, COMBINED WITH INSTINCT.*

Apart from a uniformed Assistant Commissioner, who sat silently throughout the proceedings, the panel consisted of lay members of the Authority, led by a middle-aged Chairman with the manner of a suave Tory politican, which he probably was. He asked Walker to take them through the salient aspects of his career: his start as a Glasgow bobby, quickly promoted to sergeant, then the move to London and the CID followed by a rapid rise to Detective Chief Superintendent and his long involvement with murder.

'Your CV is very impressive,' said the Chairman at last. 'It's a breath of fresh air to have a real murder detective in front of us. We don't get that many applying. This position tends to attract more, er, shall I say, academic types.'

Walker smiled modestly.

'Well, a good officer moves with the times,' he said. 'He learns to utilize network computer systems like HOLMES 2. I find that system, in particular, invaluable in complex, serious crimes, for gathering information and cross-referencing.'

'So, with all your years in the field, Detective Chief Superintendent Walker, how would you feel if you were sent back into the classroom for a three week course in the Hydrasuite?'

The Hydrasuite was a recently developed facility in which detectives were trained to work on complex enquiries using simulations and computer modelling. Walker had many times scoffed at it in company with Satchell. They called it Disneyland. But, as Walker knew, that kind of thinking would

148

never get him to Commander. So in answer to the question he said,

'I'd have no objections whatsoever. If any officer wants to stay cutting edge, where better to hone your investigative skills than in the Hydrasuite training simulator?'

The interview panellists exchanged glances, seemingly impressed at Walker's knowledge in this area. As they did so Walker risked a glance at the biro-scrawled notes in his hand. *INVESTIGATIVE TOOLS, COMBINED WITH INSTINCT.* He went confidently on,

'State-of-the-art technology has given us these incredible investigative tools. But the officer you need will combine those tools with his own natural instincts and ability, and his years of experience.'

'And you think you are that officer?' asked the Chairman.

Walker's face set in an expression of utter self-belief. There was nothing fake about it.

'After twenty-five years in the force,' he stated in perfect truth, 'yes, I do.'

* * *

North arrived home and locked the door securely in case Eric should renew his attentions. She even turned the mortise deadlocks, which were never normally used. Walker was still at Lynn's guarding his children and she was looking forward to a quiet evening of television and an early night.

These plans were derailed within ten minutes when the doorbell rang. Peering through the fish-eye she was unable to recognize the blond haired man whose face reared up in the distorting lens.

'Who is it?' she called through the door.

'It's me, Jimmy.'

'Jimmy? Oh! Are you Mike's brother?'

'Yeah, just passing through. I wanted to say hello.'

North hesitated and then, with a sigh, she unhooked the security chain, drew the bolt and unlocked the Chubbs. Jimmy stood relaxed beside a canvas sports bag.

'I've heard London was a rough place but this is like Fort Knox.'

He turned a dazzling smile on her.

'Now, you must be Pat.'

She nodded.

'Yes, I am. Mike isn't here. He's actually at Lynn's place.'

'Lynn? Oh, I'm sorry, got my wires crossed. I thought he was getting divorced.'

'He is, it's just a family matter.'

'Divorce usually is.'

Jimmy was different to what she expected. Walker's characterization had placed his brother somewhere between a drop-out and a toe-rag, but Jimmy was clean and obviously looked after himself. He was in his late thirties, but his dress and appearance were those of a younger man: kid leather jacket over a T-shirt, tight stonewashed jeans and trainers, spiky, bleached hair. He nodded at the interior of the flat.

'Nice place. But then Mickey always fell on his feet. You going to ask me in? I had lunch with Ma today. I'm exhausted. Did she not call and say I'd be dropping by?'

'No, she didn't. Come in, then.'

She stepped aside and Jimmy strolled easily in,

looking around.

'Hey, nice decor, very smart. Are you a police officer too?'

'That's right. Come and sit down. Can I get you a drink?'

His face lit up.

'You surely can.'

He hesitated and then his voice took on a more submissive tone.

'Erm, have you any bacon? I'm starving. I'd kill for a butty.'

For a moment North wasn't sure she cared for that tone. There was a hint of a whine about it, of the fake little-boy-lost. This kind of thing she'd heard very often in police cells and interview rooms, as petty criminals tried to justify themselves. But she knew the thought was unworthy. Just because there was a history of sibling rivalry between himself and Mike didn't make Jimmy a bad person.

'Actually, I was going to have dinner myself,' she forced herself to say. 'I've got a couple of steaks.'

So much for her quiet evening. Jimmy rubbed his hands with pleasure.

'Sounds the business! And I've got something here that'll go down very nicely with it.'

He crouched and unzipped his bag, bringing out a bottle of wine.

'It's only Californian Zinfandel, but a good one. Uncork it and let it breathe and it should go down a treat. Where's your bottle opener?'

North opened a drawer and rummaged. But before she could grab the corkscrew, Jimmy had appeared beside her and found it first.

'Did Mike tell you I ran a bar in Christchurch,

New Zealand? It was called The British Pub.'

He drew the cork and placed the bottle proudly on the counter. North had her back to him, pouring whisky. Jimmy looked her up and down. She had a nice bum, nice legs, nice blonde hair.

'I tell you what,' he said, as if the thought had surprised him. 'Why don't I cook?'

She turned and looked at him, surprised. This was confident, bordering on cocky. But North, though she meant to resist, was instantly seduced.

'Oh . . . well . . .'

'Hey, it's no problem. Where's the steaks?'

North helplessly indicated the fridge.

'And are those the spices over there?'

'Yes . . . help yourself.'

'Leave it to me! I've got quite a reputation.'

Jimmy was bubbling now. North couldn't help laughing.

'Yes, I believe you have.'

'And not just as a cook!'

North shook her head as if finally to dislodge the false notion of Jimmy that Walker had conveyed to her. Jimmy yanked open the stainless steel door of the fridge and extracted two sirloin steaks.

'What time is Mickey expected back?' he asked.

'He's not. He's staying over at Lynn's.'

'You don't say.'

Jimmy filled a pan with water and started to peel potatoes.

'I was expecting to get a flight out late tonight,' he went on. 'I'm on my way to Florida. But there's been a bit of a hitch. Well, to be honest more than a hitch. See, I can't contact the bloke I'm going out to work for. I've got my ticket. I mean there's no real problem, just means I'm delayed.'

'For how long?'

Jimmy's potato work was expert, shaving the peel into a perfect spiral in seconds.

'Oh just a night or two. Like I said there's no problem. I'll find a wee cheap hotel unless . . .'

North couldn't help smiling.

'Unless we have a spare bedroom?'

Jimmy laughed agreeably.

'Well, yes. I've got to watch the cash. Don't you?'

'I bet you know we do. And yes . . . you can stay over, if you want.'

Jimmy was plopping the last of the potatoes into the water. He smiled his broad, white, charming smile.

'That's a relief. I really appreciate this, Pat. Ma said you were a lovely lady.'

North's eyes opened wide in surprise.

'Did she now? She's changed her tune. She didn't used to approve of me.'

Busy dripping oil into the griddle pan, Jimmy clicked his tongue.

'Och! Don't you pay any attention to her. Bark's worse than her bite. She's got it in a bit for Lynn at the moment though. What's going on there?'

It was something North would like to know. She looked at her watch. She'd catch Walker now, probably. Find out how the interview went, and the latest on Eric.

'Oh, Lynn got herself involved with a real bastard. Violet doesn't approve . . . I think I'll just go and call Mike, OK?'

Jimmy looked at her. A momentary shadow of concern swept his face.

'Fine,' he said.

153

Lynn had spent the late afternoon preparing Walker a cooked meal, *lasagne al forno*, with everything prepared under the orders of Delia Smith, Lynn's favourite TV chef. Walker had reappeared at seven-thirty, still wearing his best suit. He'd hung the jacket in the hall and come through into the living room, where he'd poured himsclf a largc whisky and lit a cigarette. Then he'd thrown himself into an armchair and told her about the Metropolitan Police Authority, the interview panel, the questions and his answers.

'It went great, Lynn. I reckon I'm there. Within a couple of weeks I'll be Commander.'

Lynn felt good too, in spite of her battered face. The thing with Eric had been horrific but it had brought Mike and her closer than they'd been for years. It was like the days when he was a Detective Inspector making a name for himself as a murder specialist. Every evening he'd come home in just this way, hang his coat, pour a whisky, light a fag and tell her about the triumphs and disasters of the day. She'd felt proud of him then, proud to be a policeman's wife, proud to have borne his children. Perhaps—just perhaps—it could be that way again.

There were a couple of nagging problems, though. Pat North was still her rival, still on the scene. And then there was Eric. Was he still on the scene? For a moment, the thought made her guts contract.

While the children watched end-to-end episodes of *The Simpsons*, their parents sat down together to eat the lasagne, which had come out exactly as Delia predicted. As she mopped the last of the sauce from her plate with a lump of olive bread, Lynn asked Walker about his brother.

'What's Jimmy doing in London?'

Walker refilled both their glasses.

'He's on his way to some job in Florida, or so he told Ma. But you know him. Remember when he said he was working down the Glasgow docks as president of a tobacco import company, and all he was doing was nicking fags and selling them in the pubs?'

Lynn laughed then lifted her wine glass.

'To your new job.'

Walker beamed and raised his own glass.

'To you, Mike,' she went on. 'No—I mean, to Commander Walker!'

Richard and Amy came in just as they were drinking. *The Simpsons* was over.

'Hey, kids,' Walker called out jovially. 'You want Commander Walker to tell you a bedtime story?'

*   *   *

By the time North returned to the kitchen, the table was set, the candles lit, and a delicious smell of fried steak filled the air. Jimmy did all the table honours, sitting North down in her seat and plating her food before laying it with a flourish in front of her. They ate the steaks with scalloped potatoes, glazed carrots and lightly buttered peas.

Jimmy, she discovered, could talk for Scotland. He told her his life story in reverse, first about New Zealand, then his time in London and finally his upbringing in Drumchapel, one of the poorest districts in Glasgow. It was a tale of woe, of being let down, taken advantage of, disregarded and cheated.

'Mike was always Ma's bonny blue-eyed boy,' Jimmy told her. 'He could do no wrong. But me, everything I did was wrong. When Dad walked out, that was my fault. She thought everything was always my fault. Haven't seen her for ten years and all I got was "Mike's going to be a Commander, Mike's going to be a Commander." Like a bloody parrot.'

In spite of Jimmy's almost complete self-absorption, North was interested in the details of the Walker family's home life. They were matters Walker himself rarely talked about.

'So, why did he leave?' she asked.

'Dad? Well he'd got some little waitress. Like Mike, he'd always got some skirt in the background.'

'Oh yeah? Thanks for that!'

Jimmy laughed, drained his wine and refilled. North, going easy, placed a hand over her own half-empty glass.

'When we were kids,' said Jimmy, 'I remember wanting to kill Mike for stealing this girl that I was crazy about. I think if anything you really care about as a kid gets taken away from you, it seems bigger, you know? It gets blown up. Things like . . . like Dad going.'

North suddenly thought of Donny, weighed down in the photograph by his guitar.

'I met this little boy recently,' she said, 'only very little he is. But he's *unbelievable* on the guitar. Incredibly talented, but he's all messed up. And his Dad's going away too, though not with a piece of skirt. For murder.'

But Jimmy did not respond and she wondered if

he was even listening. A few seconds passed as they both sipped their wine.

'Are you and Mike thinking about having a family?' asked Jimmy then.

She looked at him steadily.

'No,' she said.

That shut-out was enough, really. But Jimmy had been bleating so much about the injustice of life, she had the urge to even things up, to blast him with a piece of her own experience, something he couldn't possibly cap, as he had capped everything else she had told him.

'I had a miscarriage last year,' she said simply.

That certainly shut Jimmy up. He stared intently into his glass, nonplussed.

'So,' said North brightly, glad to have regained the intiative. 'Are you married, Jimmy?'

Jimmy sniggered. He felt better to be back on the subject of himself.

'No, no. I'm between wives at the moment . . . and neither of them is mine. Aren't you two getting hitched then?'

'Yes, we are.'

'He's a very lucky man.'

He raised his glass and drained it. North acknowledged the compliment with a narrow smile and pushed back her chair. She picked up her plate and, as she reached over to pick up Jimmy's, he grabbed her hand.

'Hey, I'm sorry if I got a bit personal back there, about kids . . . the miscarriage.'

'Oh! That's all right.'

'I remember Ma having one. Dad didn't just leave, he left her up the spout. She said a few Hail Marys when she lost it.'

'Well, I didn't. I wanted mine more than anything.'

She turned abruptly and carried the plates into the kitchen. Jimmy followed.

'Look, I'll wash up,' he said. 'Pay for my bed.'

'No, no, you did the cooking.'

She dumped the plates in the dishwasher and went back to the table, with its remaining debris, and hesitated over it. She suddenly felt utterly exhausted, pulled between the varying demands made on her by Bob Brickman, Walker, Walker's mother, Eric and now Jimmy. She decided to postpone the clearing up.

'I'll do the dishes . . . tomorrow.'

Jimmy shrugged.

'Whatever you say. Mind if I take a shower?'

'No, no, go ahead.'

'You want me to lock up?'

'Yes, thank you.'

She was at the bottom of the stairs.

'Good night.'

'Good night, Pat.'

As she started up the stairs, she glimpsed Jimmy casually reaching into the drinks cupboard. He brought out an unopened bottle of single malt whisky. As she reached the bedroom she heard the metal seal crack as he twisted the top.

Walker chatted with Richard and Amy in Richard's room for half an hour, tucked Richard under his duvet and was taken by the hand into Amy's room to meet her tribe of soft animals, arrayed in a mass around her bed-head. Shortly afterwards Lynn, still aproned after the washing up, found him sitting at the bottom of the stairs, reflectively smoking.

'I've made us some coffee. Do you want a slice of cheesecake?'

He shook his head.

'No, sweetheart. Dinner was lovely. I miss sitting down with you all. They're good kids, Lynn. It's not fair to them really, me not being here.'

He sighed and took another drag on the cigarette. Lynn slipped her apron over her head.

'I don't know what you want me to say to that!'

Walker smiled wryly.

'Nothing. *You* don't have to say anything. But *I've* got to find more time to spend with them.'

'Oh yes?' she said lightly.

'Yes. It'll be good for them to come and stay more weekends—with me and Pat.'

Lynn took this in, then turned on her heel and carried the apron back to the kitchen, hiding her disappointment. She had thought the point Walker wanted to make was that the *family* should get together more often. But it appeared she, Lynn, was not included in the equation. It was more a matter of assuaging his conscience and getting the children to accept that woman as part of their lives, as a stepmother to them.

The man had no bloody idea how she felt, had he? Or, if he had, he didn't care.

CHAPTER THIRTEEN

THURSDAY, 27 MARCH, MORNING

North by no means wanted to see Jimmy in the morning, and nor did she, though she heard his snores forcing their way beneath the door of the spare room. It sounded remarkably similar to his brother's snoring, which she knew so well. It was half-past eight already and she'd overslept. She drank a hurried mug of tea, picked up her keys and snapped open the door of the flat. As she stepped outside and half-turned to close it behind her, she gasped.

The words in big, red, spray paint letters began on the wall about a yard to the left of the doorframe, continued across the door itself and meandered untidily along the right-hand wall towards the top of the stairs. She took a couple of steps back to take in the full effect of the graffiti artist's message.

WHORE. BENT COPS LIVE HERE. WALKER IS A BASTARD ON THE TAKE.

Within seconds she had grabbed the telephone from her bag and dialled Walker's number.

'Where are you?' she said, her voice trembling with anger.

'School gates. I brought the kids.'

He sounded quite proud of himself for performing this routine task.

'Well you're needed back here, Mike. You're needed *right now* back here!'

'Just calm down, Pat. What is it?'

'Not only is your brother in residence, but someone's been outside our door with a spray can.'

'What?'

'A spray can, for God's sake.'

She read him the words on the wall and door.

'So for Christ's sake, come back home, Mike. I'm late for work and it's a really important day, and I—'

'Listen sweetheart, I'll handle this, OK? You just leave it. Go to work.'

'And I want the locks changed. Will you get that done?'

'I said I'll *handle* it, Pat.'

North burst into her office at the Incident Room and dumped her bag on the desk. She had bundled off her coat, and was hurriedly threading it into a hanger, when Satchell tapped and entered. He was carrying a bundle of documents which all appeared to be on fax-paper.

'Gov, we need to talk. Have you seen these?'

He dropped the faxes on her desk.

'They're spewing out all over the station. Some sick pervert's got hold of our fax numbers.'

North hung the coat on the hook behind the door.

'And? Why are you telling me?'

'Because they're about you. They've got your face all over them. And Mike's.'

North picked up the bundle. The top sheet showed a photo, obviously from a porno magazine, of a well-endowed naked woman, with a cut-out of North's face pasted on to it. The crudely written inscription said, simply, *SLAG*. The second sheet did roughly the same job on Walker, with the caption *SHIRT LIFTING SHITHEAD*. The rest were all variations on the same theme.

'What!'

In her shock, the words came out as an enraged whisper. She looked at Satchell.

'Why in God's name . . . ?'

'Like I said,' Satch repeated, 'some real sicko.'

'Are they still coming in?'

'Apparently they all arrived overnight.'

161

North waved the faxes angrily under Satchell's nose, as if he were responsible for them.

'I want a watch put on the fax machines.'

'But we've got a murder invest—'

North interrupted savagely.

'And if any more of this filth comes through, trace the call! Now, we've got more important business in hand today. We're charging Robert Brickman with murder . . .'

*   *   *

'You're sure you didn't hear or see anyone?' Walker shouted, rolling up his shirt sleeves as he passed the bathroom door, in which Jimmy was showering. Walker ran down the stairs and fetched a plastic bucket with a scrubbing brush from beneath the sink. He was filling the kettle as Jimmy appeared on the stairs with a towel around his waist.

'I told you. Nothing. I was asleep.'

Walker jabbed his finger at the half-empty bottle of malt whisky on the kitchen counter.

'Yeah, I bet you were. I thought you were going to Florida. You got some problem with the job?'

'No, no,' said Jimmy. 'The job's fine. It's just there's some hitch with the ticket.'

The kettle boiled and flicked itself off. Walker poured boiling water into the bucket and pulled on a pair of rubber gloves.

'When did you not run into some hitch? Go and get some clothes on, will you? Hey, and those are my slippers!'

'All *right*!'

Jimmy retreated a few steps towards the stairs

162

then turned back to his brother.

'Will it be OK to shack up here for a couple of days, then? Just until the end of the week, then I'm gone.'

'To Florida?' Walker asked satirically. He shook his finger at his brother. 'What happened in New Zealand, Jimmy?'

'That was the problem! Nothing. Nothing ever happens there. That's why I quit.'

Walker was banging more cupboard doors, pulling out soap powder packets and bleach, and pouring liberal quantities of both into the bucket.

'Why did you stay there so long then, if it was that boring? You think I'm dumb or something? What have you done this time, Jimmy?'

His brother was indignant.

'What have I done? Got a good job offer, that's what I've done, all right? Why have you always got to insinuate something's bent?'

'Because where you're concerned it normally is.'

Walker picked up thc bucket and strode to the front door, slopping a trail of soap-suds across the carpet. With an aggrieved air, Jimmy followed and hung idly in the open doorway, watching Walker get to work on the graffiti.

'And don't think I won't check up on you,' Walker was saying as he worked. 'Nothing happened in New Zealand? Bullshit. Two days, Jimmy! Then you're out.'

Walker was scrubbing the wall in circles. The soapy water spread the paint around in pink spiralling smears although the original words could still be easily read.

'You'll never get it off like that,' put in Jimmy. 'You want to repaint. That's what I'd do.'

Walker gave his brother a filthy look and continued doggedly scrubbing.

'This guy's obviously nuts,' he said. 'He's beaten my wife, terrified my kids, and now this.'

'Why can't you pick him up?'

'Because,' Walker snarled, 'we don't know who the bastard is, OK?'

*   *   *

Lynn hummed along with the Harry Nilsson anthem playing on the radio as she got started on tonight's supper, chopping the fresh steak she had bought yesterday. It was still only eleven but she wanted to have the aroma of home-made steak and kidney pie, a great favourite of Walker's, filling the house by the time he came back.

She heard the letterbox flap rattling and expected it was the postman. Wiping her hand, bloody from the steak, across her apron, she went through into the hall. There were no letters on the mat. The flap rattled again and she glimpsed fingers poking momentarily through. She recognized them at once by their bitten nails.

It was Eric.

The fingers disappeared and were followed by an almighty crash, and another, the impacts accompanied by the sound of splintering wood. Eric was trying to kick down the door.

'Open the door, Lynn. Open . . . this . . . DOOR!'

Lynn felt her stomach lurch.

'No! Go away! Eric, go away. I'm calling the police.'

Eric's fist began battering the coloured glass that

164

was inset into the door. He hit it again and again. She ran back to the kitchen and, scrabbling for the phone, managed to press the number nine three times.

'Emergency services,' came the voice. 'Which service do you require?'

In the hall the door glass shattered and shards fell inwards.

'This is Lynn Walker of 46 Har—'

'Which service do you require, madam?'

'What? Oh! Police, I want the police. There's someone breaking into my house.'

'What is your name, please?'

She edged into a position that gave her a sightline to the front door. Eric had made a jagged hole in the door glass and his hand had pushed through to release the chain and the spring-lock. Now he was pushing, kicking and yelling again, but the closed bolts at top and bottom of the door had for the moment defeated him.

'My name?' said Lynn. 'It's Lynn, Mrs Lynn Walker, 46 Harcourt Green.'

'What postcode, please?'

'The *postcode*? Look just send me someone to help me. My number's 020 8543 7007. Yes, that is my phone here, I am at home, I—'

There was an ominous silence in the hall. Eric's shadow had disappeared from behind the glass.

'Please,' begged Lynn. 'Dear God, *please*.'

'We are doing all we can, madam. Please stay on the line.'

She hung on, cramming the phone against her ear as if this gave her more safety. She kept her eyes on the hall door, watching for any flicker on the glass, any sound. But the sound, when it came, was from another direction. With a shuddering, shattering concussion, the garden door exploded through its frame and crashed to the floor.

Lynn dropped the phone with a shriek. Her only thought now was to get outside, to avoid being trapped inside these walls. She ran into the hall and fumbled at the door bolts. The lower one drew back but the upper would not move, bent out of shape by Eric's earlier assault.

'LYNN!' roared the intruder from the rear of the house. And then his voice changed to sing-song, like the parody of a child playing hide and seek.

'Lynn! I'm in he-ere! And I'm co-oming for you!'

Reaching up on tip-toe, and with all her strength, she dragged at the upper bolt until it shifted a little, then a little more, then shot back with a sound like a rifle-crack. Heaving the door open, she looked round. Eric was in the house. She heard a cutlery drawer clatter, and then saw a shadow move in the dark rear of the hall. He was advancing on her, hunting her. Suddenly she saw his outline, large and looming, with some metal object glinting in his hand. It was a blade. It was her long kitchen knife.

Lynn screamed. She yanked the door back and it juddered against the wall. She hurled herself across the threshold.

'LYNN!'

She ignored the voice behind her. As she passed herself through the half-open front gate, she barked her shin cruelly against the gate-post, but hardly felt the pain. Eric's footfall was slap-slapping behind her as she ran clumsily along the street, still screaming with all her strength. And then in front of her was the wail of a police siren, the squeal of tyres and the click of the squad-car's doors springing open.

Eric's steps behind her faltered and without looking round she knew he had turned back. The police officers saw him as they reached Lynn, disappearing back through the gate of number 46. One of them stayed with her, holding her by the shoulders and making reassuring noises while she babbled that he was a maniac who wanted to beat her and kill her. The other officers sprinted after Eric and into the house.

One galloped up the stairs, while the other rapidly searched the living room, the kitchen, the passage and at last went into the garden through the smashed back door. But by the time he reached the rabbit hutches lined up below the far garden wall, Eric had gone. All there was to find was the big carving knife on the ground. Eric had dropped it in his scramble to get over the wall and away.

CHAPTER FOURTEEN

THURSDAY, 27 MARCH, AFTERNOON AND EVENING

North had not seen Walker since Tuesday morning, but she was not at all pleased to find him now, at four o'clock, in her Incident Room, crouched over a computer terminal with Detective Sergeant Dave Satchell. He, on the other hand, greeted her arrival with a cry of triumph.

'Pat, Satch has nailed the bastard! Fingerprints on the knife from Lynn's house! Look.'

He pointed to the screen, where the computerized fingerprint-matching system was up and running.

'Eric Fowler. Two prison terms for aggravated assault. Psych report says he has a severe personality disorder and has suffered from violent schizophrenia.'

He held Fowler's sheet in the air between finger and thumb in front of her face. She did not hide her irritation.

'Mike, this is not your case. You're on leave. You shouldn't be here.'

But Walker in this mood was unstoppable. He read from Eric Fowler's chronological record.

'Last known address, Ramsfield mental institution, Brighton, discharged '96. Howe Hospital, discharged ditto. Sussex neurological hospital, discharged.'

'Mike!'

'They don't know where he is now, though. Bloody Social Services have lost him.'

'Mike!'

'But am I worried? No way, because I've got an address for his Ma.'

North stood slack-jawed, unable to believe that Walker could hijack her facilities like this.

'Oh, by the way, Lynn and the kids are OK,' Walker told her. 'But I'm moving them into a hotel for safety while this bastard's still at large. Come on, Satch.'

Beckoning he made towards the exit, then checked and spun round, indicating Satchell with his thumb.

'Oh, do you need him today?'

'Yes, I bloody well do!' said North. 'And you

have to back off, Mike. There's already an officer in charge of the Fowler case.'

Walker scoffed openly at this.

'Yeah, yeah, I hear you. But you and I both know that the locals won't dig shit. I am not wasting any more time. I want this bastard off the streets.'

'And I don't?' challenged North, her eyes flashing.

'Come on, Mike,' urged Satchell. 'If you go out like some vigilante you'll only make a lot of trouble for yourself.'

Walker wiped the air with spread hands.

'I don't need your advice on this one Pat, or yours, Satch. I'm taking care of it because these are my kids, and my wife. Oh, sorry. My *former* wife.'

North grabbed his sleeve.

'You're a police officer, Mike. I'm a police officer. This is going to—'

But Walker was not to be denied. He shook himself free.

'Just back off me on this one, Pat, I mean it. And you too, Satch.'

Walker shoved the paper with Mrs Fowler's details into his pocket and strode towards the exit, banging out through the swing doors. As his footsteps faded down the stairwell the team stared after him. North looked truculently from one to another.

'And what are *you* all staring at? He shouldn't be in *my* Incident Room!'

One by one, exchanging knowing grins, they returned to their allotted tasks. Satchell pointed to the orders, lists, rosters and photographs pinned to the Incident Room wall-boards.

'Should we take these down, Gov?'

North still felt angry and frustrated. Unable to control Walker, she barked at Satchell instead.

'No. Brickman's not been in bloody court yet and, until he has, they stay!'

*   *   *

Bob Brickman had already been charged with abduction. Now he was also formally accused of murder and removed from his police holding cell to the remand wing of Brixton Prison, where he would await a bail hearing. He could also now receive family visitors and, at four-thirty, his brother Alan presented a Visiting Order at the main gate and was escorted through.

In the Visiting Suite there was no physical separation of inmates and visitors, just low tables and easy chairs. Everything was unthreateningly functional, like the public areas of a district hospital with the one difference that, here, every angle, every view across the room, was covered by a security camera. And the input of every camera was continuously recorded. In an adjoining control room, prison officers sat in front of a battery of monitors, watching every move.

'I brought fruit, grapes and nuts and stuff,' said Alan in the church-whisper instinctively adopted in prison visiting-rooms. 'And some chocolate bars. They took them off me at the gate. Said you'd get them later.'

Bob sniggered.

'Probably checking every grape for a file. How's Mum?'

'She's coping. But you know her. She's more interested in her dinner than anything else.'

170

'And my lovely boy Donny?'

'I've kept him off school. It's in the papers you've been charged, so I thought it best.'

Bob smiled, thinking of his son.

'I want to see him, Alan. I've worked out some lessons for him. You got to keep him practising, Alan.'

He looked at his brother, but Alan wouldn't meet his gaze. He concentrated moodily on the low tabletop between them.

'It was in his guitar case,' he said in an even more subdued voice. 'In his guitar case, you *bastard*!'

Bob was confused. He frowned. Alan looked up and caught his brother's reaction.

'The baseball bat,' he said.

Bob did not move a muscle, except for his lips which seemed to be shaping unspoken words. Then he said,

'You've got nothing to worry about, Alan. They'll never find nothing out from me. Get rid of the bat.'

'Oh, I already did. I cut it up and shredded it.'

Without warning Bob reached across with both his hands and grasped Alan around the neck. He pulled him towards him, shaking with emotion, until their foreheads touched.

'I love you Alan. Remember that. So you take good care of my boy. Nobody's going to take him away from us.'

He let go of Alan's neck and dropped his head almost to the table. Alan's hand lay there and Bob held it and kissed it.

'Nobody,' he repeated.

Alan withdrew his hand, embarrassed.

171

'Look Bob, it's not as simple as that. So . . . this isn't permanent, nothing like that, but I think I should get Sharon back.'

Abruptly, Bob shook his head.

'No,' he said. 'No way.'

'It's for Donny's sake. Then if anyone comes snooping round, we'll look like a happy family.'

Alan couldn't tell if his brother was considering this, or if his mind had wandered off on some other tack.

'I also need you to countersign some cheques,' he went on, 'and we've still got to get a lawyer to give me power of attorney over the business and custody of Donny until you get out.'

Casually, Bob leaned back and rubbed his finger down his chin.

'Bob?'

'I'm thinking about it.'

Alan leaned forward and spoke in a near whisper.

'Yes, well, after what I've done for you, you'd better think about it, and fast. That was the deal—right?'

*   *   *

The address on Walker's piece of paper was a fifties' block of flats in Shoreditch, a solidly built but now heavily scuffed council development. Walker made his way up some dank outside stairs, along a deck walkway and past a succession of front doors until he reached Mrs Fowler's flat. He sounded the bell with a long ring.

He listened carefully. There was shuffling within and a worn, overweight woman of about sixty, in a

172

pale blue cardigan, opened the door. Walker held up his warrant card.

'Mrs Fowler? I am a police officer. May I come in?'

He looked past her into the tiny, passage-like hall. Rooms led off it to left and right. All the doors but one were shut.

'What's the trouble? Where's your mate? You lot usually come in pairs.'

'It's about your son, Eric. Just a quick word, eh?'

With a sigh she stood aside and Walker marched through into the sitting room. Here the television was on, midway through one of those daytime lifestyle programmes that claim they can make you wealthier, healthier, trendier, sexier or just happier. Mrs Fowler, on whom this output had never had any discernible effect, followed the policeman through and lowered herself into the chair she'd clearly been occupying most of the day. An empty mug, an ashtray full of stubs and the TV remote control were balanced in a line on the chair's arm.

'So what's he done now?' she asked wearily.

Walker made it a general rule never to answer questions when he himself had more important ones to ask.

'I need to contact Eric, Mrs Fowler. Where is he?'

She picked up the remote and upped the volume as Walker looked around the room. He noted a mid-range desktop computer standing in front of the window. It was turned on and the screen saver was of a well-endowed, bikini-clad female posing on a beach.

'He's not right in the head you know,' Eric's mother said above the TV chatter. 'He never was.

173

Anyway, whatever he's gone and done, it's nothing to do with me.'

'When did you last see him?'

'Oh, I don't know, he comes and goes.'

She continued to eye the screen, peering round Walker, who tried to stand in the way.

'Where is he now?'

'I never know where he is. What do you want him for?'

Walker grabbed the remote from her and zapped the programme out of existence. He broke his rule about questions and answers, as was sometimes necessary to get to the next question.

'He's been making threats.'

'Threats? He's getting married, that's what he told me. Got a new girlfriend.'

She pointed at the television.

'And *you've* got no right to do that!'

'Are you expecting Eric here?'

She shook her head.

'No, no. I don't know where he is. He's not been here for, oh, a long time.'

Still holding the TV control unit, Walker crossed to the PC and slapped it with the flat of his hand.

'But he *has* been here recently. This computer is his, for instance, isn't it? He's living here isn't he?'

The old woman scowled.

'No, he's not. And if you lot would just leave him alone he'd be a sight better off.'

'Mrs Fowler,' said Walker, coming back to her and leaning down until his face was just an inch from hers. 'I wouldn't try to protect him. We really need to trace him, it's *very* important.'

His voice was low and menacing, but Mrs Fowler was impervious to his tone. She simply plucked the remote control from his fingers and zapped the television back on. Walker hesitated, then went to the front door and let himself out.

He had, in a sense, got what he came for. Eric had obviously been holed up with his mother and had brought his computer with him. There was a modem connected, he'd noticed. And if they looked into the Internet application he'd been using, they would surely find evidence of his membership of the sensualsingles site and his many visits to it, including yesterday afternoon's. Eric had not disappeared into the hinterland. He was still in London, still close at hand, and still a threat.

*   *   *

When North reached her front door, at the end of a day of end-to-end paperwork, she saw that Walker had managed to create a huge pink and red smear, like an action painting, across the wall and door. But at least he had succeeded in obscuring the words of Eric Fowler's nasty message. She made a mental note to contact a housepainter and let herself in.

Jimmy was lying on the sofa, barefooted and half-dressed, watching *EastEnders*.

'Hi,' he said, as she came in. 'Had a good day?'

'I've had better.'

'Did you find the phantom paint sprayer?'

'Not yet. But at least we know who he is now.'

'How are Lynn and the kids?'

'They're fine. Though it feels like I'm seeing a little too much of Mike's family these days.'

She hung her coat and went to fill the kettle at the kitchen sink.

'Speaking of which, just how long do *you* intend staying, Jimmy? This really isn't a hotel, and—'

'Don't take it out on me,' protested Jimmy. 'It's no my fault. Couple of days, till my ticket comes through.'

She snatched a mug from the drainer and dropped a tea bag into it.

'Ticket? I thought you had your ticket. I thought the problem was with the job offer.'

Jimmy forced his eyes open wide and shook his head.

'No, no,' he said, 'it's just the ticket. The job's sorted. Where's Mike?'

She tried to remember if what he had just said about the job was what he'd originally told her, but quickly gave up. So much had been happening lately.

'Mike? He's staying at a hotel, with his wife—his ex-wife—and his kids.'

'So it's just you and me tonight, then.'

Jimmy allowed a pause to lengthen over a few beats while she made herself tea. Then he said, like one having a surprisingly good idea,

'What do you say we go out? An Indian, maybe, or Chinese? My treat.'

North stirred semi-skimmed milk into her tea.

'I don't think so. I'm really tired out.'

Jimmy came over and stood within touching distance behind her.

'All the more reason, Pat,' he said, wheedling now. 'You don't want to cook. Come on girl, comb your hair, slap on a bit of lipstick, let's go eat!'

North sipped from her mug as she moved away from him towards the stair.

'No thanks, Jimmy. I'm having a bath.'

176

The bath was delicious, warm water seeping into her limbs, the fresh scent of her bath salts reviving her spirit. She was soaping her neck and shoulders when there came a tap on the door and almost instantaneously it clicked open. It was Jimmy, looking down on her with a grin. Gasping, she crossed her arms across her breasts.

'I'm no going to take no for an answer, Pat,' he said, goggling at her soapy body through the steam. 'I've booked us a table at the local curry house. My treat and I've pre-ordered, so chop chop! Hot, hotter and scorching for me!'

Then he was gone and she sank back under the water, dazed and astonished at his sheer gall.

*   *   *

It clearly was not the Savoy, but the chain hotel was clean and reached acceptable roadhouse standards of comfort and décor. Walker had taken a family room, which meant the kids were bundled together, fast asleep at ten o'clock, in a collapsible single bed, while the double was there for the parents. This apparent arrangement had not escaped Lynn's notice.

'What, we're going to share are we?'

Walker was sitting up with his back against the headrest, smoking.

'I mean I don't mind,' she went on, 'but the kids could have had the double . . .'

'They still can if you like, sweetheart, because I'm not staying. It'll be perfectly all right. You'll be safe. He doesn't know you're here.'

He patted the mattress and she sat down beside him. He put his hand on hers.

'Anyway, I'll kill the bastard if he tries to contact you or the kids again. I mean it, Lynn. I'll kill him.'

Her face creased in distress. The bruises were now a deep mottled purple, giving her a new, more sinister appearance. 'Don't say that. Don't *do* this to me, Mike. What the hell, you know you've got me. All you have to do is . . .'

Walker gave a single splutter of laughter.

'You stop it, Lynn. Don't twist things around. I'm talking about protection, that's all.'

*   *   *

It was raining on the way home, which at least helped to cool the effects of the spiciest curry North had ever tasted—if 'tasted' was the word. Her tongue felt swollen and ravaged.

'My God, when you said hot . . .' she remarked as they reached the front door and Jimmy lowered the umbrella they'd shared. 'I'm still weak at the knees.'

'Are you sure it wasn't all those lagers?'

She waved the suggestion away.

'No, don't be daft. It takes a lot more than that to put me under the table.'

She keyed in the entry code and, pushing into the main building, they made their way up the stairs. For some reason, a question she'd been meaning to ask all evening now came to the fore.

'Jimmy . . . Mike paid for you to go to New Zealand, didn't he?'

Jimmy didn't like the question.

'He told you that, did he?'

'Yes, sort of. Said you were in some kind of trouble and—'

178

'Well, let me tell *you*,' he interrupted, speaking savagely for a moment. 'My brother is a liar, he always was. He wanted me out of the way, so he'd have no competition.'

'Oh yes?' she asked innocently. 'What kind of competition was that?'

They were at the flat door now. Jimmy touched with his fingertips the garish smears of paint on the wall.

'Och, you name it. That's Mike, isn't it?'

Jimmy hadn't been bad company during the evening. He had a way with words and had told one or two good stories. But now, quite suddenly, North realized that she didn't like him. She didn't like him at all. She rammed her key into the lock and twisted it round.

'Well it couldn't have bothered him that much,' she said. 'He never even mentions you.'

She led him into the flat, not displeased with the put-down. But she might have known he would have a comeback. Jimmy always did.

'I'm actually not his problem, Pat. He's his own worst enemy, and I don't why *you're* defending him, with his playing around.'

'Playing around? What's that supposed to mean?'

'Shacked up with his ex-wife is what I mean.'

She knew this had to stop, and now.

'I don't like what you are inferring,' she said stiffly. 'Now, if you'll excuse me, I'm going to bed.'

But Jimmy was barring her way to the stairs. He was smiling in a sickly way that he mistook for seductive.

'Why don't I come with you?'

He took her upper arm, grasping it tightly, and

179

drew her so close she could smell his curried breath.

'You've been flirting all night. Come on Pat, what's stopping you?'

With a convulsive movement she shrugged herself out of his grip and stepped back.

'Listen, *Jimmy*. I didn't tick you off earlier about walking into the bathroom. Maybe I should have. But you just try one more move on me and I'll—'

'You'll what? Nobody's here, darling. Loverboy's with his cuddly little wife.'

North stepped forward and landed a stinging slap on Jimmy's face. He staggered slightly and put a hand to his cheek.

'I want you *out* of here, Jimmy,' hissed North. 'Right now.'

She turned away and started up the stairs. Jimmy stood with his hands spread in a gesture of baffled innocence.

'Hey, come on Pat, I was only joking. We've just had a bit too much to drink, that's all.'

North turned.

'No. I mean it Jimmy. I want you out of the flat, tonight.'

'But I've no place to go! Pat, please. I'm sorry. I'm really sorry, all right?'

But she ignored him.

In the bedroom she picked up her mobile phone from the bedside table and checked the display. There were no messages. She sighed, sat down at her dressing table and keyed in Walker's number, unhooking her earrings as she waited. He answered almost at once.

'Mike?'

'Yes, sweetheart.'

'OK, that's it! I've just about had enough of your *bloody* family. I've been very patient with all this Lynn business but I am NOT going to put up with it any more.'

She unhooked her silver necklet and flipped open the jewel box, which she kept on the dressing table. It was a neat little leather-covered box that her father had given her many years ago. She was about to drop the necklet and earrings inside when she realized the box was strangely empty.

'Oh my God!'

She stirred the contents around. There were a couple of strings of beads and a few other bits of costume jewellery. But everything of value was missing.

'Jesus!' she said, still holding the phone to her ear.

'What's the matter, Pat?' asked Walker. 'What's up?'

She tipped the contents of the box out. There was no question. The lapis lazuli ring was missing, so was the 9-carat charm bracelet she'd had since she was twelve, and the string of cultured pearls. AND her diamond engagement ring that Walker had given her in the hospital after her miscarriage. She was sure everything had been there at the weekend, when she'd last looked.

'Mike,' she said, 'just hang on for a moment, will you?'

She stormed out on to the landing.

'Jimmy?'

There was no reply. She flung open the door of the spare bedroom and looked in. It was empty. The bed was a tangle of bedclothes, but Jimmy's bag was gone. The bathroom was empty too.

'Jimmy!' she called again.

It seemed he had heeded her instruction and already cleared out. She returned to the phone.

'Mike! You still there?'

'Pat, what's going on for God's sake?'

'Listen, Mike. Trying to make a pass at me I can deal with, but now he's stolen my jewellery. There's a whole load of stuff missing.'

Walker whistled.

'The little bastard. When I get my hands on him—'

'I want you to come home, Mike. Now. I am fed up with looking after your family. *I* want to be looked after, just for once.'

Walker's voice was soothing.

'I'm already on my way, OK? Should be with you in a few minutes.'

North was surprised.

'Oh, aren't you staying at the hotel?'

'I was, but I miss you. They'll be safe enough there, anyway.'

The knowledge that he would be back within minutes calmed her.

'Right. I'll see you in a bit then.'

She clicked off the phone and carried on undressing. She did not hear Jimmy, down in the kitchen, tip the last of another bottle of whisky down his throat, toss the empty into the bin and pick up the bag waiting by the door. Quietly, he let himself out of the flat. He had, of course, been ready to depart in a hurry. He always made sure he was.

He switched off the light, eased open the door and let himself silently out. A few moments later he was skipping down the stairs, where he met a big,

182

balding man in a beige zipper jacket on his way up. Jimmy took the man to be a resident. As they passed, the stranger lurched sideways, barging Jimmy against the wall. You might almost have said he did it on purpose.

'Oi! Wanker!' Jimmy yelled out, rubbing his shoulder. The stranger said nothing in reply but carried on up the stairs.

CHAPTER FIFTEEN

THURSDAY, 27 MARCH, NIGHT

As Jimmy stepped out into the night air, the rain had lightened but it was still drizzling. He saw a licensed taxi enter the private drive and stop. Jimmy signalled to it. At first he felt glad to see the cab, but that was before he realized it was bringing his brother home.

'Oh, er, hi,' he said, when the door opened and Walker loomed above him. 'I didn't expect you back tonight, Mickey.'

'Cut the crap, Jimmy,' said Walker, stepping out on to the Tarmac. 'We both know what this is about.'

The cabbie leaned across and called to Jimmy through the nearside window.

'Did you want this cab or what, mate?'

'Oh, no, you're all right,' said Jimmy, waving him away.

But Walker pushed between Jimmy and the cab driver, handing his fare through the window.

'Yes, he does want it. But can you just hold on

for two minutes?'

The cabbie shrugged.

'Suit yourself.'

In one movement, Walker spun round and seized the holdall from Jimmy. He dropped it on the damp ground and yanked back the zip.

'What the hell are you doing?' protested Jimmy.

He caught hold of one of the handles and pulled hard. Walker chopped his arm.

'Pat's jewellery. Get your hand off!'

He rummaged around inside the bag.

'Give me my bag,' Jimmy shouted. He sounded suddenly desperate, which convinced Walker he was on the right track.

'Pat's jewellery,' repeated Walker. 'Where is it?'

'What? What are you talking about?'

'I mean it Jimmy. I want that stuff you stole back. Now.'

'You're fucking crazy,' said Jimmy. 'Get the hell out of my bag.'

The more panic there was in Jimmy's voice the more certain Walker was that he would find the jewellery in the bag. The bag was off the ground now, as he and Jimmy, holding one handle each, were pulling and twisting to gain advantage. Suddenly the bag swivelled over and much of its contents tumbled out on the glinting Tarmac: passport, a pair of jeans, T-shirts, duty free cigarettes, sponge bag. With a gasp, Jimmy tried to scrabble for the spilled items while Walker thrust a hand into the bag and came out with something wrapped in oilcloth. It weighed heavy for the parcel's size and had to be made of steel. It seemed to be an angled object, one end being longer and slimmer, the other shorter but twice as bulky.

184

Jimmy, still crouching, watched aghast as Walker dropped the holdall and unwrapped the thing he'd found. It was of black metal. He dropped the oilcloth and held it up to the light. It was a Luger automatic pistol.

The first to react was the cab driver. He took one look at the gun in Walker's hand, rammed his car into gear and drove off without a word. Jimmy rose slowly to his feet while Walker stood transfixed by his find. Then Jimmy took a faltering step towards his brother.

'I can explain, Mickey. It's not mine. I'm just delivering it for a . . . a mate.'

Walker turned the piece round, examining it from every angle. Then in a burst of anger he shoved his brother hard in the middle of his chest. Jimmy staggered backwards.

'You know what, Jimmy? I don't want to know. I'm tired, and I need to see Pat now.'

Jimmy held out his hand.

'Mike, give me the gun.'

Walker didn't react and Jimmy lunged forward to grab what he wanted, but Walker stepped back, lifting the gun out of reach. Then he stuffed it into his jacket pocket.

'Give it me back, Mike.' Jimmy was pleading now. 'Mike, please! It doesn't belong to me. If I don't hand it over, I'll get my legs broken.'

'Oh yeah?'

Walker stood for a moment and watched as Jimmy bent to gather up his passport, sponge bag and cigarettes.

'For Christ's sake,' Jimmy went on. 'What were you *doing*? Do you think I'd nick Pat's stuff? I swear I didn't, I swear on Ma's life. Come on Mike,

I'm your brother.'

Walker's face was set hard as he looked down at Jimmy.

'Yeah, you're my brother. But let me tell you, if you weren't I'd have you arrested. Just like I should have years ago.'

He reached into his breast pocket and pulled out his wallet, which he flipped open. There was a wad of notes he'd earlier extracted from a cash dispenser and this he tossed on the ground at Jimmy's feet.

'Go to Florida, or wherever you were going. I won't look after you any more Jimmy.'

Jimmy crouched and pulled the holdall towards him as he quickly picked up the money. He stuffed it into the holdall as Walker turned and marched towards the door of the flats. His brother looked up desperately as he reached for the pair of jeans tightly rolled up around a T-shirt. As he pushed this too into the bag, the roll loosened and an earring dropped out.

'Look after me?' he shouted, not noticing the spilled piece of jewellery. 'That's a good one. You never did, Mike, you never did. You only ever looked after number *one*.'

Walker was at the entrance now, pressing the access code on the keypad. Jimmy stood up again.

'And I never touched Pat! It was *her* wanted me!'

Violently, Walker shoved open the door and passed through. Jimmy threw himself forward to catch it before it shut again.

'Oi!' he shouted up the stairs. 'I said I need that gun back!'

But Walker kept on going upstairs.

*   *   *

Eric Fowler hadn't paid any attention to the little guy with the bleached hair and leather jacket who'd bumped into him on his way up the stairs. Eric was intent on his object, which was to punish that shithead policeman for wrecking his chances with Lynn and for threatening his mother in her own home. Eric was not going to let these serious crimes pass. Eric had turned himself into an instrument of retribution.

He noted the red paint around the door with a grim but contented smile. It looked satisfactorily like smeared blood. Producing Richard's keys he tried the lock but it wouldn't turn, which made him growl angrily and strike the door hard with his fist. He struck it again, and again, a series of hammer-blows. Then stepped back and charged it with a bull-like roar.

Carefully, as always, North was brushing her teeth in the bathroom, using the electric toothbrush which Walker had recently given her. Its buzz largely masked the thumping sounds she could vaguely hear from downstairs and she carried on with her task, supposing the noises to come from outside or another of the flats. But then a burst of enraged shouts, obviously close to her own flat's door attracted her attention. She stopped her brushing to listen. There was a crash, followed by a grunt. It was enough to send her out into the landing, where she knew for certain that someone was trying to force their way through the front door of the flat.

She hardly had time to react before the door yielded with a wood-splitting crack. It crashed

187

inwards, bouncing back against the wall, followed by the shape of a large man stumbling in through the aperture. He was carried by his own momentum into the centre of the darkened room, where he skidded on a toy police car left there by Richard Walker, and floundered into a glass-topped table, on which stood the empty whisky bottle left a few minutes earlier by Jimmy. North gave a shriek as the man lost his balance and went down heavily, shattering the tabletop and bottle and hitting the floor amongst the debris of broken glass. He did not long lie still, but immediately rolled over and sat up, looking to see where her cry had come from. She heard him mutter,

'That Walker's tart?'

Only then did North appreciate that this must be Eric Fowler. As he began to climb laboriously to his feet, she stood, rooted and appalled. Eric swung his head looking from side to side, seeming disoriented. Then he paused to examine his right arm, clawing at a piece of glass that had become embedded there. The shard fell away and a fountain of blood spurted high into the air. The glass had severed an artery.

When she saw the gushing blood North cut short a second shriek by biting her knuckles, but Eric had already located the truncated sound. With a finger jamming his wound, he bent to pick up, with his other hand, the jagged remains of the whisky bottle. Then he lumbered purposefully towards the stairs and began to climb towards her. North ran back to the bedroom and banged the door behind her, dragging furniture in front of it to make some sort of a barricade. Eric came on up, still leaking blood as he reached the top and staggered along the landing. He did not hesitate, but threw himself at the bedroom door with all his bulk and roared with all the strength of his lungs.

'Let me in, bitch!'

She resisted desperately, holding the door, pushing to keep him out and screaming. She heard his breathing, his grunts as he pushed and pushed to get in. Then she heard something else. It was another voice at the top of the stairs, a man's voice—Walker's voice.

'Eric, Eric Fowler! Get away from that door. BACK OFF, Eric!'

The pressure on the door ceased and she sank to the floor sobbing.

'Pat!' Walker shouted. 'You all right? Pat, where are you?'

She tried to catch her breath.

'I'm here,' she whispered, not loudly enough. 'I'm here, Mike.'

Through the door, she could still hear the rasping sobs of Eric's breathing, receding from her now as he moved back along the landing.

'Pat! You all right?' Walker called again, but then his tone changed.

'Hey! You bastard. Back off. Drop the bottle. You're going to hurt somebody.'

North managed to stand, using the door handle for support.

'BOTTLE?' she heard Eric scream. 'Hurt ME? You can't hurt ME!'

'Put it down, Eric,' Walker shouted. 'Get back. Put the bottle DOWN!'

North scrabbled at her makeshift barricade, hurling the chair away and shoving the chest of drawers back to get the door open.

The next few moments were jumbled together, so that when she later tried to reconstruct them for the police she became confused. The two men were shouting, yelling. She pulled the door open. There was a lot of blood as she came out of the bedroom. As she moved down the corridor, she screamed.

'Oh my God! Mike! Mike, NO!'

But it was much too late. It had already happened. Eric was down and she was kneeling beside him. He was half-sitting, half-lying, like an unstrung puppet against the wall, a smear of blood behind him where he had slithered down. His plump face had taken on a look of intense amazement. The look lasted only a few seconds, then vanished, to be replaced by no expression at all, just a vacancy, and Eric slumped forward, his head hanging lifelessly away from the wall. She felt for a pulse on his jugular while Walker stood waiting, breathing heavily. She kept her fingers pressed against Eric's neck for many seconds, then took them away and slowly rose to her feet.

'He's just died, Mike.'

She looked at Walker. He did not seem to hear but continued to stand there, glowering down at Eric's lifeless body.

'Mike, he's dead,' she repeated.

And at some point, somewhere in the middle of all the yelling and shouting, in the three or four seconds between her pulling down her barricade and dropping to her knees beside Eric Fowler's body, there had been a very loud noise—a crack, report, bang or shot, it was hard to choose the best word. Now, kneeling beside Eric, she looked down at the floor and saw the handgun lying where it had fallen. And she understood.

CHAPTER SIXTEEN

FRIDAY, 28 MARCH

'You're in a certain amount of shit here, Mike—I'd say about up to your eyebrows.'

Walker, still covered in Eric Fowler's blood, had arrived at the police station at around midnight, in the custody of local uniforms. Now he was in conference with Andrew Pinton, the solicitor who had left a dinner party to respond to Walker's call.

'Yes, Andrew,' he sighed, smoking as he paced up and down the police cell. 'I do know how it looks.'

Walker was exhausted and desperate for a shower. He stank of human blood but he couldn't wash until forensics had seen him. The arrest of a police officer suspected of murder was no different from that of any other mortal, except that he *was* a police officer—a senior murder detective to boot. Walker was therefore in no doubt that the Serious Crime Group would be playing this case as straight as the crease in the Commissioner's trousers.

'But I wonder if you do really, Mike. You see, they got the victim's mother down to formally identify him, and she's given a blistering statement about you being at her flat yesterday, threatening to kill him.'

Walker swung round.

'She's bloody lying!'

'Sounds pretty believable, though.'

'But I *didn't* threaten to kill him. I had this from the CID prat in here. It happened while I was being attacked. When am I going to find someone who believes me?'

Pinton smiled in an attempt at reassurance.

'We all believe you, Mike. But you can see how they might try to steer it: no accidental firing, and no self-defence because the defendant's armed himself with an illegal gun and shot the man dead. You've got to think clearly.'

'I don't need to think clearly, it was an accident. The bloody thing went off, bang! How was I to know?'

Now Pinton's smile broadened, pleased that Walker had provided him with an opening.

'Exactly, Mike. You wouldn't expect an *imitation* firearm to go off, now would you?'

Walker frowned.

'Who said anything about an imitation firearm?'

Pinton raised his finger in the gesture of a lawyer arriving at a significant juncture in the argument.

'Ah, well now, let's just see where this takes us. The last thing you'd expect is for your own brother to be carrying a loaded gun—correct?'

Walker's lip curled.

'That piece of shite would be capable of carrying anything.'

But Pinton did not want to hear this. He put his finger to his lips.

'Mike, listen to me. The last thing you'd expect is your own brother, staying—remember—in your own flat, to be carrying a loaded gun. Am I right, or am I right?'

Walker sighed, going along with the lawyer.

'OK, you're right.'

'Good! So when he tells you it's a toy gun, you believe him. Correct?'

192

'When he tells me—*what*? Where did you get that from? I don't remember him saying anything about—'

Pinton was smiling again.

'Quite, quite. You've had one hell of a shock. Just give yourself a chance to reconstruct it all so that it all makes sense. A man who thinks he is holding an imitation firearm is unlikely to have the necessary intent for murder, d'you see?'

Pinton waited a moment to let this sink in, before going on in a low, confidential voice.

'Now, if your own brother tells you it's a toy gun, you're going to believe him, aren't you? Of course you are. And no doubt that's why you didn't arrest your brother isn't it?'

'Oh! Right . . .'

Walker had begun to understand where this was going.

'So,' the lawyer went on smoothly, 'what do you do? Why, the sensible thing, of course. You just take it off him, no fuss, and put it in your pocket. You know what, Mike? I'd have done the same thing myself. See?'

Walker broke the filter off a cigarette, jammed it between his lips and lit up. Yes, he saw.

'Now, you've interviewed enough people in this sort of situation. You know the form. Just take your time, tell the truth and you'll be all right. I'll be in there with you.'

Walker inhaled smoke sharply.

'Just get me out of here, will you?'

Pinton patted Walker on the shoulder.

'As I say, Mike, you know the form. They can't let you out tonight. Tomorrow they'll take statements and all that, and then I think we'll be able to have a pretty good shot at getting you bail.'

'I should bloody well think so,' commented Walker dryly.

But after Pinton had gone, he thought to himself,

'If I was investigating this incident, would I support letting me out on bail?'

Like bloody fun he would! He'd fight it with every weapon he had.

*　　　*　　　*

The cabbie at the small suburban station felt warmly towards his fare. She was a curly-haired blonde with a fantastic figure, and a nature so open and friendly that you couldn't help liking her. She was the kind of person who'd talk to anyone, about anything, not least the topic that was his own personal hobby-horse, true crime or, to be more specific, true murder. It was when she'd told him her destination, Brickman's Sawmill, that the hobbyists's enthusiasm overcame his professional reticence.

'Bad stuff been going on over there, right?' said the cabbie.

'Oh, yes,' Sharon agreed. 'It's been in all the papers. They found a body. God, how could somebody? Poor woman.'

By the time she stepped out of the cab wearing her long leopard-pattern coat and high heeled leather boots, they'd ranged conversationally over the whole spectrum of murder, from Crippen to Christie, from the Ripper to Shipman. But it was a funny thing. Try as he might, the driver couldn't get her back to the subject of the murder of the music teacher Jane Mellor, even though it happened at the very same address he was taking her to. It was obvious his fare was no fool, whatever she looked like.

Alan Brickman was waiting to greet Sharon in the yard, not quite warmly though he seemed pleased enough to see her.

'Hello, Sharon,' he said, standing back while she paid off the cab from a flashy snakeskin purse. Sharon pulled a suitcase followed by a brand new skateboard from the back seat and sent the cabbie on his way. She turned and looked at Alan with that open smile he had known so well. With Sharon, what you saw was the whole deal. She held nothing back.

'I thought you'd at least meet me at the station,' she said.

Alan looked her up and down. Christ, he thought. And she was every bit as sexy as he remembered.

'Good to scc you, Sharon,' he mumbled.

And he meant it.

'Well, this is going to cost you, Alan Brickman. Have you told Donny I was coming?'

'No, not yet. Come in.'

Alan took the suitcase from Sharon's hand, but left her with the skateboard.

'You mean you haven't told him? And here's me come all this way to play Mummy.'

Alan gave her a twisted, shy smile.

'And to see me,' he suggested.

He made to put his arm around her shoulder but she performed a quick sidestep.

'Don't think you can start all that again!'

As they passed into the house, Donny was

standing at the top of the stairs, looking down.

'Donny,' shouted Alan, 'look who's here.'

Donny's face remained impassive.

'I got you a skateboard, Donny,' cooed Sharon. 'Do you like it?'

But Donny didn't even look at the gift his mother had brought, he simply eyed her suspiciously for a moment, then turned and ran back up the stairs.

'That went well!' said Sharon.

*   *   *

It had been a restless night followed by a difficult morning for Walker. He had a forensic expert crawling all over him. He gave up his clothes for examination. He was grilled for an hour by a juvenile Detective Inspector. He ran out of cigarettes. And, in the end, he was charged with murder.

A suspected murder by a service London police officer, whether on duty or not, is a matter for CIB3—the Complaints Investigation Bureau of the Metropolitan Police. Now a CIB3 Inspector in a blazer and grey washable trousers sat opposite Walker, staring into his eyes. He hardly looked a man yet, despite his confident command of the interview room and his use of Walker's familiar name.

'You understand, Mike,' he was saying, 'our hands are tied. In cases like this, we've got no option but to prefer charges.'

Prefer charges. Walker smiled grimly at the dated phrase. What was preferable about being charged with murder? Yet he understood all right. He knew exactly how much this infant DI wanted him to be a murderer. Most CIB3 cases were about grubby junior officers on the take from drug dealers and loan sharks. In any police station they landed, CIB3 officers were treated with suspicion and only grudging cooperation, because they were charged with nosing into all the scabby corners of the place. Then the lives of all the officers came under scrutiny. They find out all the local gossip, the feuds, who's sleeping with whom, who's having emotional, marital or money problems.

But the local station Superintendent would be giving them all assistance in this case. Michael Walker was, after all, not one of his own. And having a top-flight investigator from the SCG actually facing a murder rap on the Super's own patch must give a certain satisfaction.

Walker even knew what the red-cheeked young Metcalfe, his constant minder, thought of it all. It was exciting. It was drama. It was what the whole of thc Mct was talking about. And he, PC Brian Metcalfe, was right at the centre of it.

By six in the afternoon Pinton had been as good as his word and secured bail, under which Walker was released on his own recognizance if he stayed at the address of his friend Detective Sergeant David Satchell. He knew he'd have to keep away from the flat and, for the moment, from Pat North, the prime witness to the death of Eric Fowler. But he was granted permission to go back home briefly, under the escort of PC Metcalfe, to collect some clothes and personal items.

He was not surprised to find three Scene of Crime Officers still in the flat, combing the landing and stairs for evidence. He really wanted to see

North, but had little hope of it. Yet she arrived all the same, while he was making a final check of his bag in the living room, to see if he'd forgotten anything. The two stood and looked at each other. They seemed a trifle sheepish, though not as embarrassed as young Metcalfe.

'I, er, have to be here,' he explained apologetically to North. He was well aware of the relationship between Walker and North, two of the SCG's finest. 'It's . . . well, you know.'

'Yes,' said North. 'It's quite all right.'

But it wasn't for Walker. He said, under his breath,

'Brian, do us a favour. Give us a couple of minutes alone, will you?'

Metcalfe looked from one to the other. It was against all regulations.

'You know me, Brian, eh?' urged Walker again. 'This is our home.'

'OK. A couple of minutes then,' Metcalfe whispered finally, after a struggle with his conscience. Hoping none of the SOCOs would notice he withdrew into the hallway, leaving the door slightly ajar.

'You shouldn't be here,' murmured North.

'I'm just getting some things.'

'Mike, you've been charged and I'm the main witness.'

'I left in a bit of a hurry, if you remember.'

There was an awkward pause, then Walker went into the kitchen area.

'SOCOs have finished in here. You want a drink, or anything?'

She shed her coat as Walker poured two whiskies.

198

'Satch called me to say you'd been granted bail. Said you're staying with him.'

'Yeah. Cheers.'

He handed her the glass.

'Did Jimmy get to the station for you?' she asked.

Walker nodded.

'Yes, gave a statement.'

'Did he say where he got the gun from?'

'No, clammed up when they asked him that.'

'Oh.'

'But he confirmed events, I believe, and he'll stay around until the trial.'

'Yes, I should bloody well hope so! Where's he staying?'

'A b&b over at Paddington. Lynn offered to let him stay at the house, but . . .'

'Oh, that *would* have been cosy, wouldn't it? Jimmy at Lynn's!'

'Just don't start, Pat.'

'They could have gone to the trial together, hand in hand.'

Walker ignored the sarcasm.

'I'm hoping her statement's enough and she won't have to go to court. I don't want her being put through that.'

North bridled.

'You don't want *her* to be put through that! Mike, it's her stupidity that got us into this mess.'

'Yeah, but that woman's going to have a nervous breakdown if she's put under any more pressure. I won't do it to her.'

North finished her whisky in one gulp and put the tumbler down with heavy emphasis.

'My God!' she said. 'Please don't give me the

"she's the mother of my children" routine, because it makes me bloody sick.'

'Drop it, Pat. I mean it. I don't want to talk about Lynn.'

'Oh, so you mean *I* can't. So where am I in this, Mike? We're supposed to be getting married. But never mind. Don't look out for me. Don't worry about protecting me. I *am* going to give evidence, but you're not worried what this might be doing to me, are you?'

'What?' snapped Walker. 'You worried it might affect your career?'

North tossed her head and returned the gibe with interest.

'You saying it hasn't affected *yours*? You know as well as I do, this has screwed any hope you had, any hope at ALL, of making Commander.'

Walker could hardly credit she had said this. He flushed with anger.

'You think I don't know? YOU THINK I DON'T BLOODY KNOW THAT!'

He was suddenly overtaken by rage. He swung round and hurled his tumbler at the wall. Bits of glass flew back at them. Some landed in North's hair.

Brian Metcalfe was back in the room instantly, his eyes wide. But North remained calm.

'It's all right,' she said quickly. 'We're all right. An accident.'

This time the PC did not leave the room, but dropped back to stand near the door. North opened the cupboard under the sink where the dustpan and brush were kept.

'Leave it,' said Walker. 'Just leave it! Leave all the mess. You know Pat, I wanted to see you. I *wanted* you to come through that door. You know why?'

He moved towards her, and was whispering now.

'I just needed you to put your arms around me, tell me it's all OK, make me feel that you're here for me.'

North immediately melted. Afterwards the question occurred to her, why are women such suckers for this kind of thing? Why does it never fail, a man appealing for tenderness, wanting to be mothered? But now, she took his hand.

'You know I am. I'll be in court for you as well.'

Walker held on to the hand for as long as he could without Metcalfe feeling obliged to look. Then he picked up his bag and headed for the door.

'OK, I'm at Satch's,' he called.

He nodded to Metcalfe on his way out.

'Thanks, son,' he said, with a wink.

*   *   *

Sharon had borrowed Alan's car and gone to the superstore, returning with sausages, chips, baked beans and ice cream for Donny's tea. 'Playing Mummy', she called it. Going towards the barn, where Donny spent most of his spare time these days playing the guitar, she was startled to hear Bob's voice inside.

Practice makes perfect, so they say, Donny. And it's true. This needs dedication, so keep up your scales, there's my boy. You've got to do them over and over.

She pushed open the door and saw her son with the big Gibson guitar slung from his neck and a

201

cassette player by his side, where Bob's voice was coming from. She stood for a moment as Donny played scales. When he hit the 'Pause' button, she said,

'For a minute I thought he was in here. Gave me a bit of a turn. Of course he couldn't be, could he?'

Donny said nothing. He played another run of notes and stopped again.

'Do you like sausages?' Sharon asked. 'I've got sausages for tea.'

Donny pressed 'Play' on the cassette machine.

Fifth position now Donny, Major in A, up and down, up and down . . .

'Do you want them with chips?' asked Sharon, raising her voice to override Bob's. 'Or mash? How about baked beans? You like them?'

Donny was working his fingers up and down the fretboard as he picked the strings, watching where they pressed, following his father's instructions.

Now reverse it, back down in Minor, one fret at a time, keep it fast and neat . . .

Sharon smiled. What Bob had done was insane, disgusting, psychotic. But she'd loved something about him once and you could never completely erase that feeling.

'Teaching you to play, is he?'

Back on Major A . . . remember the C Sharp is on the fourth fret . . .

Donny played a fast series of fast arpeggios.

'He would never play for me,' Sharon said, with a touch of ironic regret.

Don't try to stretch to the ninth with those little fingers of yours!

The boy was not looking at his mother but Sharon persisted.

202

'Bob got a record contract when he was your age, you know? Do you think you'll ever be as good as he was?'

Donny paused the tape again and, for the first time, met his mother's gaze. He might have been looking at a member of an alien species.

'No, better,' he said, flatly.

Sharon, unfazed by Donny's coolness, laughed.

'Well, I'll be seeing you on *Top of the Pops*, eh? Meantime, tea'll be ready for you in a minute.'

As she left, Donny let go with some fancy runs of notes, played so fast they blurred into each other.

*   *   *

Satchell's flat was in a high-rise block, with views over a sunlit south London. Walker was out on the living room balcony having a smoke and a can of beer when Satchell came in from work, carrying two paper bags with looped handles.

'I've been busy,' he said, looking into the living room, then hurrying back to the kitchen. 'It took some rapping in the right places but, anyway, I got something for you.'

He placed the two paper bags carefully on the table.

'For a start, I got chicken tikka masala, biriani, pilau rice, couple of naans and poppadams.'

He wandered back to the living room, where Walker was looking morose in the face of Satchell's flippancy.

'OK,' said Satchell throwing himself on to the sofa with a deep sigh. 'This is what I've found out. That brother of yours is in deep shit, if he hadn't scarpered out of New Zealand he'd have been arrested for dealing in heroin, and he's in serious trouble with a bunch of hard men from Sydney. My guess is he had the gun for his own protection.'

Walker rolled his eyes up to the sky.

'Oh, Jesus!'

'Listen Mike, we've got to keep an eye on him.'

'He's my brother, Satch.'

'Well he's getting pissed off about that cheap b&b we've got him shacked up in. AND I'd say showing his face in a court is the last thing the punk wants.'

Walker shook his head.

'He's not going to walk away. He knows how much I need him and . . .'

He raised his beer can in a gesture of defiance at the fates.

'Blood's thicker than water!'

He finished the beer in a series of rapid gulps and wandered inside to fetch another one from the fridge.

CHAPTER SEVENTEEN

MONDAY 21 APRIL

The Plea and Directions Hearing at the Crown Court is normally a preliminary affair, an appetizer to the main course of the murder trial itself. But, like some appetizers, the PDH can suffice on its own. Its business is to acquaint the accused with the full and final indictment, and to establish his (or her) plea. If the plea is not guilty, the judge then makes arrangements for the full-scale trial some months later before bringing the hearing to an end. If, on the other hand, the accused pleads guilty, there is no need for a trial at all. In this case the presiding judge pronounces sentence and everyone goes home—everyone, that is, except the prisoner in the dock. He (or she) goes to jail for life.

From the point of view of the police and the Crown Prosecution Service—if not the individual lawyers—this is highly satisfactory. A murder trial is a very expensive event and an accused person who pleads guilty saves the taxpayer several million pounds in police, legal and forensic expenses. In fact, a guilty plea is a considerable act of public service.

But it is fair to say also that other matters are at the forefront of most defendants' minds, and Bob Brickman was no exception. He kept his intended plea to himself. As his lawyer Shawlcross had told him, just because a suspect has made admissions doesn't mean he cannot retract them at his trial. He might claim they were extorted from him. He may say he was insane or didn't understand what he was doing. The most important principle, according to Shawlcross, was to keep your cards close and never help the other side unless and before you had to.

So when Brickman came to the Crown Court for the PDH, no one, not even Shawlcross, knew for sure what he would say when asked to plead. The atmosphere in court was quiet and businesslike. The press benches were full. North and Satchell were there and, in the public gallery, James Mellor and Crispin Yates sitting at a nervous distance from Alan Brickman and the bottle-blonde by his side, wearing a dress that revealed an Alpine valley of a cleavage.

'Would the Defendant please stand?' said the Clerk.

Bob Brickman obeyed. His face wore a secretive expression but his body language, thought Pat North in the police benches, was odd. He was like a big boy sidling into the spotlight to do his turn at a school concert.

'Robert Antony Brickman,' intoned the Clerk, 'you are charged with murder, in that on 19 March of this year you did murder Jane Susan Mellor. How do you plead—guilty or not guilty?'

There was a silence, a moment of genuine suspense. Brickman, milking the moment, looked around the court. He eyed Mellor and Yates. Then, swinging his large head around, he found North and Satchell. Finally he looked down at his hands, took a deep breath and muttered something.

There were murmurs around the court, and uncertainty about what precisely Brickman had said. All had heard the word 'guilty', but could not be sure if it had been prefixed by the word 'not'. Brickman smiled cunningly and then raised his head with a flourish to face the Clerk. North had the sense that all this was quite deliberate, part of his private game with the Establishment, the world at large, the people who had once sabotaged his music and his life. At last he opened his mouth and bayed a single defiant word that echoed across the court.

'GUILTY!'

It was in this way that he told the world he was a rapist, a killer, a psychopath—in fact, the worst kind of mad bastard society could imagine.

*   *   *

Pat North had been finding it hard to enjoy her work, or anything at all for that matter. She knew she was always liable to depressive moods. Now she ate sleeping pills at night and vitamin and energy tablets by day, but the results were discouraging. Walker's plight was never far from her mind. As the chief witness she had to stay away from him; as his lover, her situation was even worse. She could not keep up those vital contacts, without which the life in all relationships dries down to dust. Depression hung over her constantly, like a bird of prey.

As she crossed the hallway on her way out of the Crown Court, she heard James Mellor's voice behind her.

'Detective Inspector North!'

She looked round. Mellor approached with Yates, and suddenly she saw them as they were, a gay couple if ever there was one. It wasn't that any outsider would necessarily spot this. But North had already considered the possibility, and now she could see that all doubt and ambiguity had gone with the end of Jane Mellor.

'I just wanted—'

He looked at Yates, and went on.

'*We* just wanted to thank you for finding the person who did this to Jane.'

North's original suspicion of Mellor had melted away, but it was replaced by a lingering resentment at the way he had obstructed her inquiries. The resentment chose this moment to come pouring out.

'Well it would have been a lot easier,' she said

207

tetchily, 'if you two had been more forthcoming about where you were the day Jane was killed.'

Mellor exchanged another quick look with Yates.

'Actually, we were together. You understand? We kept it quiet because we'd already lost Jane, we didn't want to lose anything else.'

'I don't want to know about this,' said North stiffly.

'And nobody else needs to know about us, do they?' asked Yates.

'Mr Yates, no one cares! This case is closed. What you two do in your personal life is none of my business.'

She turned and began to walk away but was stopped by an angry shout from Mellor.

'Hey, wait a minute!'

Mellor took an angry step towards her, his voice shaking, only just under control.

'You've no right to speak to us like that. It may be none of your business, but from the first moment you came to my house, I tried to explain. I was honest with you.'

She thought it was a strange kind of honesty. All right, he'd told her he and Jane didn't have sex. But he'd left the reason open to all kinds of speculation.

'Not entirely honest, I think,' she said.

This tart reply did not help. Mellor was really angry now. He jabbed himself in the chest with a thumb.

'I allowed my daughter to be traumatized all over again when YOU requested taking her back to where her mother was kidnapped. I even agreed— against my better judgement and against my instincts as a father—when you asked for Tara to identify Jane's killer.'

'Mr Mellor, I—'

'You'll have the courtesy to let me finish. Not *once* did you have any compassion. At least I've learned one thing. My personal life really is my own, and I will never be frightened of what other people think.'

He turned on his heel and walked away. Yates looked hesitantly at North, then scurried after him.

'Oh, God,' she thought wearily. 'Is he right? Did I lack compassion?'

A second insidious question came with this moment of doubt. Did she deserve the equally unwelcome publicity that her own personal life was inevitably facing, once Walker's trial started? Was it a case of being hoist by her own petard?

She shook the thought off as the blonde who'd been sitting with Alan Brickman walked past amongst the crowd leaving the court. North called out to her.

'Are you Sharon Fearnley?'

The woman looked back and nodded.

'We tried to contact you,' North said, walking along with her. 'But there was no forwarding address.'

'Oh yeah?' said Sharon, half turning and calling Alan Brickman with a jerk of her head. 'Well, if you need me in the future, you'll know where. I'll be with Alan, and Donny of course. We felt our Donny needed his mother, after this terrible business.'

She hooked her arm into Alan's and they sauntered away. Satchell caught up with North in time to hear her last remark.

209

'Can you believe it?' North said to him bitterly. 'One minute he's telling us that woman's a cheap, gold-digging tart, and the next he's letting her move in.'

Satchell had been host to Walker and all his problems for the last three weeks and was evidently feeling the strain. He snapped back,

'So? I mean, Alan Brickman gets his cheap bit of skirt. Sharon gets what she wants. James and Crispin get to play happy families together in the closet.'

He held up his finger like a school teacher.

'Every relationship is dysfunctional, Pat. You, of all people, should know that.'

*   *   *

North got home early, via the supermarket. The place was being redecorated at last and, carrying her bags of groceries into the flat, the front door crashed back against a decorator's stepladder that stood propped against the wall. She was surprised to hear, next, a voice calling from within.

'Hi, Pat.'

She jumped and looked around. Walker was standing on the landing, in just the spot where Eric Fowler had died.

'Mike! You scared me.'

He was carrying an armful of shirts and a dark suit.

'Sorry,' he said.

He indicated the clothing.

'I needed this lot. I didn't think I'd bump into you.'

They looked at each other. North was conscious

210

that her face was set in a stupid, artificial grin, and she could not think of anything to say.

'I gather congratulations are in order,' said Walker. 'Brickman's pleading guilty.'

Finally, she managed to speak.

'Oh, yeah. Thanks.'

'Your first murder inquiry done and dusted. Well done.'

He gestured towards the bedroom behind him.

'I'll just get my shoes.'

He headed back to the bedroom and North bent wearily to pick up her post. She opened the first letter, which she knew to be a statement of the joint bank account they had opened after moving into the flat. She cast her eye over it.

When Walker came back down with his shoes, she was frowning. She showed him the statement.

'Mike, don't bite my head off, but this is the joint account statement, right? So I think I have a right to know something.'

He crouched, pushing the shoes into his bag and zipping it up.

'What?'

'Well, you took out a thousand quid. What's it for?'

Walker closed his eyes briefly. He shook his head.

'It's my business.'

'No, it's mine. We're paying two mortgages, Mike. We won't have enough in the account to cover both. Was it for Lynn?'

'No. Jimmy.'

North was incredulous.

'*Jimmy?* You paid him a thousand pounds from our account? What are you playing at?'

'He's my brother.'

'He's also your defence witness, Mike! How's it going to look if they find out you've been giving him money?'

'It was for his hotel bill.'

'Why didn't you just tell him to sell off the jewellery he stole from me?'

Walker straightened and shook his head.

'No, no. That wasn't Jimmy. That loony bastard Fowler was here. He had keys to the flat, remember? And Jimmy swore he never touched your stuff.'

She did not say what she was thinking—that Jimmy's word was not worth so much as a very small hill of beans.

'All right,' said Walker. 'I'll call the bank tomorrow, and no more joint account. Will that satisfy you?'

'Fine.'

Walker's face was drawn tight with pain. He spoke in a voice so low it was almost a whisper.

'In fact, we might as well face it, Pat. There's no more joint anything any more, is there?'

For a moment she rebelled against the idea, but at a deeper level she knew Walker was right. Her heart felt like a piece of lead in her chest.

'You said it, Mike.'

It was as if she had pronounced a sentence of death on their relationship, and Walker knew it. He turned without a word, hoisted his bag and let himself out. She did not go after him.

CHAPTER EIGHTEEN

MONDAY, 21 JULY, MORNING

Walker's four months on bail dragged unbearably. He had no work, no contact with North, no focus for his life. His case might have provided a focus, but there was little enough going on. He met his legal team—the solicitor Andrew Pinton and defence counsel Willoughby Stevens QC—on a few occasions to discuss his legal aid and defence strategy. Once he attended an interview with an official of the Police Superintendents' Association to explore ways in which the PSA could help on the defence side. But because the shooting of Eric Fowler had taken place when Walker was on leave at his own address, and did not connect with any case Walker had worked on, there was little they could do. Walker met Jimmy from time to time in discreet pubs, mainly to hand over money. The two had little else to say to each other. He saw Lynn and the children odd weekends but, with the case hanging over him, he could not relax and there were rows, so he kept the visits to a minimum. In the middle of all this, the inevitable outcome of his request for promotion: it was a firm thumbs-down to Commander Walker.

He and Satchell lived together like a re-enactment of *The Odd Couple*. Walker drove Satchell mad with his untidiness, his late night drinking, his inability to work the washing machine, shop, rent videos, get in take-aways or any of the everyday tasks of a single man's life. Satchell on the other hand was busy, putting in his usual long hours at work. He could not go out drinking every night, as Walker wanted. And he insisted on having a sex life, so that most off-duty Friday and Saturday nights he didn't come home at all. Walker, frankly, was much of the time alone, unhappy and terrified at the prospect of his trial.

Yet it was a relief when the day arrived. Early in the morning Walker gave himself up to the custody of the court, dressed in his best suit and most sober tie. The Prison Officers on duty in the Crown Court cells treated him with respect. They made a distinction between a corrupt officer, who always got the cold shoulder, and a good copper like Walker, who'd taken out an undoubted villain under circumstances every man could identify with.

The presiding judge was to be Mr Justice Geoffrey Winfield, whom Walker approved of and liked, despite his occasional eccentricities. Prosecution counsel gave greater cause for concern. The Crown had briefed the formidable Robert Rylands QC, MP, who had several times crossed Walker's path. It was an interesting choice. Rylands was mainly a defence brief, specializing in social justice cases and police malpractice. Walker remembered the times Rylands had defended villains he had caught. In particular there was the child-killer, Michael Dunn, who was now serving life after Ryland's defence effort at the Old Bailey had failed by a whisker. And then there'd been Jimmy McCready, put away by Walker for murdering his gay lover and represented by Rylands on appeal. The appeal had failed. It would not be normal, and certainly not professional, for a barrister to have it in for a policeman who might be thought to have bested him. But Rylands was different. He had never liked Walker. In the McCready appeal he'd accused him in open court of being a bad policeman, driven by prejudice and ambition rather than professionalism and public service. It would be childish to say Rylands wanted revenge. But, in trying to have Detective Chief Superintendent Michael Walker banged up for life as a murderer, he had a point to prove, and it made him doubly dangerous.

At ten o'clock Walker was brought up from the cells, feeling keenly the humiliation of being a prisoner, led everywhere, guarded, given orders. A prisoner didn't think for himself or choose for himself as Walker had done all his life. But, of course, this was temporary, it was just for the trial. Except for the little matter of the verdict . . .

They placed Walker in the dock and he listened as a jury was empanelled and sworn in. They seemed a non-descript, neutral bunch of citizens, as far as he could tell. Then the charge of murder was read out by the Clerk, and the trial proper began. Rylands got to his feet, introducing himself to the jury and naming with the other counsel in the case. Then he began his opening submission.

He told them about the victim, with his history of mental problems and his unconventional life. He told them, too, about the defendant, a man who held a highly responsible position in public life, but who was also something of a maverick. In addition, he emphasised, Walker's private life was in turmoil, after an acrimonious split with his wife of fourteen years. Finally, he sketched the evidence he would be bringing before them of how the victim Eric Fowler's path had crossed with that of Walker, through Fowler's relationship with, and behaviour towards, Walker's estranged wife and children, and how Walker, out of jealousy and uncontrolled anger, had intentionally shot Fowler dead.

'A husband and father who believed himself and his family to be threatened, accused of killing the man who he thought was the threat: it is, you might think, a fairly unsurprising scenario. But, members of the jury, what renders this case of murder particularly unusual is that, at the time of the shooting, Michael Walker was, and indeed still is, a senior police officer with the rank of Detective Chief Superintendent and by all accounts is a highly regarded and very experienced police officer. Against that background, however, you will hear that he is not, and never has been, an authorized shot, that is a police officer with the specialist training required to be issued with a firearm whilst on duty.'

Rylands paused for effect, raking the jury box with his gaze.

'No gun had been issued to Detective Chief Superintendent Walker in the course of his duties.'

Rylands paused again and looked over his spectacles towards a court official. By prearrangement a board of thick card, with the handgun attached to it, was passed to him. He seemed to weigh it in his hands.

'Indeed, the firearm in question, a Luger pistol, was not of a type that the Metropolitan Police Force issues to its officers. Quite apart from the circumstances in which a shot came to be fired, you will be concerned, no doubt, as to how *this* gun . . .'

He held up the exhibit so that the jury, and then the entire court, could see it.

'. . . ever came to be in the possession of Michael Walker. Well, you will hear that it all began with an apparently amicable weekend in the Peak District of Derbyshire . . .'

Rylands did not try to minimize the extent to which Eric Fowler had attacked Lynn Walker. In fact he described it in detail, how she'd slipped away to the telephone box, he'd followed and subjected her to a frenzied attack, using the phone receiver itself to batter her face.

'When she returned to London alone on the Sunday and contacted her husband, she had a swollen eye and a bruised cheek where she admitted he had hit her. By the following Tuesday Eric Fowler had also returned to London, and here he attacked Lynn Walker again, leaving her even more badly beaten.

'She did not then want to tell her ex-husband, Michael Walker, how these latest injuries had occurred, nor did she wish to involve the police. As you might expect his first concern as a father was to take the children away from the house. He left them in the care of his fiancée, who was a colleague in the police, Detective Inspector Patricia North. Michael Walker then stayed with Lynn Walker at her house to look after her. He spent the night there.

'But, at around eleven-thirty that night, Eric Fowler went to the defendant's flat in Barnes, shouting and trying to gain entry, disturbing Detective Inspector North and the two children who were staying there. You will hear from her the details of his bizarre behaviour which must have been terrifying, particularly in the dead of night. She alerted the local police—a call timed at

217

11.36pm—and contacted Michael Walker by telephone shortly thereafter.

'You will hear evidence from a computer analyst that at 12.14pm on the following day, Wednesday 26 March, Michael and Lynn Walker used Lynn's home computer to enter the chat room sensualsingles.co.uk, through which Lynn had first met Fowler. Michael Walker pretended to be Lynn and eventually they made contact with Fowler whose response was . . .'

Rylands looked at his notes, after adjusting the glasses on his nose.

' "Hi, Mike, this is Eric, Lynn's boyfriend Eric . . . I am going to make your life a living hell." '

'And you will further hear, members of the jury, that within a matter of hours Fowler tried to carry out his threat. He went back to the flat shared by Michael Walker and Patricia North and spray painted offensive and obscene graffiti across their front door. Then, during the night, he sent anonymous faxes to the police station where Ms North was working, faxes which attacked the good names of both Mr Walker and Ms North in the most obscene terms.'

Rylands picked up a sheaf of papers and waved them at the jury.

'You have copies of these faxes in your evidence folders under references 3(a), 3(b), 3(c) and 3(d). The next day, Fowler returned once again to Mrs Walker's house. He tried to persuade her to open the front door, and when she refused he began kicking the door. She dialled 999 and, while she was speaking to the police, the attack resumed at the rear of the house. Here the man, whom Lynn Walker has confirmed in her statement she knew as

218

Eric Knowles, broke in. I refer you to photographs five and six in your folders. He at once tried to attack her in the kitchen and then chased her, holding a kitchen knife, but she escaped via the front door and was met by police responding to her call. Her attacker made his escape through the rear garden, dropping the knife there. Fingerprint examination of that knife revealed two clear prints, and computer identification produced an exact match to one Eric Fowler, aged forty-two.'

The jury were following in rapt attention, leafing through their folders to see the photographs of Eric's entry point at the back of the house, and the photos of the fingerprints found on the knife. Rylands took a sip of cold water and cleared his throat.

'I should tell you that, following this knife attack on Lynn Walker, an officer from the local station was assigned to investigate the case, Detective Sergeant Babbington. Any unilateral actions taken by Michael Walker outside Detective Sergeant Babbington's inquiry would therefore be unofficial and clearly contrary to good and proper police practice, however understandable they might seem to be. Nevertheless, that Thursday evening at around five o'clock you will hear that Michael Walker visited the address of Mrs Fowler, Fowler's mother, in East London, looking for her son.

'Mrs Fowler will tell you that Michael Walker made a threat to find her son and kill him, and that he then left. If that is what he said, was it a case of an unfortunate choice of words in the light of such traumatic events? Or did he, as the Crown will argue, mean every word of it?

'I turn now to the events of that fatal evening.'

Rylands took another sip of water, replaced the glass and began to make eye contact with one juror after another in turn until he had met the gaze of each one. As he did so he recounted the sequence of events, with Walker arriving by taxi and, on his own account, meeting his brother and finding the gun. Then, on climbing the stairs, he discovered that Fowler had just broken into the flat and was threatening North.

'The defendant said in interview,' Rylands went on, 'that when he went into his house with the gun in his pocket he was quite unexpectedly confronted by an extremely aggressive and violent Fowler. He said that he instinctively produced the gun from his pocket in order to keep Fowler at bay, shouting that he was an armed police officer. Now, the burden remains on us, the prosecution, to prove every element of the case against this defendant, and in particular two vital elements—firstly, that the shooting of Fowler was not an accident but a deliberate act, and secondly that it was not an act committed in lawful self-defence. You may think that his account of how he came into possession of that gun, that very evening and at that very location from his brother in an episode wholly unconnected with Fowler stretches credulity beyond breaking-point. You may indeed. We shall see.'

*   *   *

Dave Satchell had had his frustrations living with Walker, but he considered him one of his closest friends and was damned if he was going to watch the man go down for killing a scumbag like Fowler. He had taken the week of the trial off work so he could be available to do anything that needed doing. One key job was to make sure Mike's friends were there for him, and, realizing Rylands's opening was drawing to a finish, he'd left the court looking to see if Jimmy had turned up. He was not to be found either in the witnesses' waiting room or the reception hall. Satchell phoned Jimmy's hotel but got no reply from the room.

Next, he thought of Lynn. It seemed she had got out of giving evidence for Mike on the grounds of being clinically anxious and emotionally overwrought. But Satchell thought the least she could do was appear in the relatives' benches in court. He keyed her number on his mobile phone and stood waiting for an answer. It was then he saw Pat North coming through the security checks at the entrance to the Crown Court. She waved at him and hurried over.

'Bloody traffic. Has it started already?'

Satchell nodded.

'Damn, I was hoping to see him before he went in. How is he, Satch? Is he OK?'

'He just needs a bit of TLC right now, yeah?'

North felt his tone was critical, implying she was falling short in the Tender Loving Care department.

'Look, I'd be in there right now if I could, Satch. But I'm giving evidence today. You know I can't go in until I'm called.'

Satchell was busy with his phone, refusing to look at her. North was not prepared to dance attendance, so she walked crisply down the hall and away from him.

Satchell's call was answered at last.

'Lynn? This is Satch. Mike's in court today and I

221

just wondered if you were going to show.'

'No, Dave. I'm not coming down.'

Satchell thought for a second.

'Right,' he said. 'I'm coming over.'

He disconnected and ran out of the court towards his car.

Twenty-five minutes later he was standing by Lynn Walker's kitchen table, watching as she sat and drank a cup of tea. The two of them had never seen eye-to-eye. Lynn thought Satchell typical of Walker's friends in the Job, men (and now increasingly women) who drank late into the night, got up to all sorts of bad behaviour and kept a decent man from being a home-maker and father. Satchell, on his part, saw Lynn as Walker's worst mistake. She knew nothing about police culture and had never done anything but complain about the work that he loved and was so good at. She had been a drag on him in every way, but she *was* the mother of his children and right now he reckoned Walker needed her.

'Lynn, I think you should be in court. Mike needs all of our support right now.'

She sipped her tea and shook her head.

'No, I can't. I really can't.'

She turned to look up at Satchell.

'Is he all right?'

Satchell shook his head grimly.

'It hasn't even started yet!'

He looked her up and down. The facial damage was all repaired and she looked dimpled and well.

'For someone who's supposed to be having a nervous breakdown, Lynn, you look all right.'

She shook her head defensively.

'It wasn't my idea not to give evidence, it was

222

Mike's.'

Satchell was surprised.

'Was it?'

'Yes. I'd be under oath you see. I might say things I shouldn't.'

This was news to Satchell. They'd been living together and got drunk together regularly, but Walker hadn't mentioned it.

'Say things? Like what things?'

'What he said to me.'

'What did he say to you?'

Lynn sighed. She didn't know if she should tell Satchell this. She'd not told anyone else, but she had to unburden herself.

'He said he'd kill Eric if he tried to see me or the kids again. Not just once. It was scary. He said it over and over.'

Satchell's mouth dropped open.

'Oh, come on, Lynn, he just said that in anger. We all say it. He didn't *mean* it.'

'But he wasn't angry Satch, that's what frightened me. He was so calm.'

'OK, when did he say this?'

'That night. That same night that he . . . that Eric died.'

CHAPTER NINETEEN

MONDAY, 21 JULY, AFTERNOON AND EVENING

Satchell was considerably shaken by what Lynn had told him and immediately gave up any idea of bringing her with him to the Crown Court. Arriving back himself half an hour later, he regained his place on the police bench and winked at Walker, who was looking isolated and diminished in the dock. By this time Pat North was giving evidence and the suffering on Walker's face was palpable as he listened.

'When I left home that morning,' she was saying, 'I saw obscene and personal graffiti painted all over the landing and across the front door. I reported it at once to the local police who came round and took photographs. Mike cleaned it off the same day. I found it very upsetting, we both did.'

'Did he appear to know who was responsible?' asked Rylands.

'Well, it was obviously his ex-wife's new boyfriend Eric, who had threatened Mike.'

'What was Michael Walker's reaction to the threat? Was he angry?'

'Annoyed more than angry. Annoyed and concerned.'

'Concerned, would you say?'

'The man was clearly unstable and he had access to two very young children—he had keys, you see. The obscene faxes that had arrived at the station later were pretty frightening as well. Mike said to leave it to the local police, and I gave the faxes to them.'

'Did the defendant mention Mrs Fowler to you at any stage?'

North's throat was dry. She lifted the glass in front of her and drank.

'Detective Inspector?'

North wiped the moisture from her mouth with the back of her hand and nodded.

'Yes, he did. He said he was going to visit her.'

'Going to visit her? As an active police officer?'

'He said he was trying to locate Eric Fowler, so that the local police could arrest him. Mike did not himself want to be involved in the arrest.'

Rylands then took North through the events later that evening, as she had witnessed them. First there was the departure of Jimmy from the flat, and the phone call to Walker. Then the hammering on the door and Eric smashing his way in and picking up a broken bottle.

'What did you do?'

'I ran back to the bedroom. There's a short flight of stairs up to the corridor. I ran into my room and he followed me waving the broken bottle. Before he could get in I pushed a lot of furniture in front of the door to stop him. He was in a fury, throwing himself against the bedroom door, but I kept him out.'

'What happened next?'

'There was a lot of shouting and then what sounded like a shot, a single shot, then he was screaming my name.'

'Who was?'

'Mike.'

'Did you hear any warning shouted by the defendant before you heard the shot?'

'I was barricaded behind the bedroom door. It was hard to hear but he shouted to Fowler to put down the bottle.'

' "Put down the bottle" . . . just that?'

'No, he swore at him. He called him a bastard.'

'What? "Put down the bottle, you bastard"?'

'Something like that. I heard more shouts. You must understand, I was very frightened. And I

225

couldn't hear clearly. And then I heard the shot.'

'Between "Put down the bottle you bastard" and the shot, what sort of time gap would you say there was?'

'It all happened very quickly, a matter of seconds. I managed to get the bedroom door open and there was Mike looking very shaken. My first thought was that he'd been shot.'

'You thought he'd been shot?'

'Yes. I mean, Mike does not carry a firearm.'

Rylands turned to a court official.

'Could Detective Inspector North be given the photograph album please?'

The album, a large ring binder, was brought to the witness stand.

'Photograph number ten,' said Rylands. 'In the main album, my Lord.'

The QC waited as Winfield, the jury and the witness all found the relevant page in their albums.

'We can see,' he said, 'the top of the stairs and the landing and your bloodstained bedroom door at the end of the hall. Can you show us where Michael Walker was standing?'

'Yes, he was standing at the bottom of the stairs, just to the right.'

Winfield picked up a large magnifying glass and peered at the photos.

'Which would be to his left,' he said, 'but to your right? Right?'

'Yes, my Lord,' said North.

'And the gun?' went on Rylands. 'Where exactly was that when you first saw it?'

'That was on the floor, between Mike and the deceased.'

'Did *you* do anything with the gun?'

226

'No, my first thought was to see if the man, Eric, was all right. I went to him and felt for a pulse. But he was dead.'

'And the broken bottle, did you see that?'

North tapped the album of photographs, which was still open in front of her.

'Yes, that was in the same position as it is here, in photograph eleven.'

Again Rylands waited while the Judge and jury studied photo number eleven before continuing.

'So what happened next?'

'Mike told me to phone the station and get an ambulance.'

Rylands turned a page of his notes, glancing at it briefly, and then sideways at the witness.

'Have a look at this gun, would you?'

He nodded towards the court official and the gun was carried from the exhibits table to North.

'Is that the gun you saw on the floor?' Rylands asked.

'Yes it is.'

'Had you ever seen that gun before that night?'

'No.'

'Do you know James Walker, Michael Walker's brother?'

'Yes, I met him the day before, when he turned up on our doorstep from New Zealand.'

'When did you last see him?'

'At about eight the next night, a short time before the attack started.'

'Did he tell you where he was going?'

'I think he was going to the airport to fly off to Florida.'

'Did you see him with a gun at any time?'

North shook her head emphatically.

'No, I didn't.'

Rylands took off his spectacles and nodded his head.

'Thank you Detective Inspector.'

North made a slight move to leave the stand but immediately changed her mind and looked at Winfield. She took a deep breath.

'I would just like to say this,' she said. 'Michael Walker is an experienced, tough and extremely brave police officer. His method of dealing with the Eric Fowlers of this world would never be to take the law into his own hands, neither as a police officer nor as a man.'

She bowed her head.

'That's all I wanted to say.'

She only needed to turn her head through ninety degrees to make eye contact with Walker. She did so. He looked back at her, his lips twitching almost into a smile. Winfield on the other hand was not impressed by witnesses who volunteer their opinions.

'Thank you, Detective Inspector North,' he said stiffly, and she left the stand.

Winfield brought the day's business to an end shortly after North had given her evidence. Walker called at the pub on his way home, which he reached a couple of hours later, with a bag containing a six-pack of beer. Satchell was closing the balcony doors, locking down for the night.

'Guess what?' said Walker morosely. 'The top brass upstairs have decided that it'd be "inappropriate" to make me Commander right now.'

Satchell nodded.

'I know, I know. You told me.'

228

'I suppose I was expecting it.'

'What does Pat say?'

'She doesn't know.'

'She was there for you today, Mike. She was *there*. And she got one over that Rylands right at the end there.'

Walker nodded slowly.

'I went over to see Lynn,' Satchell went on. Walker didn't react. 'I still think you should have had her in court.'

'No, no. She'd been through enough.'

'No other reason, Mike?'

Walker knew Dave Satchell well enough to appreciate that this was leading somewhere.

'Like what?'

'Like, you didn't threaten to kill that bastard, did you?'

Walker sniggered.

'Eric? Only about a thousand times. But, hey, I've threatened to kill you a few times and you're still around.'

Satchell laughed at this.

'Yeah,' he said. 'Well, I'm going to bed. Another long day tomorrow.'

Walker waved his hand.

'You go,' he said. 'I'm going to stay up for a while.'

'G'night, then.'

Satchell mock-punched Walker's arm, then strolled out of the room. Walker stayed on, alone. He spotted his phone, which had lain unused all day. He was thinking of calling North. He picked it up and examined it, front and back, as if it could tell him what to do. It couldn't. He put it down and took another mouthful of beer.

229

CHAPTER TWENTY

TUESDAY, 22 JULY, MORNING

In the morning, Rylands wheeled out his scientific witnesses. This brought, firstly, pathologist Doctor John Foster to the stand. Foster was himself a faintly cadaverous figure—tall, skeletally thin—but he had the brusque, beady look of a rational man who is daily faced with the consequences of human unreason, violence and unspeakable cruelty. He was one of the top men in his field and had assisted Walker in several murder investigations. Now he was acting for the other side.

Rylands asked him how long he thought it had taken Eric Fowler to die from his wounds. Foster cast a glance at his notes.

'From the very extensive damage caused by the passage of the bullet through the chest, I would estimate that death occurred within a very short period of time, possibly within a minute.'

'What can you tell us about the trajectory of the bullet?'

Foster took off his glasses and gestured towards the well of the court.

'If you'll allow me to demonstrate . . .'

Rylands swivelled and addressed the Bench.

'With my Lord's permission?'

Winfield nodded. Foster left the witness stand and moved down to where an usher was waiting with a life-sized dummy, Foster's demonstration prop. Winfield knew the dummy well. It even had a name.

'Ah,' he said, beaming with incongruous pleasure. 'The oft-murdered Heidi!'

Foster smiled in gloomy ingratiation.

'I considered the position where the bullet came to rest to be here.'

He poked a finger into the back of the dummy, on a spot that would have been a few inches beneath Heidi's right shoulder blade, had she possessed one.

'The entry wound was here . . .'

He simulated a gun with the fore- and middle fingers of his other hand and pointed it at the chest.

'And the track of the bullet between those two locations. So you see with the bullet finishing just to the right of the midline of the body, it travelled to a position slightly higher within the body than the entry wound.'

He pulled back his hand from the chest still pointing his finger to make a handgun.

'That suggests the shot was fired with the gun pointing about ten degrees above the horizontal, and perhaps twenty degrees off centre to the left as it was fired.'

Rylands nodded and pointed to his own chest.

'Ten degrees above the horizontal, and twenty degrees to the left, with the entry about here?'

On the bench, the judge craned sideways to see better.

'Would you move the dummy slightly to the right,' he asked, 'so I can get a better perspective?'

Foster turned the dummy and moved it slightly. The judge peered at it intently.

'Thank you.'

Foster still maintained the position of his

231

handgun.

'This is the approximate direction the gun was pointing at the time it was fired in relation to the body of the deceased. The two parties were close together and they were facing each other.'

Rylands nodded his head.

'Thank you, Doctor.'

He sat down and made way for Walker's brief to cross-examine. Willoughby Stevens rose majestically.

'Dr Foster, I want to put to you another scenario.' He looked at the bench and gestured at his junior, Tulley, sitting in wig and gown beside him. 'If I might call upon Mr Tulley to assist me?'

Winfield smiled indulgently.

'For clarity's sake, I think we need all the assistance possible,' he said. Winfield was enjoying these mild theatricals.

Tulley, slightly embarrassed, stood up and submitted himself to Stevens's direction.

'Now, suppose the following position, as given by Detective Chief Superintendent Walker in his interview. You were provided with his statement to the police, were you not?'

Foster nodded.

'Yes.'

'Good. So, the Defendant held a gun in front of him—I am the Defendant—and pointed it at Eric Fowler—that is the esteemed Mr Tulley—less than a metre away. Thus.'

He grasped Tulley's shoulder and positioned him, turning his pen into a gun.

'All of a sudden,' he went on, raising his voice to heighten the drama, 'Eric Fowler then *throws* himself forward.'

232

He looked at Tulley, who glanced nervously at the Bench and half stepped towards Stevens, feigning an awkward attack.

'Like that, towards and against the Defendant, and against the gun, knocking it slightly sideways to the left and thus causing the gun to go off. Now, would this be consistent with what you have told us about the proximity of the shot, the direction and elevation of the shot, and the known positions of Detective Chief Superintendent Walker and the deceased Fowler? Please, Mr Tulley, do sit down.'

Tulley, by now scarlet in the face, resumed his seat. Foster, meanwhile, was considering.

'Yes, it would be consistent,' he agreed at last.

Stevens offered him a slight bow.

'Thank you, Doctor.'

But Winfield seemed anxious to prolong the fun. He said,

'I'm so glad that your junior survived the ordeal, Mr Stevens.'

'My Lord.'

With a slight bow Stevens sat and Rylands had the floor again.

'And if the Defendant had simply gone up to Eric Fowler and shot him in the chest at extremely close range, with the gun pointing upwards and slightly to the left, would that also be consistent?'

'Yes,' Foster affirmed. 'It would.'

'Thank you very much.'

Winfield was writing on his pad.

'It appears, Dr Foster,' he said, finishing his note and looking down at the pathologist, 'that you can't say for certain which of these scenarios occurred.'

Foster looked discomfited.

'No, I can't,' he agreed.

At lunchtime an hour later, taken below the court into the purdah of a holding cell, Walker felt that the morning had gone hopefully. Stevens's game of charades had easily matched the charms of Heidi, and must surely have scattered some seeds of reasonable doubt amongst the jury. With stirrings of his usually formidable appetite he contemplated the tray of canteen food he'd ordered from the list provided. Sausages and mash and a piece of lemon meringue pie in a sealed plastic box. As he speared the first sausage with his fork, he guessed that his legal team would be sitting down to lunch at a smart little place around the corner, which served some of the best sushi in town.

The star turn of the afternoon was to be the ballistics expert Major Giddings, a parody of a puce-faced, old school, ex-army type who stepped on to the stand at half-past three in a blue blazer and bow tie. He swore the oath and received from an usher the gun from the exhibits table.

For the jury's sake, Rylands took the Major through his qualifications in his subject, which Giddings confirmed in self-satisfied tones.

'So now, Major, may I ask you to consider the weapon you have in your hand? You have had a chance to examine it and subject it to tests, have you not?'

'I have.'

'And does it possess what is commonly referred to as a hair trigger?'

'It's not an unusually stiff trigger. But it is by no means what I would describe as a *feather* trigger.'

'Major Giddings, just to confirm,' Rylands went on, unruffled by the Major's correction of his

234

jargon. 'You have stated that this gun is fitted with a safety catch so that whoever fired it would have had to make two distinct movements, firstly to pivot the catch from safety and secondly to press the trigger to the requisite minimum pressure. Is that correct?'

Giddings nodded.

'That is correct.'

Winfield paused in his note-taking.

'That was assuming the safety catch was on in the first place, Mr Rylands,' he observed dryly.

'Of course, my Lord. And thank you, Major Giddings.'

Rylands gave way to Stevens, whose face had adopted the expression of an earnest seeker after truth.

'You said, did you not, that it would require a medium trigger pressure to activate the firing mechanism? Might a single jerk on the trigger be sufficient, a jerk such as could occur accidentally if someone launched themselves at the person holding the gun and knocked against him?'

Giddings replied slowly, as if explaining to an idiot.

'As long as 4.8lbs of pressure was achieved on the trigger, the firing mechanism would detonate.'

'So with a single jerking action, such as could occur accidentally, the gun might fire?'

'Yes, that is correct.'

Stevens paused to allow the information to sink in.

'Thank you Major Giddings.'

As Stevens sat down again, Rylands stood up. They were like two players in a game of darts.

'Unless, of course, the safety catch were applied,

in which case a single jerking action would not do, would it?'

Giddings looked as if the question were an affront to his intelligence.

'Of course not.'

That was good enough for Rylands.

'Thank you,' he said, sitting down again.

The judge cleared his throat.

'Well now, I think that after that exhilarating testimony and the questionable excitement of Heidi, it would be prudent to break for the day. We'll reconvene tomorrow at 10.00am.'

At which, he rose, waited for the court to do the same, bowed at counsel and hurried away to his chambers.

CHAPTER TWENTY-ONE

WEDNESDAY, 23 JULY, MORNING

Walker was a lifelong insomniac, but he had never found sleep so elusive as on the night before he was due to give evidence in his own defence. It wasn't that he dwelt on the ordeal ahead. In fact, he was thinking about almost anything but the actual trial. His exhausted brain drifted instead through his past life, recalling and reassessing events that he had almost forgotten. 'You only ever looked after number one,' Jimmy had told him. Was that true? Was he selfish and unloving? If so, where had his feelings for Lynn come from, once upon a time? And for North? And his children? God, he hated to think about the children at such a time as this.

He constantly saw Richard's face looming up before his mind, and Amy's, his princess. He wondered if they would judge their father for putting them through all of this. Or had they judged him already?

In the morning he felt as if he'd gone twenty rounds with Lennox Lewis—his head and body aching, his thoughts numb. Automatically, he dressed in the dark suit, and polished his shoes. It was nine-fifteen and they were due to leave for the court, but Satchell was on the phone.

'Jimmy,' he was saying in some exasperation, 'the taxi's on its way. I said you have to be there by ten. No, TEN! I'll see you there. Ten! Yeah, yeah, I'll pay the cab. Just *be* there.'

As Satchell hung up, Walker was preoccupied tying his shoelaces.

'You set, then?' said Satchell. He felt like a father trying to get his daughter to the church on time. 'We've got to be there by ten. Oh! You're wearing brown shoes?'

Satchell lived by a more rigorous dress code than Walker, who now looked at his highly polished shoes as if noticing their colour for the first time.

'Yeah,' he said, but then dismissed Satchell's objection. 'No one's going to be looking at my feet, Satch. Was that Jimmy?'

'Yes. Sounded in good shape.'

'Well, I hope to God he is. We're depending on him.'

Satchell nodded grimly but made no comment. Personally, he would rather depend on a paper parachute.

'Right, we done?' he said. 'Let's go.'

'So you don't think the brown shoes go, then?'

said Walker.

Satchell was already on his way out.

'Like you say, no one's going to be looking at your feet.'

But Walker changed the shoes anyway, hastily putting on the unpolished black ones from yesterday.

Walker's defence began by presenting a succession of carefully chosen character witnesses, senior and retired officers who had known him at various points in his career and were willing to say what a thoroughly good officer he was. There were no slip-ups. Walker came over as a successful, conscientious man. In cross-examination Rylands tried to spin the 'maverick' side of his character and career but Stevens's witnesses stonewalled these questions with skill. Rylands had got nowhere. Then it was time for the star witness: the defendant himself.

As Walker was swearing on the Bible to tell the truth, the whole truth, and nothing but the truth, Satchell was pacing up and down outside the court, checking his watch and peering out of the door. He punched a number into his phone.

'Hi, I ordered a taxi to collect a Mr James Walker from . . . What? No, I'm checking if a pickup was made . . . Shervais Hotel, S-h-e-r-v-a-i-s, in Paddington. Yeah, yeah.'

An usher whom Satchell recognized from Winfield's court walked past, carrying a clipboard.

'Have they called the next witness yet?' Satchell asked her.

'Not yet.'

'Good,' he called after her. 'Because he's on his way . . . I hope.'

Walker on the stand had been getting an easy, amicable ride from Stevens, being taken through his version of the events of 27 March and allowed to repeat the details of his statement to the Barnes police.

'Finally, Mr Walker, what is your assessment of how you handled the situation you faced, when you saw Eric Fowler in your flat, threatening your fiancée?'

Walker considered, then spoke in measured terms.

'I know, as an officer, I should have checked whether or not the gun was real. I know that if I'd found it was, I should have made it safe and arrested my brother. I know all these things.'

'But you admit you didn't do any of them.'

Walker shook his head briskly.

'No, I didn't. But there's another thing I know. If I hadn't by pure chance had the gun that night, both myself and Detective Inspector North would be dead.'

It was a good thought to end on, and Stevens decided to leave it at that.

'Thank you, Detective Chief Superintendent Walker.'

Rylands, with a dangerous gleam in his eye, immediately stood up to cross-examine.

'Mr Walker, let me just see if I have this right. You came by this gun from your long lost brother, literally a matter of minutes before seeing a man who posed a grave threat to your family and home. That right?'

Walker nodded.

'You then produced this gun thinking it was a harmless replica and were shocked when it went off. Have I understood your evidence correctly?'

'Yes, that is exactly what happened. And Eric Fowler clearly thought it was a harmless replica as well, judging from the way he took no notice of me holding it and just threw himself at me.'

'So *you* did not throw yourself at *him*? He threw himself at *you*, causing the gun to go off. That right?'

'Precisely. The gun was jolted straight out of my hand. I mcan, I wasn't holding it particularly tightly. In fact I was half thinking of hitting him with it if I had to. It was quite heavy.'

'And you didn't think to check that it was an imitation and not a real gun?'

Walker spread his arms wide.

'It was dark. I was worried about my kids, with this lunatic running round. And then I found this in my brother's holdall. He just laughed it off and said it was only a toy. So I said to him, "Yeah, well it's a toy you're not going to play with," and that was that. I put it in my pocket and went up to the flat.'

Winfield was craning forward to hear Walker's rapid-fire delivery.

'Detective Chief Superintendent Walker,' he asked. 'For the benefit of those making notes on your testimony, could you please speak a little more slowly. Thank you.'

Winfield nodded to Rylands to continue.

'Have a look at this oilcloth, will you?'

He held out his hand and the usher passed him the item from the exhibits table.

'You've seen guns wrapped in oilcloths like this before, have you not?'

'Yes, I have.'

'But have you ever in your twenty-five years as a

police officer come across an *imitation* weapon wrapped in an oilcloth like that?"

Walker had not been expecting this.

'Well, er, in my experience, people who carry contraband don't like their fingerprints or traceable fibres being found on weapons, and that would include on imitation guns.'

'But not an *oilcloth*, surely?' taunted Rylands. 'Imitation guns generally have no moving parts. Why would they need to be wrapped in an oilcloth?'

Walker was impatient. He said brusquely,

'I didn't see it as an oilcloth, I saw it just as a piece of material wrapping the gun.'

But Rylands wouldn't let it go.

'There is nothing wrong with your sense of smell, is there Mr Walker?'

'No, I don't think so.'

'Well, *this* . . .'

Rylands flamboyantly thrust the oilcloth into his face and breathed in.

'This reeks of gun oil, does it not? Do smell it for yourself, if you wish.'

He held out the oilcloth to an usher, who passed it to the witness stand. Walker put it to his nose. He handed it back.

'I did not notice that at the time,' he said.

'Ah! So you're saying that neither the smell of the gun, nor its weight, nor the fact that it was wrapped in an oilcloth, alerted you to the fact that it was the real thing? Because undoubtedly your brother was indeed carrying a real gun . . . if what you say is correct and the truth.'

Walker straightened his back haughtily.

'I resent the tone of your questions. You're

suggesting that I have cobbled together some false defence, lying like some cheap criminal. *What* kind of a person do you think I am?'

Rylands shook his head.

'That, Mr Walker, is a matter for the jury.'

'All right,' said Walker in a sudden outburst of anger. 'I'll tell you what kind of a person I am. I am a police officer. I uphold the law, I do not break it or take it into my own hands. And as for Eric Fowler, I feel sorry for the man. He clearly had mental problems. I take no pleasure at all in his death, none at all. I wanted him arrested and brought to court, that's all.'

Satchell stood beside a sign saying 'All Mobile Phones to be Left at the Desk'. He was working himself up into a fury, jabbing numbers into a mobile phone, but finding it impossible to get through. Then Jimmy crashed through the doors at the end of the corridor. His shirt collar was undone, his trousers crumpled, his tie halfway around his neck. Apart from that he looked OK, though very hungover. He carried a paper cup of coffee.

'Where the bloody hell have you been?' muttered Satchell. 'The taxi picked you up at ten and it's now, what? I mean, do you KNOW what time it is?'

'Hey! Give me a break, Satch, I'm here aren't I?'

He tossed the still half-full coffee cup into a wastebin. Satchell's face registered concern.

'You need another one of those before you can stand up straight? And, look, your tie's halfway round your neck.'

Satchell pulled Jimmy near enough to him to carry out some running repairs.

242

'You are NOT going to screw this up for Mike. No way. Stand still!'

Jimmy sighed theatrically as Satchell straightened his tie, then brushed the shoulders of his jacket with his hand. He pushed his face as close to Jimmy's as he could without actually touching noses.

'I know your game, Jimmy. I know who you were dealing with in New Zealand and who's chasing your arse all the way from Sydney.'

Jimmy pushed Satchell away. His 'reasonable' act was wearing thin and he felt tetchy.

'Give over, Satchell. You know, do you? Let me tell you, mate, you know fuck all. Oh, and, if the boot was on the other foot, do you really think Mike would have stayed holed-up in that flea-pit hotel as long as I have?'

Satchell was outraged by this.

'He PAID for it! And you had no other place to go! That was all bullshit about some job in Florida. I know why you had that gun, Jimmy, you were watching your own back as usual. I know Jimmy, and you'd better come clean about it in court or I'll . . .'

Jimmy turned on him.

'Or you'll WHAT! Don't make threats you can't follow through, Satch.'

The usher appeared in the doorway.

'Mr James Walker, please.'

Jimmy pulled his leather jacket down, trying to smooth out the folds and wrinkles.

'Well, here we go, eh! I'm here for him, Satchell. Just like you. You're a good mate to him and I appreciate that. I do, I appreciate that.'

The usher was still hovering, waiting for Jimmy.

243

Satchell whipped a comb from his own pocket and roughly combed Jimmy's hair. At this moment North emerged from the courtroom and nodded to Satchell.

'Mike's still giving evidence,' she said.

Satchell merely nodded but Jimmy greeted her like a long-lost friend.

'Hi there, Pat. Long time, no see.'

North ignored this and continued, to Satchell, 'You got him here OK then?'

'Yeah. You going back in?' Satchell asked.

North shook her head.

'No, I can't. I have to go back to the station.'

Satchell was surprised.

'What, now? We've wrapped up Brickman.'

'Brickman hasn't been sentenced yet. But it's not about the Brickman case. Chief Superintendent Bradley wants to see me.'

Satchell, always alive to any gossip, took instant notice.

'Oh yes?' he asked.

North nodded and walked away. Satchell and Jimmy watched her go.

'I could give her one,' whispered Jimmy, with sudden lasciviousness. 'Bet you could too!'

'Mr Walker! This way please,' called the usher.

As one last reminder, Satchell jabbed his finger into Jimmy's chest.

'Get in there,' he whispered. 'I'll be watching you, every second.'

Jimmy shook Satchell off and headed towards the courtroom entrance, where the usher was waiting for him. Getting there, Jimmy turned and gave the Detective Sergeant an odd, cold stare.

'I'd get front row seats, if I were you. It's going

244

to be worth it. It's going to be great!'

CHAPTER TWENTY-TWO

WEDNESDAY, 23 JULY, MORNING

Jimmy took the stand and looked around the court with a show of assurance. He glanced at his brother in the dock with confidence. He knew approximately what had gone before. Stevens had made his opening address, in which he had stated the kernel of his case: that Walker had come into possession of the gun from Jimmy only a few minutes before Eric Fowler was shot, and that he had had no time to examine it properly. Jimmy had been nervous on his way to court but now the butterflies settled.

'You are the younger brother of the defendant Michael Walker,' Stevens put to him. 'And you were staying with him and his fiancée in their flat in Barnes from 26 March of this year?'

'Yes, that's right,' agreed Jimmy pleasantly. 'I dropped in on him on my way through from New Zealand to Florida. I hadn't seen him in years and thought I'd look him up.'

'And how long did you stay there?'

'I was there for maybe a day.'

He laughed momentarily.

'That's about as long as we can put up with each other, know what I mean?'

Stevens nodded to the court official by the exhibits table.

'Would you have a look at this gun please?'

The Luger, still framed on its card, was shown to the witness.

'Have you seen that gun before?'

Jimmy viewed the gun with apparent interest. He paused, then again glanced across at Walker. He was a free man, wasn't he? He could say what he liked.

'No,' he said. 'I don't believe I have.'

The whole court immediately grasped the ghastly import of this statement for the defence. It directly contradicted the assertion already made by Stevens in his opening address. If true, it blew the doors off the defence case. There was a moment of stunned disbelief amongst Walker's lawyers and friends. Walker gripped the edge of the dock until his knuckles turned white. Satchell's mouth dropped open.

'I'm sorry?' said Stevens, as if he hadn't heard right.

Jimmy gave him a friendly smile.

'I said, I do not believe I have ever seen that gun before.'

Stevens took a deep breath.

'Have a look at it again, will you?'

The official raised the gun to the level of Jimmy's eyes.

'Now, take your time,' urged Stevens, 'and tell me—have you seen this gun before?'

Jimmy shook his head.

'No, I haven't.'

'I need not remind you that you are on oath, Mr Walker.'

There was a long silence as Jimmy stared back at the barrister as if playing a game of eyeball chicken. The silence extended to a full twenty

246

seconds before the judge came to Stevens's rescue.

'Members of the jury,' said Winfield, 'I think we'll have a short adjournment. Will you go to your room, please? We will call you again when we need you.'

The jury stood up and filed raggedly out. When the last of them had disappeared, Winfield spoke to the witness.

'Mr Walker, would you also wait outside, please? And, as I say to all witnesses, don't discuss the case.'

The witness left the court. He did not glance at the dock.

'Now, Mr Stevens,' said Winfield. 'I imagine you may wish to apply to me for leave to cross-examine your witness. Do you want me 'to rise to allow you to take some instructions?'

Stevens bowed.

'I'd be grateful for a few minutes, my Lord. We've been taken a little by surprise.'

'Let the Usher know when you are ready.'

He stood and the Clerk told the court,

'All rise!'

When the judge had gone and most of those present had gone, Walker, Stevens and Pinton held a huddled conference at the defence table.

'Well, at the risk of stating the obvious, the little shit has gone bent on us,' stated Pinton grimly.

Walker was shaking with rage.

'Can't I talk to him? Let me talk to him,' he asked.

'That's not possible, Mr Walker. Our only option is to apply to treat him as a hostile witness. That allows me to cross-examine him on the statement he made to the police.'

'Christ's sake! I only need two minutes with him.'

'You can't, I'm afraid. But what I need is to know why your own brother is doing this. He must understand how crucial his evidence is, surely?'

'Of course he understands. I've protected that bastard all his life.'

Walker was breathing heavily, and still shaking. Pinton poured a glass of water from the pitcher on the defence desk and handed it to him. He took it and drank thirstily. Stevens watched him.

'You know, these things can end up working to our advantage. We may yet come up smelling of roses.'

He turned to Pinton.

'I take it you've got his signed statement confirming that what he told the police was true?'

'Certainly have, proper Section 9 statement, signed and witnessed. Here.'

He opened his file and handed over the original statement.

Stevens looked at it in some relief.

'Thank God for that at least. Now, Mr Walker, let's consider. Is this sudden cowardice on his part, not wanting to face the consequences of possessing that gun? Or is it something more sinister? I mean it looks on the face of it as if he's seen the opportunity to do you down and grabbed it with both hands.'

Walker sipped more water. He shook his head helplessly.

'Do we really not know why he had the gun in the first place?' pressed Stevens.

'I told you what he said: something about delivering it to someone.'

'Nothing more than that, eh?'

Walker shook his head again and Stevens sighed heavily. He picked up his stack of notes and tapped them to align the edges tidily.

'Well,' he said. 'We'll just have to try to destroy the little beggar.'

He grasped Walker's upper arm for a moment.

'Courage, dear boy,' he said. 'Into battle.'

Word was sent back to the Judge's chambers and within ten minutes the court had reassembled. Jimmy took his previous place on the witness stand, ready for Stevens's questions. The barrister's tone of voice had taken on a new, noticeably harder edge.

'Tell me, are you fond of your brother?'

Jimmy was unprepared for this new opening.

'What kind of a question is that?' he asked.

'Well, are you?'

Jimmy shrugged.

'Of course I am.'

'So fond that you're prepared to lie for him?'

Jimmy frowned warily.

'I don't follow you.'

Stevens passed a document up to the stand.

'Just have a look at this statement you made to the police, would you? You made a similar one to your brother's solicitors, didn't you?'

Jimmy quickly glanced at the statement and knew he couldn't deny it.

'That's right, yes.'

'Are these truthful statements, or are they a pack of lies?'

Jimmy half-smiled.

'They're a pack of lies.'

'So why make them?'

'Because that's what he asked me to say. He said it would be all right. He was really desperate. Kept on saying that his whole life depended on me. So I agreed. I didn't really think about it that much at the time.'

'So you agreed to tell lies, is that what you're saying, to make a false witness statement? What has suddenly changed today?'

Jimmy moved his weight from one leg to the other.

'Telling lies to the police, that's easy enough. I've never really got on too well with them. Can't always trust 'em, can you? But coming here to court and telling a shed load of lies in the witness box, on oath, well, that's a bit different. I just couldn't go through with it. I warned him.'

'You warned him? Warned him of what? That you were going to have an attack of conscience as soon as you got near the witness box? Is that what you warned him?'

'I just warned him, that's all.'

'You are just making this up as you go along, aren't you?'

Jimmy looked convincingly outraged.

'Making it up? Look, I didn't even want to come here, they had to threaten me with a summons to get me in.'

'They had to threaten you with a summons to bring you to court to help your own brother? They had to force you here? I suggest that the reason you didn't want to come to court was that you were worried about possessing that gun, loaded with hollow-point bullets, weren't you?'

'That's rubbish. There wasn't any gun.'

'Or was it that you were worried not so much

250

about possessing it but about not possessing it, about losing it? Mmm? Was someone after you because of that gun? Is that why you wanted to get abroad?'

Jimmy now adopted a truculent manner. He clenched the edge of the stand.

'Are you deaf or what? I keep telling you, there was no gun. I don't have to listen to all this BOLLOCKS!'

Winfield, who had been scribbling busily, lifted his pen from his pad.

'Mr Walker, I would advise you to temper your comments whilst you are in the witness box.'

'Thank you, my Lord,' said Stevens. 'Mr Walker, you said that you didn't get on with the police. Did you mean in this country or in New Zealand? Or was it both?'

'I just don't get on with policemen, OK? Full stop.'

'I see. And that would include your brother, I take it? He's a policeman and a very good one at that. Does that bother you?'

'Why should it?'

'You're not jealous are you? Bitter and jealous at his success and your own failure in life?'

Jimmy suddenly released a loud mocking laugh.

'Jealous? Look, he's the one in the dock, not me.'

'You told the police the truth for once in your life, didn't you, or at least as much of it about the gun as you dared, and now you've reverted to form, lashing out at your own brother to settle what you see as old scores.'

'That's rubbish.'

'Can I have the gun again?' the brief asked the

guardian of the exhibits.

Stevens held the Luger up for Jimmy, and the whole court, to see.

'You were carrying this gun in your holdall, were you not? And it was fully loaded with hollow-point bullets.'

Jimmy shook his head, as if to dislodge beads of sweat. Stevens's steely pursuit of his lie was beginning to get to him.

'Rubbish,' he repeated.

'You had it with you in circumstances only you know about, isn't that right?'

Jimmy looked up at the judge, as if seeking support.

'Look, this is rubbish.'

'Your brother found it, didn't he, and took it from you outside his flat, just as he told the police and just as you told the police. Or that is rubbish too, I expect.'

'Yes, it is.'

Stevens regarded Jimmy as a man looks at a dog turd.

'You are, I suggest, an utterly despicable liar,' he said.

CHAPTER TWENTY-THREE

WEDNESDAY, 23 JULY

The witness evidence and expert testimony had been heard, the exhibits, photographs and statements examined. Now the two opposing counsel had nothing left to do but make their closing speeches. In the dock, Walker sat wishing desperately to smoke. He had begun to appreciate the awful consequences this trial might have. Life imprisonment. Shuffled between all the top security jails. The endless company of the very men he himself had had sent down during ten years in the murder squad. It did not bear thinking about.

He surveyed the jury as they listened assiduously to Rylands's closing arguments. They were impassive but, at least, awake. He could tell nothing else about what they were thinking.

Rylands had chosen to close by picking apart Stevens's defence case, rather than by pouring massive reinforcements into his own attack.

'Under which circumstance,' he challenged, 'is a man's word more trustworthy? That of a statement he gives to the police on behalf of his brother when, on his own admission, he has no respect whatever for the police. Or that of the evidence he gives here, amidst all the pomp and solemnity of this courtroom, after swearing an oath to tell the complete truth and at the very real risk of losing his own liberty should he be caught out in a lie?'

Rylands smiled complicitly, to indicate he knew that they knew, as everyone knew, the obvious answer.

'You see, so much of the defence's argument in this case has depended, has it not, on the errant brother lasting the course. Loyalty took him so far, but when asked to stand up in court and here stick by his wholly fantastical original story, he simply couldn't do it. So he changed that story.'

Rylands lowered his voice to that soft, sometimes almost whispering delivery for which he was famous.

' *"No"*, said James Walker. Until the moment he was shown the gun that killed Eric Fowler here, in your presence, he had never before seen it, let alone had it in his possession.

'Members of the jury, I want you to remember the most important thing about your difficult task. There is, in a murder trial, place neither for sympathy nor for prejudice. There is place only for the cool, dispassionate weighing of evidence heard. Your task is not to judge this experienced, high-flying officer on what he did during his career to date, impressive as that no doubt has been, but to judge him on what he did on the night of Thursday 27 March. It may be tempting to conclude that the person responsible for these assaults deserved whatever he received. But each of you will know that taking the law into one's own hands can never be justified in a civilized society. On the evidence you have heard, there is really only one verdict that you can reach in this tragic case. And that is one of guilty.'

Rylands sat down and Willoughby Stevens rose. He looked concerned, even worried, at what the jury had heard from Rylands over the past few minutes. His tone suggested that he wanted above all to correct any possible misconceptions they may have formed as a result. He was very reasonable.

'The Crown have presented you with a single snapshot of the scene that greeted police the night this shooting took place. They've described Detective Chief Superintendent Walker standing over his dying victim, the traditional smoking gun lying on the carpet, the body slumped, covered in blood, a fatal wound to his chest. The Crown have built their entire case around this snapshot, pointing to it and saying: Michael Walker had the motive, he had the killer weapon in his possession. A clear case of murder.'

Stevens drank from his water glass thoughtfully and glanced at his notes.

'That snapshot, that two-dimensional picture, tells you nothing of what went on two minutes earlier, however. It tells you nothing of what was going on five minutes earlier out in the street with Detective Chief Superintendent Walker's brother. It tells you nothing of what really happened that evening. And, above all, it tells you nothing of the people involved.

'On the one hand, you have Eric Fowler. This was a dangerously unstable man. He had attacked Lynn Walker on more than one occasion, the last time with a kitchen knife, and had then transferred his murderous rage to Detective Inspector Pat North. He burst into the flat she shared with the defendant and, already covered in his own blood, he threatened her with a broken bottle.

'On the other hand, you have the defendant, Detective Chief Superintendent Michael Walker himself, a man with twenty-five years service with the Metropolitan Police, twenty-five years dedicated to upholding the law. Well, I hope you, instead of being distracted by the sensational snapshot the Crown has presented you with, will ask yourselves the following crucial question. Would Michael Walker, the measured, dedicated man you have seen in the witness box, and been told about from so many impressive sources, suddenly give in to raw hatred and base revenge, emotions no one has ever known him to possess?'

'Would this man, on the threshold of

255

appointment to the very top echelon of the Metropolitan Police Force, and moreover about to be married, even be tempted to do what the Crown has suggested, that is, kill a man in cold blood?

'Michael Walker, the man in your charge on this indictment, is a police officer whose every instinct that night was to bring this man to justice. To subdue him, arrest him, bring him before the court and see him sentenced according to law. But NOT to kill him! So it is on behalf of this man that I invite you to return what is in my view your only conceivable verdict of not guilty.'

Walker had liked the speech. If he'd been a juryman he felt he would have been convinced by the truth of it. But then, what did that matter? He *knew* the truth.

With a good deal of coughing and shuffling, the court settled down to hear Winfield's summing up. There was no need for an adjournment first. Years of experience and a razor-edged legal brain had given Winfield the ability to sum up relatively simple cases like this at a few moments' notice.

'Members of the jury,' he began, 'you and I have our separate and distinct roles. We are both judges. I am the judge of the law and you will take the law from me. You on the other hand are the judges of the facts. And the facts remain entirely within your province. If in the course of your deliberations you detect some view that I may have formed on the facts, you are at liberty to follow it if you agree with it. If, on the other hand, you disagree with it, it is your duty to reject it. As I say, you are the sole judges of the facts, which I shall now attempt to summarize for you as we have heard them given in this court. And I turn first to the testimony of

Detective Inspector Patricia North, who was the nearest witness to the crime . . .'

Winfield spoke for less than an hour. When he finished, the arguments were over and the business of reaching a verdict was begun. Walker, removed from the dock to the holding cell, sat staring at the wall. It was a white wall. And on it he kept picturing the faces of those he had loved. His mother, years ago when he was young. Lynn, his wife, the mother of his children. His children Richard and Amy. Pat North, the object of his late-flowering lust, his strongest and neediest love. By the end of this they might all be lost to him. He knew what it was like for long-term prisoners. One by one those closest to them fell away. One by one they stopped visiting, writing, until there was no one left, no one at all to love.

The jury had been sent out at twelve-twenty. At one, the cell door opened and a prison officer entered with a tray bearing Walker's lunch.

'They're still out. Lunch has been taken in for them so we filled your order too.'

Walker shook his head.

'No thanks, I'm not hungry.'

The officer hesitated for a moment. He was tempted to leave the tray anyway. There'd been times when a prisoner claimed to have no appetite but, left alone with the food, he'd wolfed the lot. But there was something about this guy that said he really couldn't eat.

'I often wondered what it felt like, the waiting,' Walker told him. 'Even wondered how it must feel to be locked up, to be put away by people like me. Well I know now, don't I? I know now.'

He sat despairingly still, never removing his eyes

257

from the wall.

'Shouldn't be long, Sir,' the officer said cheerily. 'Mind you they always say, the longer they take . . .'

Walker smiled a little sourly.

'Well, thanks for bringing the tray. I appreciate it. You've all been good blokes.'

'Right sir. Good luck, then.'

Back in the dock, Walker viewed the people gathering like a theatre audience for the final act. He did not see many friendly faces. North wasn't there. Lynn wasn't there. His mother—if you could call her friendly—had gone back to Glasgow weeks ago.

At last he found Satchell. Faithful Satch. What he'd put his friend through in the last few weeks didn't bear thinking about. The damage to their livers alone must be frightening. But Satch had stood by him, when so many others had fallen away. The disgrace—even the potential disgrace— of a policeman tended to make his colleagues run from him as if from the plague. No one wanted to be associated with professional disgrace. But that wasn't Satch's style. He believed in nothing so much as loyalty.

'Would the foreman please stand,' intoned the Clerk. Walker jumped. For Christ's sake, not now! He wasn't ready! But this wasn't being done on his timetable. He had to be ready.

As the jury foreman, a woman in early middle age, prepared to stand up, a noise made Walker look round, a small scuffling effect as a latecomer entered the gallery at the back of the court. He saw it was Jimmy. Their eyes locked for a moment, then Walker turned back to stare at the foreman. Jimmy was irrelevant now. It was this ordinary looking woman that he'd never met and never would meet who held Walker's future in her hand.

'Madame Foreman,' continued the Clerk, 'please answer this question yes or no. Members of the jury, have you reached a verdict on which you are all agreed?'

The foreman acknowledged the question with a bob of her head.

'Yes,' she said.

'Do you find the Defendant, Michael Walker, guilty or not guilty of murder?'

He imagined there were the faintest traces of sweat on her brow. But there was no tremor in her voice as she spoke out quite distinctly,

'Not guilty.'

And, as in every big case, the verdict was met by a collective exhaling of breath throughout the court. In the dock, Walker bowed his head, and he suddenly realized this was probably the first and only time he'd ever actively longed for a not guilty verdict. In the scores of times he'd attended Crown Court trials, he had always been the one pushing for guilt, and for retribution.

'And that is the verdict of you all?' asked the Clerk.

'It is.'

Discharged immediately by the judge, Walker, whose face had never been a good barometer of his emotions, expressed a confusing mixture of triumph and humility. As the freed man stepped from the dock, Stevens was looking expensively pleased, like a man who'd seen his horse win at Royal Ascot. Rylands, gathering his notes and stuffing them into a file, showed no emotion.

Walker was about to speak his thanks when he

reacted to a movement in the public gallery. The court door banged and, turning, Walker caught a momentary glimpse of Jimmy slipping out of the court room. He mumbled something inaudible and scrambled for the door, swinging it open and careering away after his brother, across the marbled halls of the Crown Court.

'JIMMY!'

Jimmy heard his brother coming for him, the echoing cry and the running feet. He tried to make himself small, to disappear into the crowd, but Walker caught up with him and pounced, gripping the lapels of his brother's jacket and shaking him violently.

'Just tell me why, Jimmy. *Why?*'

Jimmy was backed up against a wall. He cowered. Mike had always done this. Thrashing towards him, blaming him. His hatred of Mike knew no bounds.

'You're my brother,' hissed Walker, so close that the spittle bounced off Jimmy's face. 'So *why?*'

Jimmy worked his mouth until he had a decent sized gob of spit. This he tried to launch in the direction of Walker but his aim was askew and it passed harmlessly over Walker's shoulder.

'Why?' he said, trying to summon all his powers of scorn. 'All right, I'll tell you why. Whatever you've done, all your life, you've got away with it. But not me. I never did.'

Suddenly, Walker's face smoothed over, the grimace melting away. He relaxed his grip on the leather lapels.

'You're a loser, Jimmy. You always were.'

Walker turned and, casually now, walked away.

'Goodbye Jimmy,' he said over his shoulder.

'We're done. We're done for ever.'

He did not look back. Jimmy suddenly felt trapped, panicky.

'Mike!' he shouted.

Jimmy was thinking of the gun. The case had gone against him. He had not been believed, and now he would have to pay for the gun. Not with money. It was too late for that, even if he had any. He would pay in some other way. He was fucked.

'Well go on then!' he screamed at Walker's back. 'Go on, walk away! You always did.'

Walker did not turn round. He reached into his pocket for his smokes. He selected a Marlboro and tore off the tip. He lit up.

CHAPTER TWENTY-FOUR

THURSDAY, 24 JULY, EVENING

Bob Brickman had been under psychiatric assessment for weeks and he was enjoying playing the game. Visions, delusions, dreams, fantasies—he manufactured them in wholesale quantities for analysis by the clinicians and therapists. But, now sitting at a canteen-style table in the prison visiting suite, there was more practical business on hand. With his arms resting on the plastic veneered tabletop, Bob constantly glanced towards the visitors' entrance, alerted by any coming or going. He otherwise did nothing except lace and unlace his enormous fingers. He was waiting for Alan to show up.

At last his brother appeared, with Donny in tow,

to Bob's surprise and pleasure. Alan was holding Donny's hand as the two of them threaded between the tables. Donny was looking around him with genuine interest, intrigued at being, for the first time in is life, in a roomful of criminals. He also noticed the hatch in the wall where drinks, biscuits and chocolate were sold.

Bob's face broke into a joyous smile as they arrived at his table.

'Say hello to your Dad then, Donny,' said Alan.

Donny didn't speak. He just stood by the table, shy, his head down. Bob reached up and ruffled his hair affectionately.

'How you doing Donny? You practising the chords? Need a lot of dexterity, got to keep your fingers nimble.'

Alan sat down, pointing at his brother, jabbing the air enthusiastically.

'Yeah, you used to do that trick, remember? Flicking a coin through your fingers, like a magician.'

He tipped his head towards Donny.

'I tried to show him, but I wasn't much good.'

Alan was digging in his pocket.

'Here.'

He pulled out a fifty pence piece from his pocket. Bob took it and began rolling it dexterously along the tops of his knuckles, rolling it from one end to the other and back, then covered the coin with his other hand, waved both fists in the air and said,

'Which hand?'

Donny leaned down, his elbows on the table, grinning while he chose. He pointed.

'That one.'

'Right,' said Bob, opening the fist to reveal its treasure. 'It's yours. Go buy yourself a Mars bar Donny, from the lady over there, or you can get a Coke. You want anything, Alan?'

'No.'

Both men watched as Donny threaded his way to the vending area.

'Any date for the sentencing yet?' asked Alan in a low voice.

Bob shook his head slowly.

'Soon, that's all I know.'

'Has Shawlcross said how long they think you're going to get?'

'I don't know what Shawlcross says. I only see shrinks, a different one every day.'

He tapped himself on the temple.

'According to them, sane or insane, I'm looking at twelve to fifteen years.'

The two brothers looked at each other steadily. Bob looked across at Donny, still queueing at the hatch, then went on in a very low voice.

'It's all right, Alan, it's over. You got nothing to worry about. I said it would be all right, didn't I? And we have no problem with the Social Services any more so you can kick the slag out.'

Alan blinked, straightened in his chair. He'd been enjoying having Sharon. He'd not been getting anywhere with her, that was true. But she'd been company.

Bob saw what he was thinking.

'Oh, don't tell me,' he jeered. 'You're shagging her again, aren't you.'

Alan scowled.

'No, don't be daft, she's got a bloke.'

Bob laughed.

'So you'll have no problem kicking her out then!'

Alan deflected the conversation along other, and to him more necessary, lines.

'Did you contact the solicitor, Bob? About the business?'

'Yes, he'll have the papers ready for you, give you legal guardianship of Donny and power of attorney for the business. But not for ever.'

'What do you mean, "not for ever"?'

'Exactly that, mate. It's the deal. You look after him and you get to live in the house and run the mill. All profits are yours until my boy turns eighteen and then I'm giving it all to him.'

Alan looked at Bob like he'd been smacked in the mouth.

'Give it all to him? You've got no right to do that. I'm the one who built up that business. My whole life!'

Bob regarded Alan's agitation complacently.

'You don't want me to suddenly remember who helped me bury her, do you?'

Alan's face was all anger and grievance now. He spluttered.

'*I'm* the one you came running to after you'd snatched her from the woods. Me! Looking out for you, all the time. I'm the one who got rid of the baseball bat you killed her with. I'm the one who found it in the guitar case and put it though the shredder. That was a crap hiding place, Bob.'

Bob was all smiles as he shook his head slowly and inscrutably.

'Well *I* didn't put it in the guitar case! Think, Alan. The cops were swarming all over our place like flies. Why didn't they find it?'

Alan frowned.

'I don't understand.'

'Because *Donny* hid it.'

Bob looked around at the two or three nearest groups of visitors, then went on. 'He took his case to school so they wouldn't find it.'

Alan jerked forward, almost rising out of his chair.

'My God, Bob! You've got your own kid involved, your own boy protecting you.'

Bob was still smiling his Fu Manchu smile.

'Wrong, Alan. I'm protecting *him*.'

'What do you mean?'

'That night, remember? When I came running to you, after I'd grabbed her from the woods. I didn't know why I'd done it. I didn't know what to do. So I'd left her tied up in the barn, still alive.'

'Stop lying to me, Bob,' warned Alan. 'Don't say this.'

But Bob could not be stopped.

'No, listen. You're going to hear this. When we got back, she was dead, whacked. Head smashed. But I never killed her.'

He inclined his head towards Donny, who had reached the front of the queue at the sales counter.

'He did it. Found her lying there. Found the baseball bat. Bashed her.'

Alan was chalk white. His mouth was slack.

'I don't believe it,' he said. 'He couldn't have.'

'Well, he did.'

*   *   *

Satchell had agreed to help Walker move the last of his things from the flat—the final act in the break-up of Walker's relationship with North, the ultimate finishing touch in which he removed every trace of himself from her life. He packed slowly, methodically, and with the heaviest of heavy hearts. He knew she could be back from work any time. On the other hand, she might deliberately stay out of the way, knowing he was there. He wished she would stay away. Then he wanted to see her and wished she'd show up.

As he brought down his last two suitcases the doorbell rang.

'You want a hand with one of those?' Satchell asked, indicating the suitcases.

Walker was distracted, only half listening. He looked at his watch.

'Pat not here?' Satchell asked.

'No. She's heading up another murder inquiry.'

'Oh yes? Bit of a rising star, that girl.'

Walker turned away. Emotion, his old enemy, welled up inside him. He buried his face in his hands, his body shaking. Satchell put down the case he'd hoisted and crossed to Walker, placing a hand on his shoulder. Walker slid away from the hand and waved Satchell away.

'Hey! Don't you go all pansy on me. Just get me and my stuff the hell out of here.'

Satchell doubled back to the door.

'Fine, right,' he said good-naturedly. 'I'll just schlep another bloody suitcase out of here weighing a ton. You get your wash bag and we're on our way.'

Satchell banged out with both cases while Walker stood for a moment, looking around him at the half-empty bookcase, the denuded shelves, the space on the wall where his police college class photograph had hung. Then the front door clicked and squeaked.

'Mike? MIKE?'

It was North. She came into the living room and let her coat drop on the sofa. The light was off and, in the relative gloom, she didn't see Walker at once. When he moved, she started.

'Oh! I thought I'd missed you.'

Walker moved towards her and stood close.

'I'm all packed up but I wanted to say something before I left.'

North was suddenly crying. He put his hand to her cheek, the thumb wiping away a tear.

'Look after yourself,' he said. His voice was choking. 'And if you need me, you know I'll always do anything for you.'

He leaned forward and kissed her cheek with extraordinary gentleness.

'And thank you for what you did in court.'

Walker turned away and made for the door. He wanted to be out of there before he started crying again.

'I'll be with Lynn and the kids . . . So you know where I am, yeah?'

Then he shut the door behind him.

North was alone in the silent flat. She looked around, noticing the denuded shelves and stripped walls, just as he had done. Her eyes filled again. She hoped it was not going to be one of those evenings when she did nothing but cry.

'Thanks for what you did in court,' he had said. What had she done in court?

She was thinking about this, standing on the very spot where she had witnessed the death of Eric Fowler. The succession of events that night had remained imprecise in her memory all through the build-up to the trial and the trial itself: the spurting blood of the intruder, the broken bottle, Walker's warning voice, the fear, the barricaded bedroom door, the passage, the gunshot, the dead man.

'Thanks for what you did in court.'

No need to thank her for doing her duty, telling what she saw . . . But what had she seen?

The phone in the hall rang. She went through and picked it up.

'Ah, Pat,' said a voice she knew. 'It's Frank Bradley . . .'

But other voices than the Chief Superintendent's were already crowding her head, first Eric's and then Walker's.

'BOTTLE? Hurt ME? You can't hurt ME!'

'Put it down, Eric. Get back. Put the bottle DOWN!'

And quite suddenly that night was re-running in her head like videotape.

She got the bedroom door open. There was blood all over the passage, from Eric's cut artery. The two men were shouting, close together at the far end, where the stairs were. Eric was above, still bleeding profusely, and Walker was below, glowering furiously up at him. They were shouting, their faces distorted in fury, and Eric waving the jagged broken bottle in his fist. She moved down the passage towards them. They were both charged up, on fire, yelling. She went on towards them as they seemed to close on each other . . .

'I'm sorry, sir . . . what did you say?'

'Just that I'm delighted you're on the Wapping case. The body in the white van?'

Walker was below Eric, standing on the lowest stair of the three. She was close enough, now, to see that he

*was holding something in his hand, but Eric was
between them, swaying this way and that.*

'Ah! Yes, sir, I've ear-marked the team.'

She sat on the top stair.

'I, er, was just going to get back to you . . .'

*She saw the sheen of black metal and knew,
without comprehension, that it was a gun. Had
Walker's thumb moved across the safety catch? Had
he pushed the gun forward? This was the part that
wouldn't come into focus.*

'Good,' said Bradley. 'I haven't seen the list of
names yet. Who are you putting forward?'

North touched the wall behind her with her
fingers. She wasn't sure but she thought she could
still see Eric Fowler's blood under the fresh paint.

'Pat? Who have you nominated for the team?'

'What? Oh, I'm sorry, sir. Well, I'd like with me
DC Lisa West, DC Doug Collins, most of the team
I used on the Brickman case, in fact. It worked
well.'

'No doubt you'd like Detective Sergeant
Satchell, then?'

She thought for a moment.

'Er, no,' she said. 'No, not Dave Satchell. Who
else is available?'

'Well I'm sure we can find you a capable
Detective Sergeant, Pat.'

'And the victim was found near Tower Bridge?'

'Yes—I've got a preliminary pathologist's report.
She was strangled.'

'Strangled?'

'That's right. I'll pop into the Incident Room
tomorrow. See you then.'

Bradley hung up and North sat for a moment
staring blankly ahead of her. She heard Walker's

voice again.

'Thanks for what you did in court.'

So what, exactly, had she done? She'd lied, of course.

She was there when the gun went off. The bullet threw Eric back. He grunted, eyes wide, disbelieving. He staggered back, and seconds later was slumped in a twisted sitting posture against the wall, with a smear of blood on the paintwork behind him where he'd slithered down. Walker stood by the stair, panting and staring at Eric as if in a trance. It was only then that she saw what had happened to the gun. It lay almost exactly where North was sitting, where Walker had dropped it.

She'd lied, but how big was the lie? He might have done it. He might have deliberately moved the safety catch, deliberately pulled the trigger and taken a life.

'Oh my God! Mike! Mike, NO!'

But she couldn't be sure. She'd been there but she hadn't seen, with Fowler in the way, bleeding in spurts, swaying from side to side, obscuring her view of Walker. To kill like that, to kill on purpose, was against all the instincts of a good cop. And she knew he was a good cop. She shut her eyes, seeing only the spray of Eric Fowler's blood. Only Walker knew what she'd really done for him in court. No one else would ever learn the truth. But he was a good cop, a good man, so it didn't matter.

She'd lied for him in court, but it wasn't a big lie. She'd been there but she hadn't seen. She didn't know. Only he knew for sure.

*   *   *

Back in Alan's car on the way home, Donny pulled a two pence piece from his jeans. A moment later his uncle realized he was rolling it along the top of his knuckles so smoothly that it seemed to ripple.

'The slag leaving soon is she, Alan?' he asked.

'Sharon? Your *mum*? Yeah, Donny. She's only staying with us for the Social Services to check us out and then, well, it'll just be you and me Donny. Just . . . you and me.'

Donny rolled the coin up and down his knuckles, then slapped his other hand over it.

'Which hand, Alan?' he asked.

CHIVERS
LARGE PRINT
–direct–

If you have enjoyed this Large Print book and would like to build up your own collection of Large Print books, please contact

Chivers Large Print Direct

Chivers Large Print Direct offers you a full service:

• Prompt mail order service

• Easy-to-read type

• The very best authors

• Special low prices

For further details either call Customer Services on (01225) 336552 or write to us at Chivers Large Print Direct, **FREEPOST**, Bath BA1 3ZZ

Telephone Orders: **FREEPHONE** 08081 72 74 75